based on a real-life story of heartbreak, horror and hope

THE BOY
in the
YELLOW
HOUSE

RAY SANDERS

LUCIDBOOKS

NOTE: <u>Reader discretion is advised</u>. This book includes themes of domestic, emotional, sexual, and alcohol abuse that may serve as triggers for some readers. It may also be considered profane, vulgar, or offensive to some. The publisher believes removing such realities would diminish the gravity of the story and ultimately chose to present the story in the spirit by which it would have been actually experienced.

To Stephanie.

You are my biggest fan, cheerleader, and confidante. You are my best friend, the love of my life, and the one I am privileged to call my wife. Without your encouragement and support, this book would have remained a good intention. Because of you, I have stepped out, bared my soul, and opened my heart to all who care to read this little bundle of words.

Thank you, Stephanie. You are my everything. You share in this labor of love. It is dedicated to you and the Lord we love.

AUTHOR'S NOTE

Behind every great story is an evil villain, a damsel in distress, and a charming hero that sweeps in at just the right time to save the day.

Great storytelling captures our imaginations and helps us escape the realities of everyday life. As we get lost among the pages of a good book, we settle in and forget the worries of our world as we are drawn into the lives of the characters who capture our hearts and minds.

Everyone loves a great story, especially when the story is rooted in the lives of those who lived to tell about it. Such is the basis for this story. It weaves together a cast of antagonists, women and children, yearning for rescue and countless heroes—ordinary people who can only be described as angels in disguise.

I have done my best to capture the heart and spirit of a real-life story where I am but one among many colorful characters. Certainly not everything portrayed in this book is exactly as it was, but it is incredibly close to the reality and spirit of the moment in time.

Names have been changed to protect the guilty and innocent as well as to lighten the load of those who might have hoped for a better depiction of the role they played.

My hope is for readers to become so involved in the story that they too experience the emotions, feelings, and stress that were part of everyday life for a young family suffering severely from generational curses, dysfunction, as well as sexual, domestic, and alcohol abuse.

As in any tragedy, there is light — moments of joy, adventure, and inspiration. I should know, I lived it. I am the boy in the yellow house.

P.S. I would love to hear from you. My prayer is that in some small way this story brings hope, healing, and inspiration to anyone whose life has been intense. Let's connect! Please send your thoughts to me at ray@raysanders.com or call me at 405-640-3235. Don't be surprised when I answer.

TABLE OF CONTENTS

Chapter 1	1
Chapter 2	4
Chapter 3	8
Chapter 4	12
Chapter 5	19
Chapter 6	24
Chapter 7	27
Chapter 8	36
Chapter 9	40
Chapter 10	46
Chapter 11	50
Chapter 12	53
Chapter 13	57
Chapter 14	62
Chapter 15	65
Chapter 16	71
Chapter 17	75
Chapter 18	84
Chapter 19	88
Chapter 20	95
Chapter 21	104
Chapter 22	110
Chapter 23	113
Chapter 24	118
Chapter 25	122
Chapter 26	128

Chapter 27	133
Chapter 28	137
Chapter 29	141
Chapter 30	146
Chapter 31	151
Chapter 32	157
Chapter 33	163
Chapter 34	169
Chapter 35	175
Chapter 36	181
Chapter 37	190
Chapter 38	197
Chapter 39	201
Chapter 40	207
Chapter 41	215
Chapter 42	221
Chapter 43	235
Chapter 44	241
Chapter 45	244
Chapter 46	249
Chapter 47	255
Chapter 48	270
Chapter 49	272
Chapter 50	276
Epilogue	282
Acknowledgments	284
Special Thanks	285
Helpful Resources	286
About the Author	289

CHAPTER 1

The sun shone in on the new station wagon making Anna more than hot. She was wilting in the crowded back seat from all the sunshine and body heat. The station wagon was new but wasn't equipped with the much-coveted air-conditioning.

Unfortunately for Anna, she had drawn the short straw that landed her on the bright side of the vehicle. Nonetheless, she made the most of it by improving her tan as she reached out the window riding the wind, moving her hand up and down over fence posts that skirted the new two-lane state highway, Route 66.

Anna's family was well-to-do. Her daddy, Woodriff McMillan, "Riff" to all who knew him, was an up-and-coming banker. A big promotion had him heading to a small Oklahoma town as the manager of the local branch. Not bad for a kid with a spotty past and prone to making bad decisions.

The family of six—three adorable daughters, one mischievous, nose-picking son, and their loyal standard poodle—made their way to Junction City. As the dog panted, desperate for a drink of water, Mom and Dad put a bow on yet another family feud along the way.

Riff was laying into his wife Maggie about a molehill he had turned into a mountain. It seemed she could never do enough to please him. Everything about Maggie grinded his last nerve. If you asked Riff, he was the smartest person in any room, and he sure as hell was smarter than the godforsaken woman he'd chosen to make his wife. Putting her in her place was his favorite pastime.

The kids had grown numb to the chaos, the shouting matches, the knock-down drag-outs; but their parents' civil war was nothing new. They may have been headed to a new opportunity, but it seemed as though they had packed up their old problems and brought them along for the ride. Anna laid her head against the warm glass of the back window and with a heavy sigh closed her eyes, trying to imagine what her new life in Junction City would bring.

* * *

Dwight Sanderson was the youngest of five children, four boys, and one girl. His oldest brother, Sam, left home years ago, and his next oldest brother, John, was somewhere on the other side of the world fighting a war in a jungle. That left Dwight and his one older brother, Gene, to work the farm. But Gene was gone a lot in the Marine National Guard, and hard work wasn't exactly Dwight's best skill. Truth be told, at twenty-three, he felt stuck in a life he didn't want. But, he didn't seem to be in too much of a hurry to grow up, and that was just fine with his momma.

There was no doubt Dwight was a momma's boy. He could do no wrong in her eyes, but the rest of the Sanderson family and friends saw the truth. Trouble seemed to follow Dwight Sanderson wherever he went, but his momma, Naomi, had a way of rewriting the narrative. She could twist any situation to paint Dwight as either the victim or the hero, depending on what suited the moment. Her rose-colored glasses tinted his perception of reality as well, a self-distortion that stayed with him for the rest of his life. If Dwight had a talent, it was his ability to use his good looks and warm smile to get anything he wanted. But his charming personality wasn't much good to his daddy or to their failing farm.

Farm life wasn't easy. Liam, the patriarch of the tribe, had developed heart issues. And with only one son who was willing to put in a day's work gone half the time to serve his country, keeping the farm going simply became too much. Liam fell further and further behind in his payments to the bank. So when foreclosure forced his hand, he packed up their old truck with what was left from the auction and headed to town—Junction City.

The farm truck and the station wagon were both heading towards a crossroads, both hoping for a new life.

CHAPTER 2

J unction City was smaller than expected. The name made it sound much bigger than it actually was. The two-lane road into town was the first clue that city lights wouldn't be keeping everyone up at night. There was one stoplight in the center of town. Anna noticed it as the sound of the tires stopped slapping the seams of the highway. It was the weekend, so most of the town was closed. There was some activity at the grain elevator as a late harvest had farmhands filling silos with freshly cut wheat. Dust billowed from the back of their wheat trucks as huge augers sucked the grain from the boarded truck beds into the tallest structures for miles around. They weren't high-rise office buildings like Riff had expected, but they were considerable. They weren't filled with men and women in fancy suits and leather satchels, but these massive round tubes in the sky were filled with millions and millions of wheat grains.

It had been a bumper crop. The weather had cooperated, and the sun did its part. Farmers from miles around arrived to unload their harvest, filling the grain elevators before sending their hard-earned yields by rail to larger flour mills. There, the key ingredients for fine breads, pancakes, and other baked goods were processed, packaged, and eventually stocked on local grocery store shelves.

The name was starting to make more sense. Junction City was a gathering place smack dab in the middle of seemingly endless farmland. Surrounded by dirt roads, a few fences, and even fewer neighbors, Junction City was where things came together. A small general store, dairy mart, gas station, tavern, Methodist church, Baptist church, Catholic church, liquor store, grain elevator, and the bank where Riff would serve as the chief officer, all made this little town more than just an intersection between gravel roads and a paved state highway.

Before stopping by the new house, Riff pulled the car into the bank parking lot. The movers had gotten to the house hours earlier and were busy unloading the family's earthly possessions. He didn't drive straight home because he said he didn't want to interrupt the movers, but the truth was Riff couldn't resist the chance to show off a bit and let Maggie and the kids see where the new branch manager would be hanging his hat during the workday. He turned off the ignition, leaned back in the front seat, stretched his arms, and stepped outside the station wagon to take a closer look. He had taken the job at the rural branch sight unseen. It was smaller than he expected, but it was certainly the nicest building in town.

The bank dealt mainly with farmers and local folks who commuted to work in factories in Oklahoma City. But for Riff, this job was a step up. In the big city branches, he'd been a small fish in a big pond. Here, among farmers and factory workers, he would be the one wearing a suit and tie, with his polished wing-tipped shoes and knee-high stockings. He would hold power over these local yokels, and he liked to be the one holding the cards.

The family ran to the front of the building, happy to finally be out of the car. They pressed their faces to the glass front of the bank, the kids laughing and elbowing each for a better position. Riff held his hands around his face as he peered into the bank's lobby. There were two teller windows, a small loan officer desk in the lobby, the bank vault, and there in the back, almost beyond where his straining eyes could see, was his office. His very own office. The place where he would make decisions about the futures of other people's lives. He reached for Maggie's hand and gave her a playful wink. Then he gave a sharp whistle, indicating it was time to go, and everyone needed to fall in line.

As he guided the family around the corner of the bank, Max, the standard poodle, was relieving himself on the back tire of the station wagon. Riff was too tired to care. Rather than having to wrangle everyone back into the car, he promised them the opportunity to see their bedrooms and play in their big new yard just down the street and around the corner from the bank. His plan worked. Any desires for a bathroom break or complaints of being hungry were overcome by the excitement of seeing their new home.

The house was beautiful. It was bigger than the one they had lived in before. Best of all Nathan, Anna's only brother and the baby of the family (affectionately called Booger Man for obvious reasons), had a room off the back porch all to himself. It was more like a large utility room with a bed in it. He didn't care if he shared the space with a broom and a mop bucket, at least he was alone without the girls.

The girls shared a room. Betty, the oldest daughter, was assigned the single twin bed, while Anna and Lindy were delegated the bunks. Anna was on the bottom bunk by the window, and Lindy was on the top bunk. Taller than her 14 years would imply, Anna had to be careful getting in and out of bed or she would hit her head on the ceiling, a fact she knew from experience.

Maggie surveyed the kitchen and learned that propane would heat up the stove. Other than the slightly pungent smell that was omitted when the burner was lit, she saw little difference in how a natural gas stove operated. Most of all, she was hopeful the new town would bring a new beginning.

Life with Riff was hard. He was a difficult man with a bit of a chip on his shoulder. He was charming in public, but he was a completely different man at home. He had wandering eyes as well. Maggie had good reason to believe they did more than wander, and more than once she looked the other way as Riff acted like he was a bachelor and not a family man. Maybe this time, in this town, things would be different.

CHAPTER 3

After the excitement of arriving in Junction City, then seeing the bank and the house, Anna realized just how tired she was. The soft sounds of Nathan and Max playing in the backyard and the movers finishing up their work had lulled her into a cozy afternoon nap. The sudden sound of a pickup woke Anna up from her slumber. She sat bolt upright and banged her head on the bunk, then swore under her breath, rolled over onto her belly, and looked out the window at the source of the noise.

She wasn't sure what they were called, but the pickup she saw was noisier than the cars she was used to. It was loud and sounded like thunder as it rolled into the neighbor's driveway. Lying on her belly with her chin resting on her pillow and her arms tucked beneath her, she caught sight of the driver. She had expected an older man to step out of the truck, but instead, a younger man emerged—not quite her age, yet not old enough to be the homeowner.

By the looks of it, he was probably already out of high school. Anna had just made it through the ninth grade and would be starting at the new high school in the fall. She didn't look her age, a fact that caused Riff to have his shotgun always at the ready. Puberty had come early for Anna, and she had a well-developed, womanly figure, even in her early teens.

Often mistaken as a senior in high school, Anna wasn't just mature for her age, she was beautiful as well. It wasn't something she flaunted or was arrogant about, it was just true. For as far back as she could remember, people had commented about her beauty. Although her beauty sometimes caused tension with her sisters, attracted unwanted attention from boys, and was an even greater concern for her father, Anna refused to let it define or limit her life.

Maggie was a natural beauty as well. She'd felt the admiration of older guys and had used her beauty to get them to do whatever she wanted. Ultimately, she'd fallen for the wrong man, a history she was determined not to let Anna repeat. "Remember Anna, beauty is skin deep, but ugly is to the bone." Anna always laughed when her mama said that, taking it as a joke. But Maggie knew that beauty was a fading privilege, and it was important to have the lasting beauty of a kind heart, a gentle soul, and a sharp mind. Her life with Riff had taught her how much more important those things were.

Her eyes drifted back to the window. The neighbor boy... *man?* was smoking a cigarette as he attempted to remove a push mower from the truck bed. The smoke from his cigarette drifted into his face as he tilted his head, squinted his eyes, and slightly grimaced to avoid the sting from the smoke that burned his pupils.

Anna knew her daddy would take an immediate dislike to this young man. Her daddy was known to smoke a stinky cigar from time to time, with one too many shots of scotch riding shotgun, but the vices of life were not to be permitted in her daddy's house. No one missed the message that doing so would only lead to trouble and a strong rebuke.

Watching from her bedroom window, Anna couldn't help but think that this kind of trouble might be exactly what she needed. She chuckled at the thought—she wasn't the rebellious type. She knew all too well the sting of her daddy's hand for even the smallest misstep. But still, a girl could dream, couldn't she?

The hot summer heat caused the young man next door to sweat. He was shirtless, and the sun shone down on his muscles as he flexed and continued to remove heavy equipment from the tailgate of the pickup. His hair was dark and curly, a little longer than what she was used to seeing. She imagined how it might feel to run her fingers through the little spiral lockets that looked soft and playful.

She had never touched another man except for her daddy and her chubby younger brother. What would it be like to run her hand down the muscled arm of the intriguing neighbor boy who had caught her eye? Something about him made her tingle, and she didn't even know his name or why she felt the way she did. It was a new feeling, and she liked it.

The loud sound of shattered glass shook her from her daydream. She jumped from her bunk, peeked around the corner and down the hall to the kitchen. Her mom was on the floor, crying as she hovered over a broken box of dishes. The dishes had been her great-grandmother's. Carefully preserved for years, now they were broken into a hundred tiny pieces. Riff had intentionally dropped the box in a fit of rage because Maggie had put mustard on his bologna sandwich instead of mayonnaise. His fuse was short, and they never knew what might set him off. The sandwich, with one bite out of it, sat on the floor next to the box of broken dishes. As her dad towered over her mother, Maggie continued to sob in disbelief that her cherished heirlooms lay in pieces beneath her heartless husband's feet.

Anna slipped quietly down the hall and out the front door. She sat on the front porch swing admiring the large rose bushes that were in full bloom. The aroma was fragrant and stimulating to the senses. As she bent over to smell the rose petals, she got another glimpse of the certain trouble who was now pushing the lawnmower through the neighbor's grass.

He was still smoking his cigarette as he made a sharp turn in his jean shorts and bare feet. As he spun the mower around, he unexpectedly glanced her way, smiled, and offered a quick wave and a wink. The gesture was so sudden, so disarming, that Anna flinched, pricking her finger on a thorn.

Her breath caught, though she wasn't sure if it was from the sting of the rose bush or the magnetic charm of the man across the yard. She wondered for a moment if she was dreaming. She found herself awakening to feelings she'd only encountered in the pages of romance novels.

He looked her way again over the top of his bare sun-tanned shoulder as he made his way back down the row of grass. This could be trouble and Anna knew it. But this kind of trouble, albeit forewarned, was a welcome distraction from the turmoil and dysfunction that was her home. This kind of trouble couldn't be all that bad, could it?

CHAPTER 4

Anna learned his name while he was checking out at the grocery store. He wore one of those handmade, personalized western belts with the name carved out in the back. "Dwight" was etched clear as day in the leather. *Dwight*, she thought. She liked the sound of it.

The bell of the store's door signaled his departure as she navigated her shopping cart from the produce aisle to the register where he had just left. Her eyes followed him out the door.

"Such a flirt," the girl at the checkout stand remarked as Anna placed her eggs and bread on the counter. "If he didn't come in here so often to buy smokes, I might give into his little puppy dog eyes. But I'm a Baptist, and we don't drink, smoke, or dance, and I'm pretty sure he is good at all three. My daddy would skin me alive. That boy may be dreamy looking, but trust me, he's a nightmare in real life. Half-grown, still lives at home, and goes through women like they're going out of style. It's gonna take a real strong woman to turn that boy around."

Anna absorbed every word with a quiet smile. Dwight Sanderson certainly sounded like trouble, yet there was something irresistibly captivating about him, as if he cast a spell she couldn't shake. He carried a magnetic blend of charm and mischief—a rebellious allure that lured young girls in, much like unsuspecting mice drawn to a trap. Shaking off the thought, she grabbed her two bags of groceries and stepped out the door toward home.

As she walked home from the general store, she was about a quarter mile from home when she heard the familiar sounds of the deep rumbling pickup's exhaust pipes. She knew who it was, and she couldn't help but wonder if he would notice she was making her way back toward their shared neighborhood. The sound of the engine softened, and the brakes gave a slight squeak as the familiar red Chevy pickup rolled up next to her.

"Something tells me you and I are heading in the same direction. Would you like a lift, little lady?"

Anna looked a little unsure. Dwight flashed her an adorable smile, expecting, like most of the girls he gave his attention to, that she'd climb right in. "I won't bite; well, maybe just a nibble," he said, giving her a little wink for extra measure.

Anna looked down, then continued walking as Dwight slow-rolled his truck beside her. "Come on. I'm just kidding. Don't be silly. I'm heading right next to your house. How could I not offer the pretty girl next door a ride home?" His words were so persuasive and hard to resist. Despite her better judgment, Anna nodded and moved toward the door. Dwight reached across the seat to open the door and took the two grocery bags from her arms as Anna climbed in. For the first time in longer than she could remember, she felt a sense of freedom and release from the tensions of home.

It didn't take long to drive the quarter mile back to their neighborhood. Before she knew it, they were in his driveway, and he was helping her make her way to her front door with the groceries. As she opened the screen door, she turned and took the bags from his arms. He looked into her eyes, then trailed his finger across the open shoulder of her sundress.

"I've been hoping I could meet you. It was my pleasure to give you a lift, but nothing would make my day more than to know your name," Dwight whispered in her ear before she shrugged her shoulder and slipped away.

The spring on the screen door pulled the door tight between them. She looked up into his deep brown eyes, barely able to speak. "Anna, Anna is my name. Thank you for the ride."

Over the course of the next several weeks, rides to and from the grocery store became a routine part of their days. Before long they were taking the long way home, sharing soda pops, chocolate mints, and stolen kisses. Lately, he had started driving with one hand on the wheel and the other resting on her sun-kissed leg—a touch that sent a thrilling warmth up her thigh, awakening sensations she hadn't realized were possible.

Anna was falling and falling fast. On one particular drive, Dwight's hand moved up the inside of her thigh and briefly touched the outside of her panties. *Was that an accident or intentional?* Anna wondered. She grabbed his hand and moved it to a more suitable place near her knee as he flashed her one of his characteristic smiles. From that day forward, his subtle advances were met with less resistance as his charm slowly melted away her inhibitions.

One night, Anna lay awake in her bed, unable to sleep at the thought of Dwight's warm hands moving across her body. She pulled her covers over her head and let out a frustrated groan.

What is happening to me? she thought.

Suddenly, a slight scratching on her window screen brought her to her senses. Was it a nocturnal varmint prowling around in the flower garden? Or worse, was someone trying to break in and steal something? As she looked out from under her covers with one eye still hidden, she realized it was Dwight!

"Are you crazy?" Anna hissed in a whisper. "What are you doing? If you aren't careful, my daddy is going to shoot you!"

"Want to go swimming?" Dwight asked, a bright grin crossing his face in the moonlit night.

"Swimming? You really are crazy. It's three o'clock in the morning. Who goes swimming at this time of day?" Anna protested.

"Come on. Don't be a chicken. Look, I brought towels, a blanket, and a six-pack of beer," he said convincingly.

"But I don't even have a bathing suit," she countered.

"You won't need it," he said.

Before she knew it, they were running in the dark to his truck he'd parked down the street. In just a matter of minutes, she was on the banks of the South Canadian river, drinking her first beer by a campfire, and making out on a blanket with the boy next door by the light of the fading summer moon. Dwight twisted the top off two more beers, handed Anna one, and said, "Bottoms up," then drained his bottle in one drink. "Come on, girl, keep up," he teased, and Anna followed suit.

Suddenly, Dwight jumped up and ran toward the water, shucking his clothes as he entered the water's edge. He jumped in, smacked his naked butt, and whooped as he hit the water. "Jump in. The water feels great," he crooned.

"I can't," she pleaded. "I'm too embarrassed. You'll see my . . . boobs!" And as if to make her point, she covered her chest with both hands, laughing as she kicked off her shoes.

Dwight could tell the alcohol was starting to have its desired effect; he was no newcomer to this game. This wasn't the first girl he had brought to this part of the river. Nights like these were pretty common for him. He was used to getting what he wanted from women, and tonight would be no different.

"I'll look the other way! Don't be shy. I'll even close my eyes. Plus, it's just us and the moon. Come on! It'll be fun," he coaxed, his head just above the top of the moonlit river.

Anna unzipped her shorts and tugged her blouse up over her head. With a quick look over her shoulder to be sure his eyes were closed, she unsnapped her bra. Hesitating for only a moment, she slid her panties down her smooth legs, then crossed her arms over her chest. Barefoot and cautious, she tiptoed toward the murky river. Her mind urged her to stop, but the thrill pulling her forward refused to be silenced. Letting out a squeal, she leaped into the water, sinking low to shield herself beneath its surface.

Dwight swam over and held her close as the water rushed around their naked bodies. She was shaking from the cold, but his strong arms surrounded her, and the heat from his body brought warmth in more ways than one. He kissed her and held her in ways no one had ever done before. She didn't know whether it was the beer or the feeling of his hands on her that made her brain feel foggy.

He moved his hand down the small of her back and softly squeezed the curve of her bottom.

Anna gasped, then moaned. *What is happening?*

She could hardly breathe, her thoughts and her heart were racing. Dwight knew exactly how far to take her and when to pause. Taking her by the hand, he led her back to the riverbank. Their naked bodies met under the blanket as she felt the weight of his body on top of hers. He reached for a small square package in the pocket of pants that lay next to the campfire.

"I'll be gentle," he said, as he placed the condom over his fully erect penis. She was fascinated, scared, but also completely ready for what would come next.

"This must be what it's like to fall in love," she said under her breath as she felt the fullness of him between her legs. There was a sharp pain as he pushed himself into her. His movements were quick and anything but gentle, taking nothing into account but his own need.

It was over as soon as it began. Anna hadn't known what to expect, but she'd somehow expected more.

Well, this is it, she thought. *I guess I'm not a virgin anymore.* She had lost her innocence to a man who had spent the summer pursuing her and showering her with attention she hadn't even known she craved.

Dwight rolled off the top of her, and she reached to caress his back. Suddenly he cursed and stood up. "Shit! I can't believe this! It broke!"

"What broke?" she asked, quickly sensing the shift in his mood.

"The rubber, stupid!" This cheap rubber that I bought in the gas station bathroom, broke. Damn it! Get dressed."

Dwight didn't speak to Anna. He threw his stuff in the back of the truck, popped the top on the last beer, and peeled away from the lake. Anna knew from experience not to speak. She stayed as quiet and as small as she could make herself on the passenger's side of the truck. With no attempt to be quiet, Dwight pulled into his driveway, slammed his door, and didn't give Anna so much as a wave goodbye as he stormed into his house.

Choking back a sob, Anna climbed through her bedroom window, wincing as the sill scraped against her shin. She didn't bother changing out of her clothes. Instead, she collapsed onto her bed, letting the sob she'd been holding break free, accompanied by a flood of hot, fresh tears.

CHAPTER 5

Anna was late, but she tried not to worry. There was no point in jumping to conclusions. How likely was it to get pregnant the very first time? Summer had been a whirlwind of change, and with the stress of the new school year, it wasn't unusual for her to miss a period. Stress had done it before.

Then came the morning sickness. At first, she dismissed it as a stomach virus. But why did it only strike in the mornings? That didn't add up. It wasn't food poisoning either—surely the rest of the family would be sick too. Slowly, the truth began to sink in. She had only done it once, but once was all it took. The signs were clear: she was pregnant. And if the nausea wasn't bad enough, the thought of telling her parents churned her stomach even more. Sleepless nights, gnawing anxiety, and deep regret left her feeling completely overwhelmed.

"Honey, are you feeling okay?" Maggie asked as she stood in the small family bathroom with Anna. "You look like you are losing weight, you have rings under your eyes, and I heard you throwing up this morning. What's going on?"

Anna broke into tears. Maggie shut the door, and they both sank to the floor as Anna's legs gave way. She pushed her head into her mother's chest, unable to speak. Her breath was taken away. All she could do was sob uncontrollably.

"Baby what's wrong? Are you okay? Tell momma what's going on," Maggie encouraged as she pushed Anna's hair from her eyes.

"Mom..." Anna started, but found her words were stuck in her throat. "Mama, I think. I think I might be . . ." Maggie interrupted her daughter's next words. She placed her hand over Anna's mouth, then held her tight and began to weep in disbelief.

Surely this wasn't happening. She was too young. Just a child in so many ways. Who would do such a thing? One of the new boys at school? Had she been raped? Someone was going to be held accountable, but Maggie had no idea who that someone would be. "How?" was the only word Maggie could speak.

"Mom, I'm sorry!" Anna began to cry uncontrollably once again. She gasped for a breath and then explained how it all took place. She was ashamed and deathly afraid of what would happen when her dad found out.

"Dwight! Dwight Sanderson took advantage of you? That little spoiled bastard!" Maggie rarely cussed but she was fire hot now. "I am going to blow his balls off. You just wait until your dad finds out. All I can say is that boy better run for the hills. Riff will mop him up like spilled milk. He will likely be a eunuch before your daddy is done with him."

Mother and daughter held each other until they had both calmed down. "Let's not tell anyone about this until we know for sure," Maggie insisted. "I know a doctor in Minco that we can visit privately. He is used to this kind of thing. He can make it all go away, and no one will ever have to know. Clean yourself up, and I will see if I can get an appointment with him after his clinic closes on Friday. Until then, this will be our little secret. You hear me?"

Anna understood exactly what her mother was saying.

Friday came none too soon. They waited down the street from the doctor's office until the last patient left and the medical staff left the building for the weekend. Anna's mom pulled the car into the parking lot, and together they went inside. Once there, Anna was asked to sit in the lobby while Maggie and the doctor met privately in his office.

Eventually, they came out, and she was escorted into an exam room, where with little warning, she was asked to strip down naked in front of the doctor. "I'm sorry I don't have time for the niceties, and I don't have any nursing staff, so we'll just need to get through this." He handed her a sheet and asked her to get on the examining table. She scooted down to the end of the table and put her feet in the cold stirrups. This was only the second time in her post-pubescent life that Anna had been seen naked by a grown man. Quietly, she hoped this time would go as quickly as the first.

The doctor finished his exam and then removed his gloves. He looked first at Anna and then at Maggie. "I don't think she was raped," he said. "I think little Miss Anna might have been out to enjoy herself and got caught with her pants down. Let's run some tests, and I can get you the results by early next week. If she is pregnant, I'll need you to come back as soon as possible. The earlier we take care of this the better for everyone involved. Do we know who the dad is?"

Anna glowered at the doctor. "I'm not that kind of girl," she protested. "Of course I know who the dad is!" Then she turned to her mother. "And exactly what does he mean . . . 'take care of it?'" She waited for an answer as the doctor and her mother looked at each other.

"Now Anna . . ." her mom started.

"No," Anna yelled. "I know this isn't great, but no one is taking my baby from me. I will run away before that happens. You hear me? Both of you, listen to me. If I am pregnant, I'm having my baby."

Anna got off the exam table, got dressed, and walked outside the clinic. She sat on the curb and allowed the tears to slide down her face. "What in the world has become of my life?" she sobbed to herself. "Moving to Junction City has been the worst thing ever."

Maggie leaned out the door of the doctor's office and asked Anna to come back inside to run some tests. According to the doctor, 'if the rabbit died', she was pregnant. As her mom would later explain, in earlier times, they used a rabbit to test for whether or not a woman was pregnant. If the rabbit died, the woman was pregnant. Anna couldn't help but hope that the rabbit would live to see Easter.

Maggie paid the doctor with cash and thanked him for taking the time to see them so late in the evening. As they drove back home, Anna leaned her head on the inside of the car door and stared out the window. All they could do now was wait.

By the middle of the next week, Maggie made a trip back to the doctor's office to pick up a note in a sealed envelope that the doctor had left at the front counter. She returned to the car and with shaking hands, ripped the envelope open. She couldn't believe what she read. Anna was pregnant.

She laid her head on the steering wheel and cried until she had no more tears to cry. Now what? Maggie felt as though she had failed not only Anna, but all of her children. Why had she stayed in this marriage with Riff? On many occasions, she had thought of running away, but with four children and no real education or life skills, she'd felt it was better to put up with hell at home than to put everyone else at risk. So she'd stayed. But now she couldn't help but think this might not have happened to Anna if she had left Riff and never made the move to this godforsaken town.

When she got home, she told Anna the results. Anna took in the news and said, "Well, then that's that. Mom, I meant what I said, I'm keeping this baby, and no one is going to change my mind. Not you, not daddy, not the doctor, and when he finds out, not even Dwight." It was the first adult decision Anna had ever made, and the first time of many to come that she would have to protect the life of her child.

CHAPTER 6

Maggie sat on the front porch with Dwight and Riff. Anna was asked to stay inside. At this point, everyone was well aware of the predicament. Junction City was a small town. It wouldn't be long before Anna would be showing. The secret would no longer be a secret.

This wasn't the best situation for the new banker in town. He had hoped to minimize the shock as much as possible, because if things got too crazy, he might lose his job. Especially if people went digging and looked too far into Riff's past.

Since Anna refused other options, it was clear a baby would be showing up in the near future. Now the only question was whether or not that baby would be born to a mother out of wedlock

"I want to do the right thing," Dwight said. "I take responsibility for what happened. I'll get a full-time job, marry her, and take care of the kid." His presentation wasn't overly charming or convincing. There was no mention of true love or the desire to start a family. Riff and Dwight talked it over like it was a used car deal. Anna had nothing to say in the matter. It was settled. A date was set that would keep people from noticing that the baby came earlier than months would normally allow. Nonetheless, they would be married before the baby came and Riff would save face.

Anna was 15 on her wedding day. Dwight was 23. Eight years stood between them. There was a wedding cake, a minister, and family members present, but missing were smiles and the joy that normally accompanied such an event.

It wasn't a shotgun wedding, but it was close. A heavy sadness hung in the air as the once innocent, wide-eyed bride was stripped of her childhood and thrust unprepared into the unforgiving world of adulthood. She tried her best to hold it together, but she had already started getting an idea of what life would be like with Dwight. Worst of all, it looked all too familiar to the life she already knew. She had hoped to escape life at home and now found herself in a prison of her own, a child with a child and married to an immature, self-absorbed man who treated her in the same way her dad treated her mom.

One little vulnerable moment of curiosity had taken her down a one-way path with no way out. She was trapped in a life she hadn't imagined for herself with the responsibility of bringing a baby into the world.

Her new high school learned she was pregnant and kicked her out. They made it clear that her kind wasn't welcomed. Allowing girls like her to remain in school might encourage other girls to do the same. She was no longer welcome. The principal said Anna had literally made her bed and now she would have to sleep in it. No compassion. No counseling. Zero support.

Her future felt uncertain, shadowed by doubt and fear. With few options before her, she resolved to do her best to be a good mother and housewife. She would play her part, but would Dwight uphold his? What did he really mean that he would "do the right thing?" Was a wedding ring enough to seal a promise? What about honor, cherishing, and those solemn vows—"for better or for worse?" Did any of it hold meaning? She hoped so, but even Anna wasn't sure. And how could she apply those sacred words to a man who was beginning to resemble a monster far more than the partner of her dreams?

CHAPTER 7

S he didn't notice at first. It was subtle, but as her tummy grew and the stretch marks started to appear, she was already growing apart from the boyish man who had taken her innocence. She wanted to love him. It felt that way at first, but her resentment was building against him like a shadow at sunset, growing larger and darker with each passing moment.

He made it easy to hate him. He started coming home later and later each night with the smell of alcohol on his breath. The smell of the cigarettes and cheap perfume wasn't hard to miss as he crawled into bed next to her. He would pass out and just lay there with nothing on but his wife-beater undershirt.

One night Anna had to make her way outside to their gravel driveway to turn off the car and switch off the headlights. He had been too drunk to even remember the basics of driving. Dwight hated that car as much as he seemed to hate coming home. They had to sell the truck to make a deposit on their rent. It wasn't practical anyway. They were a family now and families drove family cars, not souped-up, hot rod pickups.

As she came back to bed, the pungent smell of an ashtray reminded her of what her life had become. As she bent to pick up his shirt off the floor, there it was, more evidence that she may not be the only woman in Dwight's life. Anna knew the kind of women that lounged around at pool halls and backroad shanties. They didn't frequent these establishments in pursuit of entertainment. No, they were there on business.

The thought of what Dwight might be doing all those late nights away from home left Anna unable to go back to sleep. As she lay there rubbing her belly, she wondered whether the little one who grew inside her was a little boy or a little girl.

As the first light of day, Anna got up like she did every morning and made Dwight black coffee with no sugar and a touch of cream. Getting it wrong would result in a tirade of belittlements that reminded Anna how worthless Dwight thought she was.

The eggs had to be over easy and the whites a little runny. The bacon, if not cooked just crispy enough, would be thrown, often at her, often with a reminder that she was so stupid she couldn't even cook bacon. He belittled her, reducing her to a child in his eyes—until his desires flared, and she became nothing more than a vessel for his release. To him, she was little more than an object: his sexual outlet, the mother of his soon-to-be child, and his unpaid maid.

What had she gotten herself into? No girl dreams of a life like this. It was worse than the childhood she had endured.

Who was she kidding? This was still her childhood. She was a baby with a baby. So young. So naive. She hated herself. She was embarrassed, ashamed, and on many days, she felt like dying. Maybe that would be best. End it all now rather than live a life as a domestic slave to a cruel taskmaster. She could swallow a bunch of pills, fire a bullet into her skull, or jump off a river bridge. But then she remembered that would mean taking more than one life at this point. And as she'd promised that day at the doctor's office, no one was going to take her baby's life, including her.

The sound of Dwight puking, as he ran to the toilet, rattled her from her daydream. He hugged the porcelain and blew chunks of pork rinds, peanut hulls, and pickled eggs out of his mouth and through his nose. The veins in his throat bulged, and his eyes bugged out so far she thought they would pop from his skull.

He turned and looked at her with sick, red eyes. "Get the hell out, bitch. Can't you see I'm puking my guts up," he barked before doubling over to empty his stomach of the remainder of his night's indulgences.

She pulled the door closed and left him to his misery. It felt unkind, but she actually liked seeing him suffer in this way. It served him right. If only his suffering would make him change his ways.

She had heard that only Jesus could turn a life like his around. One thing was for sure, it wasn't going to happen anytime soon with Dwight. He was on his knees begging for mercy at an altar, but it wasn't at church. Driving the porcelain bus was as good as it would get for now.

The eggs had burned by the time she made it back to the kitchen. She thought about throwing them in the trash at first, but she feared he would find them and make her eat them anyway as a punishment for her stupidity. Besides, they *were* edible. Other than tasting like charcoal, they'd serve their purpose.

Money was tight so she wouldn't let them go to waste. She started to remake his breakfast, deciding she'd eat the burnt eggs when he left for work. "I wonder if the baby likes burnt eggs?" she mused quietly to herself. "Probably not," she reflected, patting the top of her belly. "Oh well. We're about to find out, aren't we?"

At that moment, Dwight exited the bathroom, wiping his mouth across the back of his hand. He threw on some clothes, slammed the screen door on his way out of the house, and spun out of the driveway. He was late for work and didn't have time for his morning routine.

Most people would have cried. Anna just smiled, poured herself a cup of coffee, scraped the burnt eggs into the wastebasket, and sat down to the nice country breakfast he had left behind. It felt freeing to have this tiny piece of control in her life. He was gone for now, the house quiet and for the moment, peaceful.

When she was finished, she made her way back to the bedroom to get ready for the day. When she turned the corner down the hallway, she felt a squishy mess squirt between her toes. "Oh my God! He just left it here for me to clean up!" she screamed with disgust. "What an ass! Ughhhhh! I hate him!" She started to cry as the reality of her life as a newlywed was laid out before her, and it wouldn't be long before she'd bring a baby into this harsh reality.

* * *

"Dwight, the baby . . . it's time," Anna said. It was all she could do to wake Dwight up from his deep sleep. Luckily, he'd decided to come home that night instead of spending the night out carousing. He sat bolt upright, then threw on some clothes, grabbed his keys, and made his way to the front door. As he opened the door, he was greeted by an icy blast of cold, which only added to his building frustration. "Damn it to hell," he swore.

Anna made her way slowly to the front door and peered out the small window that revealed a world covered in ice. It rarely snowed in Oklahoma, but ice storms were commonplace. When they hit, they hit hard and left everything covered in inches of thick frozen sheets of ice.

To her dismay, Anna could see the porch had not been spared. Navigating her way down the slippery steps would be dangerous, especially in her condition. It was dark and deathly quiet outside. Nothing was moving. She wondered if they would be able to make it to the hospital in time, if at all.

Dwight lit a cigarette and waddled like a baby fawn finding its legs after its introduction to the world. He slipped, fell, stood up, and fell again. Curse words filled the air as he maintained the status of his smoke. He eventually found footing and pried open the driver's side door of the car. The car was slow to turn over. The headlights dimmed under the strain of the freezing temperatures. It was slow coming, but the engine eventually turned over and fired up.

She could see his figure through the frozen windshield. The cigarette provided an extra glow each time he took a deep drag as he blew smoke out a crack in the driver's side window. After about 20 minutes he emerged, shivering in the cold as he attempted to scrape near melting ice from the windshield. Typical to form, he was half prepared for the job. His shirttail hung outside his pants as he worked to open a portal large enough for him to see through the windshield and down the road.

Ice from the scraper fell into his shoes. The absence of socks made for an even chillier experience. Even from her distance, she could see his anger was simmering in the way he flicked the remains of his cigarette into the frosty air.

Anna buttoned her coat and took a firm hold of the small suitcase she had prepared for this very moment. It was happening. If they made it to the hospital safely, she would be holding her baby in a matter of hours.

"What are you waiting on?" Dwight barked. "Get your ass in the car before I freeze to death. This is going to be a bitch, especially with these damned bald tires."

Anna did not speak a word. There was no point. She made her way to the car unassisted. She nearly wiped out more than once as he stood with the driver's side door open and looked at her with disgust. So much for being a gentleman. She tugged at the passenger door and slowly turned and found her seat.

The contractions had started while she was waiting for him to warm up the car. The pain was awful, but she did not dare let on for fear of making Dwight more upset. She needed him focused and stress-free as the car fishtailed onto the highway.

The hospital was just 12 miles away in El Reno, but at their current rate of speed, and assuming they didn't get stuck or end up in a ditch, they should be there in just over an hour, two at the most.

The labor pains began to increase. She started the breathing exercises she had learned from a pamphlet she picked up at the doctor's office.

"What are you doing? Cut that crap out! You are fogging up the windows," Dwight enforced. "You sound like a bitch in heat. You're halfway making me horny."

She laid her head back in her seat and tried to stay calm. She felt an incredible amount of pain and pressure between her legs. It was all she could do not to scream at the top of her lungs. She was growing faint as the inside of the car began to spin before her eyes.

"Oh my God! I think the baby is coming! We have to pull over. I can't stop it. Dwight pull the car over!" she cried out in a panic. "You have to do something."

"Come on, Anna! I'm not a doctor for God's sake. What the hell am I supposed to do?" Dwight protested as he sped up the car. "Just hang on. Cross your legs or something. You act like you're the first damn woman to have a baby or something!"

She was in agony. She did her best to hold back the inevitable. If something didn't happen soon, she would be dropping this baby on the floorboard of the old car.

Delirious from the pain, she traveled back to a few weeks earlier when she sat in the back of the same car with her full-term belly tight under her dress. She recalled that Dwight had made her sit in the backseat after he saw what must have been one of his late-night lady friends, walking down the street.

In her memory, he pulled over and offered the lady a lift. That is when Anna was booted to the back seat and his "friend" jumped in, winked at Anna, smacked her gum, and snuggled right up next to Dwight in the front seat.

Anna couldn't tell for sure, but it appeared the hitchhiker put her hand down the front of Dwight's pants. The car swerved and the new giggly passenger said, "Easy tiger. Not so fast. Don't make this harder than it needs to be," and at that, they both laughed.

Anna looked out the window as Dwight pulled into their driveway, insisted she get out, and stated he would be back later. As she stepped out of the car, she stood alone in the driveway, abandoned and isolated, while her husband and another woman were undoubtedly on their way to the tavern to do what only God—and everyone else in town except Anna— already knew.

The flashback ended when the passenger door swung open, and an icy blast of air snapped her back to reality. Anna nearly fell out onto the pavement as Dwight jerked her from the car right as the next contraction hit.

Blood was running down the inside of her leg. She reached down, and much to her amazement, she felt what had to be a small hand or maybe a foot? Her own foot slipped on the icy pavement, and she collapsed, hitting her head on the armrest of the car door. She was out and would have no memory of what happened next until she awoke several hours later to the sound of a baby crying.

As her eyes slowly opened, she looked over at a small little crib with a precious baby wrapped in a receiving blanket. She had made it! The baby had made it. It was a miracle and the furthest thing from a mistake. Her baby was born, and life was good.

The nurse offered her ice chips and shared the news, "You gave us a real scare this morning. You are one tough lady. We nearly lost you and the baby. You were really fortunate the doctor was already at the hospital for another delivery. Otherwise, I'm not sure what we would have done."

Anna tried to speak. "What, what ..." The emergency delivery had drained her of all her strength. She finally pushed out the words. "Is it a boy or a girl?"

The nurse reached for the baby, laid it next to its momma as it began to immediately search for her breast. "It's a baby boy," the nurse whispered. "He is a big boy too. He weighed close to 10 pounds! You should be proud. He is beautiful."

Anna began to cry. This moment made it all worth it. She was growing up fast. Life was coming at her hard. She had been so naïve, but that naivety was fading as the reality of being a mother was settling into the fiber of her being.

Her husband may have been a self-centered jerk, but she wasn't going to raise her baby boy that way. She was going to raise a leader. A man that respected women, cared for his family, and made a difference in the world.

She realized it wasn't where you started in life that mattered most but where you ended up. So much as it depended on her, this child was going to rise above this hell hole and be something respectable someday.

She pulled back the receiving blanket and looked him over head to toe. She might be a bit biased, but he really was beautiful, and he was hers.

CHAPTER 8

For a while, things were better. Dwight was proud of his son. It was all he talked about. He seemed different. He drank less, came home at dinner time, and even helped around the house. He even changed a diaper or two when things were in a pinch.

"Look at that boy. Hung like a mule. Just like his daddy," Dwight would proudly announce to anyone who might be within earshot of a diaper change. Most of his jokes were poorly timed and off-color. But Anna had to admit this particular one did make her laugh.

The months passed, and her sweet boy eventually stopped breastfeeding, started eating table food, and even tried taking a few steps. Most of the days were sweet, a fact Anna held tightly in her heart. Dwight still had bad days, still came home late, still had one too many drinks down at the tavern, but for the most part, he was a good daddy.

One day, Uncle Lyle Sanderson, whom Dwight affectionately called Uncle Corp. stopped by to check on his namesake. "How's my big guy doing?" he asked. "Your mama feeding you okay?"

They all laughed at that because there was no doubt in anyone's mind, that boy was well-fed.

Uncle Corp was a veteran of World War II. He had enlisted and made it all the way to corporal before he received a Purple Heart. He had cleared a fox hole just before a grenade went off. He looked back to make sure everyone was out, and the explosion blew shrapnel into his face. He nearly lost an eye over his heroics. The injured eye was cloudy and had a murky look to it, which left him able to see out of only his good eye. The additional scars to his face made him a bit hard to look at, but when people learned how he had got in such bad shape, they tended to pay no attention to his disfigured face and took more interest in the man than his injuries.

Dwight was close to Uncle Corp. Somehow the two connected in a deeper way than most could with Dwight. It came as no surprise that Dwight wanted to name his son after his beloved uncle.

"Corp Sanderson, II," Dwight joked at the hospital. "I'm kidding, I'm kidding. His name won't be Corp. I do want to name him Lyle Sanderson, II, though. What a great way to honor Uncle Corp."

Anna wasn't sure if she liked the name Lyle any better than Corp. She liked Uncle Corp as a person well enough, but the name Lyle just didn't sit well with her.

"Come on Anna," Dwight coaxed. "Uncle Corp said he would pay us $1,000 to name him after him. Besides, I would have done it anyway."

Surprisingly, Dwight didn't insist on the name Lyle, and when Anna offered an alternative, he gave little fight.

"How about Kyle Sanderson? I know it's not exact, but it's close," Anna offered with a smile. "What do you think?"

Dwight gave in, and it was settled. Kyle Sanderson, her beautiful baby boy had a name. Dwight was happy enough and Uncle Corp liked it to the point of promising another $500 after the boy's first birthday.

Kyle's birthday came and went, but with Uncle Corp rarely in town, no one expected his promise to be kept on time. But always a man of his word, Uncle Corp came to town to celebrate his namesake. He and Dwight shared a beer, smoked a cigar, and wrestled with Kyle on the floor. It was cute in a lot of ways. Seeing an old war hero and a young daddy play with a chubby-legged boy brought rare laughter to the otherwise intense setting.

As Uncle Corp left, he kissed Anna on the cheek, rubbed Kyle's curly hair, and looked Dwight straight in the eyes and gave him a direct command. "Dwight, you better take care of this boy and his momma, or I'm gonna come back here and stick a size 10 combat boot straight up your ass. You hear me?"

Dwight just laughed.

"I'm dead serious. You better get your stuff together, or she will up and leave you someday. Can't say I could blame her based on what I'm hearing around town."

Dwight looked at the ground. Uncle Corp's opinion of him mattered.

"I love you, and I'm proud of you two for doing the right thing. But Dwight, you have to do better. My suggestion would be to get out of this podunk town and start a new life away from everything that is holding you back."

Now Dwight looked him in the eye.

"One last thing. This money is for Kyle. Keep your damn hands off of it. Use it toward his schooling. You hear me?"

Dwight agreed.

And with that, Uncle Corp was gone. They didn't see him again for years. When he did show back up he always left a little cash behind for his namesake. For Anna, he always gave her hope that someone might just be able to get through to Dwight.

Dwight took Uncle Corp's advice and within a few months, they were packed up and heading to the big city. Dwight had gotten a good-paying job at a trucking company.

As it turned out, his days on the farm paid off because he knew how to handle heavy equipment. Starting out, he worked the graveyard shift on the dock driving a forklift. The hours were odd but perfect for keeping a working man out of a beer joint.

Anna never looked in the rear-view mirror as they left Junction City. So much had happened there. None of it good, except the baby. There was no denying that Kyle had brought joy into their lives, and as she touched her belly, she hoped the baby tucked away there would only add to that joy.

With another baby on the way, a new job, and a beautiful yellow house waiting for them in the new city, maybe, just maybe, things would start to settle down in Yukon.

CHAPTER 9

Timmy was born a few months after they moved into the yellow house. He suffered from colic and cried a lot but other than that, Anna's life was taking shape. She felt a sense of purpose and was becoming a great wife and mom.

No one questioned her age anymore. She looked older, acted older, and had two kids. No one ever suspected that she was still a teenager. Most of all, Dwight didn't seem ashamed of her age anymore. Nobody knew their story, and they liked it that way. Some things were just better left unsaid.

Dwight was doing well at work. He was moved to the daytime shift and his hours allowed him to come home for dinner.

There was only one problem, the drive home included passing by the local tavern. Soon enough, it became too much of temptation for Dwight to resist. Even if he had one too many, he could still find his way home, sleep it off, push through his hangover, and put in a full day's work on the dock.

It was hot during the summer and cold in the winter, but it was steady work, came with benefits, and provided a good income for a young working-class family.

Every morning Anna meticulously packed Dwight a lunch. He liked it simple. White bread, a thick slice of bologna, one garden fresh tomato with mayonnaise thinly spread on both pieces of bread. If she applied too much mayonnaise there would be hell to pay. Add in a small bag of Lays potato chips and a Twinkie, and Dwight was kept satisfied.

Dwight came home either tired or drunk. His normal routine included flopping down in his easy chair and throwing back a few beers as Anna put the final touches on a full course evening meal. He wanted it hot and on time. Not too hot. Not too cold. Plated and served fresh once the bottom of the last beer passed his tongue.

The smell of his dad's work filled Kyle's nostrils as he sat quietly beside the easy chair waiting for instruction. It was an unmistakable scent. A sort of blend between sweat, dirt, motor oil, and body odor. The bibbed overalls were patched and worn thin. They gave a clear indication that a hard day's work had been at hand.

Upon command, Kyle unlaced his daddy's tan leather work boots. The yellow laces were long and double wrapped around the tops of the boots for security. Sometimes the double knots proved to be a struggle but more often than not, the daily duty was fulfilled unassisted.

Dwight wanted his boots pulled off a certain way. Kyle knew not to just randomly tug on the work boots. The heel-toe technique was essential if success was to be properly achieved without complaint.

Next on Kyle's list of duties was to turn on the television and dial in the evening news. Sometimes the rabbit ear antennas had to be fiddled with to keep the static off the TV screen.

If there was a need for a channel change, Dwight only needed to announce his desires, and Kyle would promptly jump to his feet and turn the knob to the appropriate program.

As Dwight polished off a couple of beers, and Anna put the final touches on dinner, Kyle peeked inside his dad's gray plastic lunch box with the black handle. If he was lucky, the remains of a left-over Twinkie would still be nestled in the bottom of its plastic wrapper. Kyle would finish it off and then lick the thin cardboard insert clean of any additional cream filling that remained. It was one of his favorite things to do, and it felt like a small reward for all the help he had provided for the king of their little kingdom.

The yellow house was a 900 square-foot mansion complete with two bedrooms, one bathroom, with only a tub and no shower, a small kitchen, living room, and dining room. The one-car garage served as a playground when temperatures dropped outside. One winter, Dwight set up a swing set in the garage. It was cramped and difficult to navigate, but it was fun and provided a sense of adventure.

The wood-framed house was heated by natural gas. A large metal grill cover blew heat from the floor. On cold mornings, standing over the opening blew heat directly up Kyle's housecoat. The heat from the furnace was intense. One missed step and a person could gain serious burns and permanent scars in the shape of a waffle iron.

A wall-mounted, porcelain brick, gas heater kept the bathroom warm. Bend over too far and a butt burn would be added to match your waffle grill floor furnace scars.

For sure the heat was a bit primitive, but it sure beat loading a potbelly stove with firewood. Maybe someday they would have central heating and air conditioning like folks who lived further from the railroad tracks. For now, the clean-burning, gas-driven pilot lights would have to do the trick.

"What the hell is taking so long? Are you trying to starve me to death?" Dwight yelled at Anna as he leaned forward out of his easy chair.

Kyle jumped up and ran to the kitchen to check on his momma.

"Damn it woman, let's eat! Fix my plate. I'll be there after I take a piss, and my plate better be on the table!" Dwight growled as he walked to the back of the house.

The table was perfectly set. Glass dishes, napkins, fresh lemonade, and a single daisy adorned the table. Fried chicken, mashed potatoes, corn on the cob, black-eyed peas, and homemade yeast rolls awaited the presence of the man of the house. A lemon pie was cooling on the counter as dessert was always a necessity.

Dwight came down the hallway and entered the kitchen with a loud belch. He'd shucked his overalls and dirty shirt and sat down dressed in nothing more than his tighty-whities. No one said a word as he immediately began to shovel in food fit for a king.

Kyle climbed up in his chair as dinner was served. Anna picked Timmy up and sat him on the phonebook she'd placed in his chair so he could reach the table. He was small for a kinder-gartner, but he loved being a "big boy" and sitting at the table.

Dwight rolled his eyes as she placed Timmy in his chair. He took a bite of the mashed potatoes and then immediately roared, "What in the hell is this? These potatoes are cold!"

Anna attempted to cajole him. "Dwight, honey, I just put them on the table. They can't be cold."

Without warning, Dwight took the back of his hand and cleared the table of all the food and dishes. "Don't you talk back to me! I'll beat your ass right here and now. You understand me?" Dwight yelled. He stood up, towering over Anna with a strong grip on her head of hair. He pulled her head back and blew the remains of his mashed potatoes in her face.

"There is too much salt in this mush. It tastes like dog crap. I'm going to get a beef on rye sandwich at the bar. This better be cleaned up by the time I get home or there will be hell to pay. You hear me?" Dwight's message came through loud and clear, and it wouldn't be the last time he would storm out of the house in a fit of rage.

Kyle wiped spattered food from his face and jumped down to comfort his momma. Her mascara ran down her cheeks as she tried to hide her pain from her boys with a dishtowel.

"It's okay momma. He's gone for now. The chicken is really good, and the potatoes are yummy. It's even better than Grandma's cooking. You are a good cook momma. I think daddy is just having a bad day," Kyle said as he did his best to console his mother's aching heart.

This time was better than most. Many times, Anna would get into a full knock-down-drag-out with Dwight. Her eyes would be black for days. Her arms and back would be lined with bruises from his closed fist body punches. She didn't dare leave the house for fear of those in the outside world becoming aware of the hell she lived at home.

Together, Anna and Kyle scooped food off of the floor, mopped down the kitchen, and shared a piece of lemon pie with a cold glass of milk.

She settled the boys into their beds and read them a story, then turned out the lights and waited for Dwight to come home. For now, there was peace.

CHAPTER 10

The quiet of the night was awakened to the sound of breaking glass. Apparently, Dwight lost his keys in the middle of a bar fight, and the violence spilled over into life at home as he burst through the door. He never went looking for a scuffle, but he certainly wasn't going to walk away from a snide remark or back down from some asshole know-it-all.

He wasn't quite 5' 8" and weighed all of 120 pounds, but he never let his size get in the way of a good fistfight. He believed in the motto, "The taller they are the harder they fall." He might not always win the fight, but he left no doubt with his opponent that they had grabbed a tiger by the tail.

On this particular night, he got locked up with a hot-headed Irishman who lived up to his reputation. The two exchanged a few words around the pool table, and it wasn't too long before they were exchanging blow for blow in the parking lot of the tavern.

After about 15 minutes of scrapping, they finally wore down and ended up wrapped up in an all-out wrestling match for dominance. Dwight eventually got the upper hand and left the freckle-faced bar mate face down in a major hurt until he eventually cried, "Uncle!"

Dwight's shirt was ripped, and his body was covered in road rash from wallowing in a parking lot of dirt and gravel. Somewhere in the fight, his car keys went flying into the dark of the night. Left with few options, he dusted himself off and headed back to the house on foot.

As he stumbled up the steps of the front porch, he didn't even bother to knock or check to see if the door was unlocked. In his drunken stupor, the thing that made the most sense to him was to simply shatter the front window and unlatch the door handle from the inside.

He failed to switch on the overhead lights as he entered and ended up crashing through the living room stumbling over rugs, a toy tractor, and a magazine rack. He eventually landed headfirst into a China cabinet, shaking what few dishes they had left behind the glass doors.

By this time, Anna had rushed to the sound and flipped on the lamp that sat next to the divan.

"What in the world, Dwight! Are you okay?" she exclaimed as she noticed blood running down his arm, caused by a cut he had incurred while breaking the windowpane.

"I'm fine. I'm fine. I kicked that little Irishman's ass right up around his neck. He was squealing like a pig once I got him on the ground," Dwight proudly provided color commentary to his ringside activities.

"Make me some breakfast. I'm gonna get cleaned up and get a few hours of sleep before I have to drag my ass to the truck dock."

"I'm sorry, but we are out of eggs. I planned on getting some at the grocery store in the morning," Anna explained. "I can make you some bacon and toast. Is that all right?"

Dwight spun around and backhanded Anna in the face, then pushed her down, and kicked her in the side.

Seeing he had already removed his pants, and knowing full what was coming next, Anna reached up and grabbed Dwight where she knew she would inflict the most pain. She scratched his legs and bit his calf muscle.

Dwight screamed out in pain and began beating Anna like he had beaten the Irishman earlier at the bar.

Blood poured from her nose as it lay at an awkward angle on her face.

The kids stood in the hallway in terror as all hell broke loose in the living room. Their little bodies shook in fear as they held each other. They'd seen their daddy like this before, but it had never been this bad.

Anna screamed for the boys to run. Seeing the front door of the yellow house standing wide open, Kyle picked up his little brother and bolted out the front door, his little bare feet walking across the broken glass. Anna followed in her bloodied nightgown.

In less than a minute, they made their way safely to the front porch of Mr. and Mrs. Brown. Anna pounded on the front door hoping and praying they would answer and let them in before Dwight caught up with them and dragged them back home for round two of the beating.

The door swung open, and Mrs. Brown welcomed the terrified children and battered wife into the comfort of her home.

Anna looked over her shoulder and as lightning flashed, she saw Dwight standing in the middle of the street in disbelief. What did he expect? Did he really believe that Anna and the kids would simply sit idle as he destroyed their lives?

The realization that he was losing control over her fueled the inferno of rage consuming his twisted mind. Seething with rage, he turned and staggered back to the house, his wild-eyed rampage spent as darkness swallowed him in his drunken stupor.

CHAPTER 11

O nce inside, Mrs. Brown asked very few questions. She made a pallet for the boys and put together a make-shift bed for Anna on the couch, then tended to Anna's wounds. The Brown's house smelled amazing, the byproduct of her candle-making business, which added a warmth to her home. There was no place like it on earth. It was truly a safe house. A sheltering haven for the traumatized.

Eventually, Mr. Brown appeared. "Well, looky there," he said as he made efforts to catch his breath. "If it isn't those good-looking boys and their pretty mother from across the street." The boys both looked down at Mr. Brown who wasn't wearing his prosthetic leg. Their eyes widened.

Mr. Brown didn't offer up an explanation. He just continued, "You guys make yourselves right at home. Mrs. Brown will be making us a big breakfast in the morning. And when she is done, I'll show you my rock collection." And with that, he turned and made his way back to bed. He, nor Mrs. Brown, pointed out the obvious. Who needed to? Clearly, this little family was in crisis, and they had come to the right place.

The next morning the smell of fried bacon took the place of scented candles. Kyle found a seat next to his momma at the table. He noticed that her face was bruised and swollen. He didn't realize it, but her nose would require medical attention.

Anna took a sip of coffee and then bowed her head as Mr. Brown asked everyone to hold hands as he said, what he called, grace. It was a simple prayer and one of the first prayers Kyle ever recalled hearing. Over the years, Mr. Brown would become a special kind of friend. Not exactly a father figure, but more of a grandfatherly, mentoring figure who always made Kyle feel special and loved.

After breakfast, Anna looked out the front window waiting to see if Dwight had left for work. She had nearly forgotten that he had lost his car keys. She saw him exit the house with the extra set of keys in his hands as he walked toward the tavern where his car had been parked overnight.

They would be safe for a while. He would likely come home sober and sorry for what had taken place the night before. Things would be better for a few days, but everybody knew they would eventually be walking on eggshells again, and Dwight would be taking out his frustrations on his favorite punching bag. It was a cycle they had lived through for years.

The weight of it all was starting to take its toll on Anna. But what could she do? She didn't even have a high school diploma, let alone skills outside of being a cook, maid, and eye-candy for Dwight to parade around town when she wasn't covered in bruises.

The thought of getting her G.E.D entered her mind. Passing a general educational development test might be just the ticket she needed to provide her with the options she would need to secure her independence. She had noticed a flyer at the grocery store that advertised night classes that could help students pass the G.E.D. test. If she could pass the test, she could possibly qualify for a certificate in cosmetology at the local vocational-technical school.

It was the closest she'd ever come to actually making a plan for her and her sons' freedom.

CHAPTER 12

Weeks had passed since that night at the Browns. The knock at the door startled Anna out of daydream. At first, she thought it might have been a police officer or a state trooper. You never knew given how often Dwight would drink and drive. But the knock at the door couldn't have brought more of a surprise. As Anna opened the front door, a tall, handsome man in a uniform stood with hat in hand waiting to be greeted.

It turned out to be the last person she had ever expected to see standing on her porch. It was Booger Man himself! What was Nathan doing here? He looked amazingly fit and nothing like the chubby brother she grew up with.

She swung open the door and found herself surrounded by his strong arms in a warm embrace.

"What are you doing here!" Anna exclaimed as she squeezed her brother with all her might. "You look amazing! The military has treated you right! You have turned into a real man!"

Nathan smiled as he was welcomed into the house. Timmy and Kyle were at school, so it was just the two of them alone catching up on all that had happened in the last several years.

"Anna you look as beautiful as ever. You have beaten the odds. You are proving everybody wrong. You have a house, kids, and you and Dwight are making it work. I'm really proud of you," Nathan said as he placed his military hat on the coffee table.

"I do have one question, though, and I need you to be honest with me." Nathan's voice became serious as he placed his massive hand on his sister's knee. "What's actually going on here?"

Anna had hoped he wouldn't notice, but Nathan had always been intuitive. Maybe it was because he was her big brother or maybe it was because he'd grown up with Riff too, but either way, nothing seemed to escape him.

The medical tape that supported her broken nose had been removed a few days earlier, but she still had dark rings under her eyes and a small but noticeable abrasion across the bridge of her nose where Dwight had hit her.

"What do you mean?" Anna asked as she tried to downplay his concern.

"Come on, Sis. The boarded up front door, the empty China cabinet, the dark circles under your eyes, the cut on your nose? Cut the bull. He's pushing you around, isn't he?" Nathan asked, though he already knew the answer.

Tears began to pool at the bottoms of Anna's eyes. Nathan wasn't stupid. It wasn't hard to pick up on the signs of domestic abuse, especially when the one getting body slammed was your sister.

"You don't have to live like this. You have to think of your own safety and the kids. It's only going to get worse. You know this. Dwight has been off the rails for years." Nathan's words were tender but true.

Anna knew he was right. But she was the one with little to no options, not him. Talk was cheap. Change would require courage and most of all, money.

"Look, you can leave here today. Right now. You and the boys can load up and come live with me on the military base. He can't get to you there, and before long you will be a faded memory in his alcohol-soaked mind," Nathan stated, making it sound easier and more tempting than he might realize.

"Then what?" Anna countered, hiding her interest. "Am I going to live with you forever and get a job at the commissary as a cashier? My schedule is already filled with their activities. I won't be able to hold down a job and take care of their needs all at the same time."

"If you aren't careful you are going to raise them to be just like him. Self-centered and crazy as hell." Nathan's words cut to the quick. He was right, and they both knew it.

"There is another option," Anna said.

"What? Kill the bastard and pack him in the trunk of my car?" Nathan questioned in earnest. "Don't think I haven't thought about that a hundred times since I heard he got you pregnant. I'd do it now if I could get away with it."

"Good heavens, Nathan. You can't be serious," she said.

"Look at me. If it meant saving you and the boys, I'm all in. Just say the word, and I'll put him out of his misery," Nathan said without so much as a blink.

"Don't think I haven't thought about doing it myself. There are times he lays there in bed drunk as a skunk and snoring like a freight train. It's all I can do to keep from smothering him by putting a pillow over his face or just cutting his scrawny neck," Anna confessed.

"Then think of Kyle and Timmy. What would that be like for them growing up without either of their parents? One dead and the other on death row?"

"What if I got my G.E.D. and then became a beautician. Hairdressers do pretty well for themselves. I could make enough to support us without Dwight," Anna said as she explained the strategy. She knew in her mind she had to find a way to make it happen.

"Are you serious? You would do that?" Nathan asked.

"Yes," Anna affirmed. "It's just a matter of getting the money together to do it."

"Then do it, and have them send me the bill," Nathan stated. "You've got what it takes. If you can live with an asshole and get your ass beat for half a decade, getting your G.E.D. and a cosmetology license will be a cakewalk."

Nathan picked up his hat and made his way to the door. He loved his sister and hated the mess she was in. He wasn't there to cause a divorce, but the way Anna was talking, he might just be preventing a murder. Anna waved at Nathan as he drove away, laughing as he honked and waved back. She was finding a lot of things hard to believe of late. Booger Man had turned out to be more than a brother. He was a Bonafide superhero in her books.

CHAPTER 13

Anna was concerned about how Dwight might react to the idea of her getting her G.E.D. and cosmetology license. Surprisingly, he was very supportive. She managed to attend night classes and passed her G.E.D. with flying colors.

Once they were back in school, for at least a half a day, she started the cosmetology classes. She eventually graduated at the top of her beauty school. Anna was proud when her instructor announced her accomplishments to an audience full of fellow students and guests.

Dwight stood at the back of the auditorium with the boys at his side. He smiled at her and winked. It was a rare moment when she felt he might actually love her.

Because of her success in school, she was soon offered a job at a popular local hair salon. She wasn't able to work full-time, but they gladly offered her a stylist's booth on a part-time basis. She worked mornings and was able to be home in the early afternoon to be with the boys. Anna loved her job. Her clients loved her, and her schedule was soon full of ladies seeking haircuts, shampoos, and sets.

One morning, an elderly lady came into the salon as a walk-in customer. She looked a bit disheveled, unkempt, and smelled like she could use a warm bath. Anna gently reclined the lady at the shampoo bowl. Her hair looked more like a helmet than a hairdo. She applied water to the area but failed to penetrate the layers and layers of matted hair. Anna rubbed shampoo across the surface of the iron-clad shell.

Nothing worked. Clearly, the woman had been applying and reapplying hairspray for weeks if not months. Anna raised the woman's legs on the shampoo chair and asked if she would like to relax for a few minutes while Anna checked on her appointment book for another customer. The plan worked. After about 15 minutes, Anna returned to the sound of a woman fast asleep and snoring, her mouth drooped open and drool sliding from the corner of her mouth.

Anna giggled to herself and left the woman for another 30 minutes until the sound of the telephone ringing woke the hair-helmet lady from her nap.

"Oh, my goodness. I fell asleep," she said. "I hope I didn't keep you."

"It happens all the time. There is nothing like a shampoo and a head massage to put a person to sleep," Anna explained.

In this case, at least up until this point, there had been no shampoo or a head massage, but soaking the area had worked and the powerful sprayer attachment was able to break things loose. As Anna began to rub in hair products, she felt a lump in the front of the woman's hairline. Was it a mole or a tumor of some sort?

She leaned over the sink and pulled the hairs of the woman's head apart very carefully. Slowly and with absolute intrigue, she made it to the source of her inquiry. Surely not. Was she believing her eyes? It wasn't a mole or tumor, it was a....

The telephone rang again. Anna had been left in the salon alone while other operators ran next door to get a sandwich on their much-needed lunch break. The telephone was the salon's lifeline to the outside world, and everyone knew to miss a call could mean missing a valuable customer.

She answered the phone and the voice on the line was clearly not a customer, but it was someone she recognized.

"Hi, Sis! I have just a minute before our unit pulls out for deployment. I was thinking about you and hoped you would be the one to answer. Lucky for me you did!"

The sound of Nathan's voice brightened her day. "I'm so proud of you! Just know I love you, and I will touch base with you when I return."

And with that, the conversation ended. She hardly said hello, and he had to hang up.

Nathan was her hero. Knowing someone believed in her gave her courage and strength. It made her want to be that somebody in the life of someone else.

Anna was blessed, and she knew it. People like the Browns and Nathan were out there. She knew it because their influence and love were being felt in very practical ways. Without them, she wasn't sure where she would be.

Dark thoughts crept back into her mind from time to time, but she had a reason to live again. With two little boys and a blossoming career, she was on her way to brighter days. She had learned there was more to life than Dwight.

"Honey, are you there?" the lady at the shampoo bowl asked as she spoke out from the back of the salon. "My neck is starting to hurt from hanging backward in this shampoo bowl. Can you help me up?"

"Oh, I'm so sorry." Anna rushed over to her. "Let me rinse your hair, and we can get you that well-deserved haircut."

As she reached for the spray nozzle, the lumpy substance peeked out from beneath the tangled hairs. It was a green bean! Anna felt a little nauseous but picked the remains out from the twisted strands of hair. She suspected the woman must have fallen asleep while eating and face planted in her dinner plate. How else would a green bean have gotten embedded into someone's scalp?

She swished around water and freed any remaining green bean particles from their hairy prison. She also felt sorry for the lady. How sad not to have anyone to help her manage the duties of everyday life. No one to even tell her she had a green bean in her hair.

As the lady rummaged through her purse, she extended her arm to pay for her haircut.

"Keep the change baby. I haven't been that relaxed in months. That wasn't just a haircut; that was therapy!" the lady said with a smile.

Anna pushed the lady's money back toward her. "Thank you, and I hope you come back soon. But this one's on me. It was my pleasure to serve you today," Anna said with a smile.

It felt good to be in a position to help someone else out for a change. She knew those who had invested in her were starting to rub off. Giving back was a good thing and she liked it.

The smelly, elderly woman thanked her as she shuffled out the salon door with a beautiful head of hair and a heart full of love.

What Anna didn't know was that the lady she had served had, at one time, been a successful high school principal and had been married to a wealthy real estate developer. When he died, her world crumbled, and she became a recluse. Few people bothered to give her the time of day as her outer world declined in keeping with her broken heart. Anna had been one of just a few people who had treated her with kindness and dignity.

The next Sunday, Anna read in the newspaper that the woman had died. She was found at her dinner table with a fork in hand and her head in a plate of green beans. Next to her was a small little diary. The last entry read, "I met the sweetest young lady today. She was so kind and caring as she did my hair. I could just tell from talking to her she was smart. Like I've always said, 'Smarts can only get you so far, but kindness will take you to the moon.'"

Anna couldn't help but wonder how this former high school principal would have reacted to the news of her pregnancy. Something told her she would have never needed to get a G.E.D. if this lady had been her principal.

Seeing the note, the director of the funeral home asked Anna if she would mind fixing the lady's hair for burial.

Anna had never fixed a dead lady's hair before. But this wouldn't be the last. Anna informed the funeral home that she would be honored to fix her customer's hair, and that she wanted to donate her time in the future to prepare the hair of any other ladies who had passed and might not otherwise be able to afford it.

The bean-haired lady had changed her life. Anna discovered that helping others had a way of helping a person help themselves. Certainly, things could be hard, but even hard times were made a little easier when a person lightened the load of another hurting soul.

CHAPTER 14

Seeing Naomi always made Anna feel loved and cared for. She may have been Dwight's mother, but she was nothing like him. Naomi and Liam both had been nothing but supportive and loving toward Anna.

Naomi was proud of the woman Anna had become. She was happy she had been able to help Anna navigate the challenges of being a teenage mother and newlywed. Anna had exceeded Naomi's expectations. And as much as Naomi loved her son, she wished he had likewise exceeded her expectations and grown into someone she could be proud of. In all honesty, he was a disappointment. Naomi couldn't help but wonder if she hadn't contributed to his narcissistic mindset by babying him as a boy.

It seemed everyone was aware of the man Dwight had become. Even Dwight's dad, Liam, could hardly speak of his son without getting red in the face, not from embarrassment, but anger.

Dwight and Anna had lived with his parents for three months as newlyweds until they were able to get a place of their own. Yes, it was awkward at times, but it provided an opportunity for Anna to learn from one of the sweetest women she would ever come to know.

Naomi took Anna under her wing and taught her everything she knew about homemaking; and Naomi was a masterful homemaker. Their times in the kitchen making fresh bread, chocolate cake, and her savory comfort foods were some of the best times of Anna's life.

Anna was there dropping the boys off at grandma and grandpas for the summer. To no one's surprise, they were greeted with fresh-baked chocolate chip cookies and tall glasses of milk. Anna and Naomi walked together through Liam's strawberry patch as they caught up on life.

"It's going really well in town. The boys are doing well in school, Dwight has become a union superintendent at work, and I have some really big news!" Anna shared with excitement. "I'm pregnant!"

Naomi stood up from picking strawberries and said with a bewildered look, "You are pregnant?" She was clearly surprised by the announcement.

"I'm kidding, Naomi! I'm not pregnant," she said with a laugh. "Actually, I am opening my own hair salon while the boys are with you and Liam for the summer. We are converting the garage into, *Anna's Styling Salon*. What do you think?"

Naomi dropped the basket, accidently spilling freshly picked strawberries on the ground, as she gave Anna a big hug.

"Anna, you never cease to amaze me. Liam and I are so proud of the woman you have become," Naomi said as she removed her arms from around Anna's sides and then held Anna's hands in her own. With a huge smile on her face, Naomi said, "God has his hand on you. He never wastes pain, and he never gives birth to a mistake. What the world thought for certain would never amount to much, he has turned from a sow's ear to a silk purse. This is wonderful news."

As they re-entered the house, the boys ran to their sides. "When does Grandpa get home, Grandma? Kyle asked. "He promised to show me how to drive his lawn tractor when I was here last summer."

"It's amazing what kids remember," Naomi said to Anna. Naomi turned to Kyle and explained, "He should be home around dinner time. I bet he is looking forward to teaching you how to shift gears and mow down the grass now that your feet can reach the pedals!"

Anna gave the boys a lingering hug, kissed them on the cheek, and left them in the loving care of a woman she deeply admired.

Not everything about Dwight was bad. He had wonderful parents and for this, Anna was grateful as she headed back to check on the progress of her new hair salon.

By the time she returned to pick up the boys, she would be not only a wife, mother, and beautician, but she would be a Bonafide business owner. With that thought, she tapped the top of the steering wheel with the inside of her palm and honked her car horn.

Anna grinned. Her smile was bigger than Texas. She extended her arm out the window and raised and lowered her hand in the wind over the long line of fence posts that decorated the landscape. There was something peaceful about that experience. It provided a sense of freedom and serenity.

A lot had changed since she had last done that as a child on her way to Junction City. Perhaps, this time, the change would be good.

CHAPTER 15

L iam walked through the front door with a large bag of money. The boys shot out from behind the drapes and yelled, "Surprise!" Liam played along and immediately dropped to the floor wrestling the boys, smothering them with kisses, and tickling them as they laughed for joy.

Liam pretended they were getting the upper hand and cried out for Naomi. "Grandma! Get in here and save me! There are a couple of robbers in here trying to steal my money!"

Naomi hurried in from the kitchen where the unmistakable aroma of a delicious dinner was permeating the air. With her favorite, yellow, daisy and bumblebee apron tied around her waist, she crawled into the middle of the testosterone-filled battle for power.

Liam rolled over and held Naomi down and gave the command, "Get her boys!" The boys shifted their efforts to Grandma and started tickling Naomi under her arms as Liam kissed her on her lips and all over her face. He pressed his lips into her neck and blew hard. Naomi was helpless to the onslaught. The boys fell backward in laughter as Grandpa and Grandma crawled into each other's arms with a warm embrace.

Kyle and Timmy looked on in amazement at such an endearing display of affection. They weren't used to seeing adults be so intimate and loving in their presence. Among all the things they loved about being at their grandma and grandpa's house, they loved how safe and loved they felt at all times.

Grandma filled the table with mountains of all their favorite foods, and Grandpa said, "Dig in!" If this summer was to be like previous stays at their grandparents, the boys would be adding a few inches to their waistlines.

After dinner, Liam dumped the big bag of money from the liquor store onto the living room floor. He managed access to adult beverages for the local liquor store owner. When Liam worked the night shift, he was responsible for bringing the cash from the register home from the store. The boys loved it when he did because Liam had come up with a fun game he called the "coin train."

For the coin train, Liam set aside the paper currency and worked with the boys to line up coins all around the house. The coin train could stretch from ten to twenty feet depending on how business had been for the day. It wrapped around the legs of end tables, floor lamps, throw rugs, and the piano which Grandma was known to play from time to time.

When coins from the liquor store weren't available, following the evening meal, Grandpa would pull out checkers and take on all challengers. Dominos were their other favorite. Not so much the game itself but stacking them up in a row on the linoleum floor in the kitchen, then flicking them and watching them fall.

Visiting Grandpa and Grandma's was as much about time with them as it was about being with the extended family. Riff and Maggie had moved away years ago, but Dwight's side of the family, other than Dwight, never moved further than five miles from town.

West of town is where Kyle's cousins, Tyler and Robby, lived. They were among the oldest of the grandchildren. Tyler and Robby were farm kids. They raised cattle, grew and harvested wheat, chopped cotton, and hauled hay to make extra money when they weren't sweating it out on their family farm.

Their mom was Dwight's sister, Lue Ann, and she had never lived in the city. She loved the country, and she planned on dying there. She worked hard keeping the farmhands fed and her husband, Leo, happy at home.

Directly across the road from their grandparents were Dean and Chubs, Aunt Adeline's boys. They were a few years older, but not so much older that they didn't enjoy spending time with the boys from the city. Chubs' real name was Ren, but he was so chunky as a toddler that the name Chubs stuck, and for the rest of his life he rarely answered to Ren. When he did, it was because he was in trouble, and his mom was yelling, "Ren Alan Sanderson!" Failing to heed his three-name warning would result in a twisted ear or a hot bottom. Chubs was keen on not letting either of those outcomes make their way into his orbit.

Dean and Chubs were first cousins but as far as Kyle and Timmy were concerned, their cousins were aliens from another planet. Though they lived in a small town, their yard looked more like a small zoo. Pigs, sheep, chickens, and rabbits everywhere.

They even had a horse and bird dogs! Keeping up with all the animals fascinated the city boys.

The morning after they arrived at Liam and Naomi's for the summer, they ran across the road to visit their cousins, arriving just in time for the morning chores. As they came upon Chubs slopping the hogs, he looked at Kyle and then stuck his fingers into the nostrils of a huge boar hog. The monstrous pig didn't even flinch as it stuck it's head into the pig slop. He removed his fingers from the holes in the pig's head as slimy snot dripped from the tips of his fingers, then he slung the snot in Kyle and Timmy's direction.

Kyle was so disgusted by Chub's actions that he gagged. It was so gross and totally unnecessary.

Is this all country boys have to do for entertainment? Kyle wondered.

Once the morning chores were finished the boys gathered around the kitchen table for a country breakfast complete with buttermilk biscuits, gravy, fried eggs, and mounds and mounds of bacon.

"This here was Leonard. I won first prize on him at the county fair," Chubs said as he reached for a handful of crispy bacon. "If Dean hadn't backed the tractor over Leonard's leg, I'd be showing Leonard again this year. But he's pretty tasty, so, win-win."

"Chubs, did you wash your hands before sitting down to eat?" Kyle inquired. If Dwight had done anything right he had insisted that his boys practice good hygiene. He was so obsessed with cleanliness that he made his sons carry little rose-shaped balls of hand soap in plastic sandwich bags to school.

Without a word, Chubs licked the fingers he had buried inside the pig's head and then fondled all of the bacon that remained on the platter. "Who needs to wash their hands when finger licking will do?" Chubs said with an evil grin and one eyebrow turned up. "Toss me a couple of biscuits will you, pretty boy?"

Kyle and Timmy looked at each other repulsed. As good as that special "Leonard" bacon looked, they would be sticking to the biscuits and gravy. Chubs could have all the bacon he cared to eat.

As their Aunt Adeline came to check on her hungry little tribe she asked, "Don't you boys like bacon?"

Kyle gave Chubs a hard stare and lied, "Our daddy doesn't let us eat bacon. Sorry, Aunt Addie." He crossed his fingers under the table and felt sure the good Lord would forgive this one lie.

After breakfast, the boys went out back behind the barn. "Want a chew?" Chubs asked. "I bet you city boys can't handle it," he taunted. Chubs pulled a white pouch from his back pocket. The image of an Indian chief adorned the outside of the packing.

"This here is chewin' tobacco. Tough cowboys put it in their cheek and chew on it as they pulled their hats down right before spurring a bucking bronco," Chubs explained. "You gotta be tough to handle it. It ain't for sissies. Are you able?"

Without thinking, Kyle grabbed the bag out of Chub's hand a shoved a wad of the leafy tobacco into his mouth.

Chubs laughed and explained, "If you are really tough you won't spit. Just swallow the juice. Once you've ground those leaves into powder, that's how you know you are through."

It wasn't too bad at first. The burn was subtle but in a matter of minutes, Kyle's mouth was full of spit. He swallowed in gulps with pieces of tobacco leaves sliding down the back of his throat as well.

Within minutes he was green and puking up breakfast. Timmy ran and hid behind a sheep shed as Kyle lay on the ground, praying his cousin wouldn't make him eat it too.

Kyle was seeing double as Chubs approached him with a bucket of water. The water came crashing down on Kyle's face as Chubs laughed uncontrollably.

"Damn, cuz. You are tough. I ain't never seen nobody put that much chaw in their mouth at one time."

Needless to say, Kyle didn't eat much for dinner that night. He told his grandma he was just too hot from a day of playing under the sun. He slept well that night as the gentle breeze made its way through the screen window and danced lightly across the crisp cotton sheets his grandma had ironed before he arrived.

"You showed them today, big brother. You sure showed them," Timmy said with pride in his voice. "Daddy would have been proud of you standing up to them." And with that, Kyle drifted off to sleep, feeling certain of two things: he would never chew tobacco ever again, and he would never trust Chubs again.

CHAPTER 16

Later in the summer, Kyle and Timmy were fishing on a farm pond just west of the home place with Tyler and Robby. Tyler had dropped them off with Robby while he drove into town for more live bait.

The fish were hitting the minnows hard, and supplies were getting low. Crappie, largemouth bass, and catfish were jumping on the fishing lines as fast as the boys could reel them in.

The air had been muggy for most of the day. There was a stillness about the atmosphere that was complicated by an almost sepia-tone glow. In a matter of minutes, the sweltering air turned cold, and the wind picked up fiercely. Dust was blowing everywhere as Tyler came racing back over the top of the dam.

"Come on boys. We've got to get out of here. Now! Leave your fishing poles and come with me. That thunderstorm is blowing in fast, and a funnel cloud is starting to form," Tyler said in a panic as he tried to corral his brother and little cousins. "This is getting serious, and we have to get to the house!"

Tyler floored the old Ford pickup and spun the tires in the gravel as he turned onto the main road. What had been a bright sunshiny day had turned to an ominous darkness.

Hail began to fall as they ran into the house. Lightning struck an old cedar tree, and it immediately burst into flames. It was barely ablaze before a torrential downpour swiftly extinguished it. And suddenly, everything was calm, and the air pressure dropped causing everyone's ears to pop.

"Get to the cellar everyone. Get there now. A tornado is about to hit, and if we aren't underground soon we are as good as dead," barked Uncle Leo as he rushed everyone underground.

The door was pulled down over the cellar opening just in time as the sucking winds began to vacuum up everything in its path. The rope holding the cellar door down broke from its latch as the door was sucked from its hinges.

Uncle Leo grabbed an old bed box spring, which had been used as a makeshift bench, and placed it against the opening of the cellar.

Outside it sounded as if a freight train was driving its way down the middle of the farm. Crumpling sheet metal could be heard ripping away from the barns. Tree branches broke and the earth appeared to moan and ache as the guts of the farm were being ripped apart.

No one could tell for certain, but it sounded as if one of the dairy cows literally flew by overhead wailing with a terrible and distraught "moo."

The sucking wind began to draw dirt and debris from the only shelter the family had from the massive storm. Uncle Leo placed his huge body up against the opening and spread his long arms and legs across the stairway in an attempt to keep the wire bed frame in place as the family's last line of defense against the raging tornado.

He yelled at the top of his lungs, "Stay low everyone and hold on to each other. I'm not sure this frame is going to hold."

And then, just as quickly as it had started, it was over. No rain. No wind, and no tornado. The sun was shining as before as the tornado just danced along the edge of the house and away from the farmyard.

As they stepped outside of the cellar, they surveyed the damage. One barn was down flat, and a few trees had blown over, but other than that, they had survived and everything else had fared pretty well, all things considered. The door to the cellar ended up on top of the house and curtains flapped through windows where glass panes had broken due to the enormous change in air pressure that had taken place.

When Aunt Lue Ann made her way above ground, she looked east and gave out a cry, "Oh Lord. Leo, it is heading right for Junction City. This is going to be terrible."

While things were calm and clear on the west side of the tornado, darkness prevailed as the back of the tornado was visible from their vantage point.

The wall cloud was massive, and the tornado funnel had to be one of the largest in history. Leo estimated it must be nearly a mile wide. It was relentless and was pounding everything to shreds as it pulverized anything standing above ground.

Leo and the boys loaded up the pickup and headed to town. They were afraid of what they might find once they got there, but they had to do what they could to take care of their family and friends. Lue Ann was left behind to gather chickens, cows, and other livestock that somehow braved the storm.

As they neared town, it was obvious much of the town had been leveled. It looked as if everything had been put into a blender and spit back out. They drove as far as they could until the roads were impassable, then jumped out of the pickup and began running to each of their relative's houses.

Thankfully, they had all made it underground before the tornado gutted Junction City. Everyone that is except Uncle Corp.

Uncle Corp had moved into the childhood home where Kyle had spent his early years as a baby. Unfortunately, Uncle Corp had grown deaf and failed to really appreciate the severity of the growing storm. Neighbors indicated they had tried to gain his attention, but he waved them off as he sat on his front porch in his overalls and no shirt rolling himself a cigarette. It was to be his last.

He was sucked from the wood-frame house in an instant. He was found alive, buried in rubble about a mile from his house. He suffered from severe lacerations and blunt force trauma. Rescue workers said all he kept saying when they found him was, "Round and round. Round and round. Round and round."

Uncle Corp had clearly gone for the ride of a lifetime. Sadly, he lingered for a few days, but his injuries were too severe to survive. Lyle Sanderson was buried a week later, and though Dwight and Anna didn't make it for the funeral, Kyle knew the future he had been given was a credit to the man whose name he bore in part.

CHAPTER 17

As the sun was beginning to set on the summer, Kyle made the final lap mowing his grandfather's acreage. He had been mowing the parcel all summer long after having received his grandad's approval to operate the lawn tractor. It was his last day there, and he couldn't wait for his mom to see how great he'd gotten at driving the tractor.

"Great job, Kyle! I might make a farmer out of you yet!" Liam bathed his grandson in praise.

Kyle grinned under his grandfather's adoration. When it came to Dwight, whatever Kyle did, wasn't quite good enough. When Kyle mowed the lawn with a push mower, Dwight would stand at the end of the row in his shorts and work boots smoking a pipe and barking orders at Kyle, pounding him with put-downs and pointing out rows of cut grass that weren't straight enough.

One day when Kyle was turning the soil in the garden, Dwight yanked a shovel from Kyle's hands and threw it across the yard. "Damn it, boy! Can't you even turn dirt? Sometimes I think you were just born stupid," Dwight barked at Kyle. Dwight was a professional at pointing out everyone's faults except his own.

Kyle jumped from the lawn tractor when he saw Dwight pulling in his grandparents' gravel driveway, immediately wondering why his mom wasn't the one picking him up.

The car ended up being parked halfway on the grass and halfway on the drive. Kyle knew something wasn't quite right, and it didn't take long to figure out the problem as Dwight staggered out of the front seat of the car.

"Come here, you little shit! Come and give your daddy a hug," Dwight slurred.

"Looks like you did a pretty damn good job cutting the ole' man's grass. Sure, wish you would uncross your eyes when you mow ours!"

Then he turned his gaze to the tractor. "Were your eyes closed when you parked that tractor for your grandpa? Hell, a drunk sailor could have docked a boat better than that."

Dwight's words stung and Kyle's spirits sank. Why couldn't his dad be more like his grandpa? The summer had been so fun and full of adventure, but here was Dwight ready to push Kyle back down under his thumb where he belonged.

"Cut the cow manure, Dwight. Leave the boy alone. He has done a great job," Liam said as he stepped next to Kyle and put his hand on Kyle's shoulder "Besides, who are you to judge? Look how you parked your car."

He took a step toward Dwight then said, "Good God, Dwight. How much have you had to drink?"

"Not enough considering how much that bitch I'm married to is driving me crazy. She opened her business, and it seems half the town is coming to her place to have their hair handled," Dwight said with resentment.

"Sounds like somebody might be jealous. You should be proud of her," Liam protested. "You should be proud of these boys too. They work hard, are polite, and everyone enjoys their company. I hate to say it, but you could learn a lesson or two from them."

"Kiss my ass!" Dwight yelled. "Who the hell are you to be telling me how to live? Blame yourself. You are the one who raised me."

Liam turned and walked away. As much as he hated to admit it, he and Naomi felt a deep sense of responsibility for who Dwight had become. He was an embarrassment to the family and a deep sense of shame for them.

Instead of coming up to the house, Dwight yelled out for the boys to pack their bags, load up, and get in the car.

"You are too drunk to drive, Dwight," Naomi said as she came outside to appeal to her red-eyed son. "It's too dangerous. Come inside and sleep it off. I'll make you a big breakfast, and you can leave in the morning."

"Like hell!" he yelled back at his mother. "I'm fine. Boys, get your asses in the car before I whoop'em," Dwight exploded.

Boys in tow, Dwight swerved out of the driveway and onto the main road.

Naomi wrapped her arms around Liam's side and began to cry. "Liam, what have we done? What have we raised? He needs help. We have to pray that those boys make it home safe," Naomi whimpered as the car drove out of sight.

Dwight pointed the car in the right direction to get back home, but he couldn't resist making a stop at his old watering hole.

"Come on you little shitheads. Let's go get a soda pop and a few beers," Dwight insisted. He laughed and rubbed their heads. "The beers are for me, and the soda pops are for you!"

As they walked into the dingy room, the smell of the bar slapped them in the face. There was a sour, yet sweet smell that filled the air. Old beer bottles filled trash cans to the rim and oozed a rancid odor.

The boys' eyes widened as they took in everything before them. This was a full-out honky-tonk. Bar stools were packed with working-class men in trucker's hats while scantily dressed barmaids slithered amongst the patrons.

A pool table and shuffleboard caught the boys' eyes as the sound of a dart hitting its target on the wall drew their attention.

Country and western music blared on the jukebox where a cowboy was grinding his hips into a barmaid who had her leg lifted over his hip.

Kyle and Timmy were getting an education that was normally reserved for men of drinking age but for some reason, Dwight gave no attention to how inappropriate it was to have two young boys in such a hell hole.

"Well, I'll be damned if it isn't Dwight the Dirty Dog," came the greeting from an older lady of the night. Her lipstick was bright red, her eyeliner extra thick, and her hair stacked high like cotton candy on a stick. It was clear the two had known each other for years as she leaned in and kissed Dwight straight on the lips with an open mouth. Dwight didn't pull back but instead slapped her on the butt and returned the gesture.

Kyle and Timmy looked at each other with disbelief. What would their mother think of this? Should they tell her when they got home? Dwight disappeared behind a red velvet curtain as the older barmaid switched on a red light above the entrance to the so-called men's lounge of the speakeasy.

"I'll be back in a minute, girls. I've got some catching up to do with an old customer," she said as she looked over her shoulder and kicked up the high heel of her left foot. "Keep the boys entertained for a bit. Will ya?"

Two younger barmaids escorted the boys to a booth and offered them small bottles of Coca-Cola and a small metal pail of salted beer nuts. "You two boys have a favorite song? We will play it for you on the jukebox," the younger of the two barmaids offered.

Kyle spoke up. "No ma'am. But thank you. We will be fine right here. We appreciate the drinks and peanuts."

"You sure are cute," she replied. "I hope you will come and see me again once you get your first hair." She giggled and walked away smacking her gum and swinging her bottom like a peacock spreading its feathers.

Dwight finally reappeared through the curtain with his hair disheveled as he tucked in his shirttail trying to hold two bottles of beer in one hand and a lighted cigarette in the other.

For the next two hours, Dwight sat on a bar stool pouring beer after beer down his throat and blowing smoke rings from the cigar he bought from the bartender.

Timmy fell asleep on the red upholstered bench seat of the corner booth as Kyle kept his eye on his daddy in awe of how comfortable and happy he appeared to be in this setting and with these kinds of people. Eventually, Dwight spun on his barstool, looked straight at Kyle, and pointed to the front door with his cigar glowing between his fingers.

Kyle felt a sense of sadness for the people he'd watched all night. Looking at life from the bottom of a bottle was something Kyle knew he never wanted to experience or endure.

The fresh crisp night air was a welcomed relief from the thick smoke that infested every crack and crevice of the bar.

Dwight tossed Kyle the car keys. "If you can drive that damned tractor, you can drive this car. Crawl your ass up in that seat and get me home, boy," he said with an awkward wink. "I'm gonna lay down in the back seat and catch a few winks. Just keep your eyes on that yellow line on the right side of the highway, and you'll do just fine."

And with that, Dwight stayed true to his promise as he passed out face down in the back seat with a bottle of beer in his hand.

"Well little brother, get in. I'm gonna need your help keeping this old Ford on the road," Kyle said as he looked over at the terror-filled eyes of his little brother. "We can do it. We're a team, you and me." Kyle had never driven a Galaxy 500 before. His feet barely touched the pedals, and his eyes barely peered over the top of the steering wheel.

He turned the ignition key, and the engine came to life. The car creeped out into the darkness, and slowly they made their way down the winding, two-lane, blacktop road.

Soon, they were all alone on the road, passing through the darkness of the night as the dual exhaust from the tailpipes rumbled across the asphalt. The smell of a woman's cheap perfume filled the cab of the car as the remnants of Dwight's close encounter lingered longer than he might have expected.

The boys rolled down the front windows and welcomed in the fresh night air that smelt of fresh cut wheat and sunflowers. Cicadas cried out in search of their mates.

There was an unexpected calmness between the boys as they worked together to navigate two thousand pounds of steel between the white and yellow stripes that lined the road back to home.

There were a few times the car's tires rolled off the edge of the pavement and the bright lights from an 18-wheeler caused Kyle to take a firmer grip on the steering wheel. Other than that, Kyle took command of their little ship like he had learned to do in so many other ways in his life.

The boys made it to their neighborhood without one wrong turn. The many summers of making this drive had served their memories well. As the lights of the car shined on the front of the house, Anna ran frantically from the front porch.

"Oh my God, where have you guys been? I have been worried sick! Your grandma called hours ago to see if you'd made it home yet." As she looked at the boys who had just stepped out of the front seat of the car, reality set in. "Kyle! What are you doing driving this car, and where is your daddy?" Anna asked, her voice draped in panic.

Dwight raised his hand from behind the driver's seat, then he pulled himself to a semi-upright position and grinned. "We're fine. The boy's a hell of a driver."

The boys grabbed their belongings and ran into the house. Anna followed and Dwight wobbled his way up the steps and into the living room.

"Dwight! What were you thinking! All of you could have been killed! I am not living this way! You need help!" Anna screamed at Dwight like never before. "This is ridiculous. You put the kids' lives at risk. This is just stupid!"

Dwight doubled up his fist and smashed it full force into Anna's face. "Shut up and get out of my business."

The force of the blow cracked Anna's nose for a second time. She stumbled backward into the hallway as blood immediately flowed from the front of her face. Dwight came at her with a vengeance, but this time Kyle stepped in between his parents.

The intrusion caught Dwight by surprise.

"Stop it! Leave her alone. She is just trying to help you," Kyle said with a commanding voice, twice the level of a boy his age. "No more. I'm not going to watch this! Never again!" Stop!"

Dwight paused, looked Kyle in the eyes, looked at Anna, then laughed and turned and walked away.

Timmy was balled up in a corner screaming, crying, and cranking a wire hanger in his hands in absolute terror. The mental scars were growing deep as the emotional and physical abuse appeared to have no end.

The sound of the car leaving the driveway brought much-needed relief.

Kyle helped his mother make her way to the kitchen. He opened the top freezer door on the refrigerator and ran water over the ice cube tray. He pulled the handle and freed the cubes from their chambers, dumping them into a bowl and handing it to his mother.

Anna wrapped the ice in a dish towel and placed it gently on her now, twice-broken nose. As she began to cry uncontrollably, her boys came to her sides and leaned their heads on their momma's shoulders. Together they wept with her and held each other tight knowing the demon they called Dad had left them for the time being.

"We can't live like this," Anna whispered under her breath. "I can't let you boys grow up like this. Dwight is going to turn on you next, and I won't stand for it. I'll kill him before I let that happen."

Anna and the boys slept together that night. She hardly moved as she held each boy under separate arms. They were what made life worth it. She was living for them now.

In a few hours, the dawn of a new day would bring drastic changes, changes for the better, but changes that weren't without consequence. Anna was determined to make the break. Nothing would stop her now.

CHAPTER 18

"Dwight?" asked the stranger who appeared unannounced on the truck dock.

"That's me," Dwight replied as he backed a forklift out of the semi-trailer.

"Have a nice day," came the reply as the man handed Dwight a manila envelope. "You've been officially served."

Dwight tore open the package as he saw the stranger drive away in a county sheriff's patrol car. "What the hell is this?" Dwight asked as he read the headline of the first document.

"Restraining order?" Are you kidding me?" Dwight spoke out loud as he read the news. "What does she think she's doing? This is bullshit." Then he roared with laughter. "Divorce! She's filing for divorce too? After all I've done for her?"

I'll show that little bitch," he said with rage as he crammed the documents in his lunch box and walked off the job site. "If she thinks I'm going to put up with this sack of rocks she has another thing coming."

Dwight drove straight from work to the house. Much to his surprise, the sheriff's patrol car was parked in the parking lot of the hair salon.

Dwight was tempted to walk in and raise some hell. Instead, he drove around the block and headed to the bar to gain some counsel from Mr. Jack Daniels. A six-pack wasn't going to take the edge off of this kind of news.

The hours began to add up as the shots of whiskey kept coming. The longer he drank, the madder he became. By the time the bar closed, he was fit to be tied.

Fueled by an ungodly amount of liquid courage, Dwight wheeled into the driveway and stormed to the front door of his house.

"Restraining order my ass. I'm about to kick some ass right here and now," Dwight fumed as he tried his key in the door lock.

"Are you kidding? She changed the locks!"

"If she thinks I'm going down without a fight, she's in for a show." Dwight made his way to the trunk of his car, a string of expletives exploding from his mouth.

He pulled the spare tire from its rack and made his way back to the front door.

Dwight didn't know it, but Anna and the boys were peeking through a bedroom window and watching his every move.

If Dwight was anything, he was predictable. Give him one too many beers and the slightest reason to be agitated, and he would go into a fit of rage. His favorite target was Anna. But this time she was ready. She called the police the second he pulled in the driveway. The police were on their way and prepared to take matters into their own hands.

Dwight raised the spare tire above his head and pounded it into the front door. The impact shook the house. Anna and the boys ran to a closet in fear that the door might not hold.

Again and again, he beat the spare tire against the front door. Eventually, he succeeded, and the deadbolt shattered the doorframe. Dwight turned around and threw the spare tire onto the front yard. When he did, it bounced right in front of two armed police officers with handguns drawn.

"Put your hands above your head and get on your knees," came the strong and forceful command from a massive, six-foot-five, rookie police officer.

"You are under arrest for breaking and entering and for violating your restraining order."

Dwight liked a good fight, but this time he was outnumbered, overpowered, and looking down the barrel of not one, but two 38 specials. He complied as the officers cuffed his arms behind his back and escorted him away in the backseat of the patrol car.

Once the emergency lights quit flashing throughout the house and the entire neighborhood, Anna stepped out on the porch just in time to see a tow truck back up to Dwight's car and pull it away.

She looked across the street and saw Mr. and Mrs. Brown standing on their front porch waving at her. Mrs. Brown was in her nightgown, and Mr. Brown stood on his good leg, leaning on crutches to keep his balance in the absence of his prosthesis.

"You alright Anna? You and the boys okay?" Mr. Brown yelled from across the way. "You are welcomed here tonight if need be. You know we love you guys."

Anna choked back tears and responded as best she could. "We're going to be okay. It will be alright. Things will be better soon," she said as she blew them a kiss and stepped back inside the house to comfort her boys who were obviously wide awake from all the excitement.

They looked so cute and innocent standing there in nothing but their tighty-whities. It was nearly three o'clock in the morning, but the band of three were too wired to even think about sleep.

"Who wants some cookies and milk?" Anna asked with enthusiasm.

"I do!" came the simultaneous replies.

"Let's do it! I want some too," Anna proclaimed as she switched on the kitchen light.

Timmy pulled ice cold milk from the refrigerator and Kyle brought the cookie jar from the countertop. They sat there drinking milk and eating cookies until there were none to be had. It was hard to tell whether they were mourning a loss or celebrating a victory. Based on the smiles and the laughs that started to push away fears, it was definitely the latter.

There was no turning back now. The cat was out of the bag. Dwight the wife-beater, domestic-abuser, and alcohol-dependent man of the hour was officially behind bars, finally facing the consequences for his actions.

CHAPTER 19

After his visit to the county jail, Dwight decided it might be in his best interest to comply with the law. He didn't like it one bit, and more than once he started to stop by and rip Anna a new one, but his better judgment prevailed. Not to mention the threat of a regular police presence in the neighborhood as patrol cars made regular routes between the bar and the house.

It seemed the whole town had taken an interest in the story and were rallying behind Anna and the kids. It was embarrassing to Anna, but helpful in many ways. Dwight was losing control over more than just Anna and the boys. He was losing control of his life. His lack of self-control was about to make matters worse for him and anyone that got in his way.

Surprisingly, Dwight was allowed to have regular visitation with his sons, so long as he agreed to restrain himself and pick up the boys for the weekends without interacting with Anna.

More times than not, the weekends with Dad meant a trip to visit Dwight's family in Junction City. Kyle and Timmy always enjoyed spending the night at Grandma and Grandpas. Plus, their cousins could always be counted on for more than a good time.

On one particular weekend getaway, Timmy had to stay behind because he had come down with some sort of stomach bug. This meant Dwight and Kyle would be spending most of the weekend together.

Rather than lay around and watch cartoons and eat TV dinners, they decided to make the trip to Grandma's and fill up on homemade meals and new adventures.

Things had gone pretty well. Dwight surprised Kyle when he bought him a used 12-gauge shotgun. The gun was heavy and powerful, and Dwight taught Kyle how to put the gun to good use.

Kyle learned to aim, pump the chamber to load a shotgun shell, and then breathe out slowly as he squeezed the trigger and blasted fire from the end of the barrel, blowing a tin can into a thousand little pieces. It was scary and fun all at the same time.

As the weekend wound down, Dwight chose to cap it off with a visit to the local café—a small, no-frills spot where the counter wrapped around the cook's station. Customers perched on round-seated stools, their chrome-plated bases bolted to the floor. The stools swiveled with ease as patrons settled in, swinging their feet beneath the bar.

It was one of Kyle's favorite places to eat, especially at lunch. The smell of the fried onion burgers had a way of doubling your hunger, the powerful scent of onion lingering in your clothes for days.

"Double meat and cheese for my boy," Dwight said as he ordered his spin on the traditional county boy burger basket. "Make the fries extra crispy if you don't mind."

Kyle could hardly wait to sink his teeth into the huge, man-size meal, stacked high with a half-pound patty of grass-fed beef, homegrown tomatoes, pickles, lettuce, cheese, savory fried onions, and double toasted sesame seed buns that had been battered with plenty of butter before they were placed on the grill.

The hamburger sizzled on the grill as the cook pressed the patties, layering them with fried onions. Kyle's mouth watered, his eyes widening as two thick slices of American cheese slowly melted over the top. Soon enough, the burger arrived hot off the grill with hand-cut French fries and a vanilla shake with a cherry on top. It was everything a grown man could do to wash it all down with a tall glass of soda pop, but Kyle had no problem conquering the mountain of grub. One thing was for certain, he wouldn't be asking for seconds!

At the end of the counter was a display case where fishing lures, Buck knives, cigarette lighters, playing cards, ammunition, and handguns were offered for sale. It seemed like an odd place to be selling such items, but Junction City was a small town, and if there was a need, someone was always trying to meet it, especially if they could make a few extra dollars. As Dwight and Kyle pushed away from the bar, both full as summer ticks, Dwight pulled his wallet from his back pocket and asked the owner how much one of the pistols and a box of ammo would set him back.

"Including your burgers and drinks, I'd say a $100 bill would get you out of here," said the cafe owner. "And that will even cover your tip!"

"I'll take it!" Dwight said as he tucked the pistol in his waistband like a gangster about to rob a bank. "We've been blowing holes in beer cans all morning. I think I'll show the boy how the West was won before we head back to the city."

"Sounds good, Dwight!" the owner replied. "Be safe out there, and for goodness sake, don't shoot yourself in the foot."

Dwight laughed as he and Kyle made their way to the car. "What do you say we head down to the river and see if we can blow a few holes in some fish sunning near the bank?" Dwight asked as he headed toward the outskirts of town. Kyle grinned, and nodded, though a little unsure if this was actually a great idea.

"Before we do, Daddy's gonna stop and grab a little bottle of his favorite treat for old times' sake," Dwight said as he pulled into the liquor store where Liam worked.

Dwight was in and out in a flash and reentered the car with the all-too-familiar bottle wrapped in a brown paper sack.

Kyle knew that if his grandpa had been working he would have refused to sell Dwight the source of so many of his troubles. Nonetheless, Dwight cracked the seal on the bottleneck and took a swig straight from the bottle. No chaser needed.

Dwight had half the bottle drunk before they had fired three rounds from the revolver. Dwight waved the gun around recklessly firing at anything that moved. The alcohol had already started having its effect. Strangely, Dwight started talking to himself and seemed to fade off into his own little world.

He walked over to a particular place on the sandy bank and started reloading the gun as if he were shooting someone.

Kyle didn't know it, but this was the very place where he had been conceived.

Dwight was reliving the night in his mind and in his drunken stupor was firing round after round into the images from his past that danced before his mind. Dwight yelled out in a crazed rage as he shot the last round into the air, " Dammit!

Dammit to hell! I wish I had never met you, you bitch. Look where it got me! My life is a living hell."

Dwight dropped to his knees and started pounding the sand with his fists. The gun was covered in mud and grime, as he crawled toward Kyle, spit foaming from his mouth. With his eyes squinted tight, Dwight asked, "Hey! What do you think she would think if you weren't here, you little bastard?"

Dwight grabbed the ammo box and started reloading the pistol.

"What do you mean, Dad? Not here?" Kyle asked as he began to fear for his life.

"I mean not here. Not here! Don't you think that would piss her off? Don't you think she might wish she had never messed with ole Dwight?"

Dwight was coming unglued. He appeared to be losing his mind. "I bet it would make her regret ever divorcing me!"

And with that Dwight pointed the gun at Kyle, fired several rounds at his feet, and then raised the barrel directly at Kyle's chest.

"Dad! Dad! Dad! Stop it! Don't do this!" Kyle screamed as loud as he could. He wanted to run, but he was frozen in a trance of disbelief.

Dwight cocked the trigger. Straightened his arm. Looked Kyle directly in the eyes and began to weep.

He fell to his knees. Fired the gun into the rushing river and then threw the pistol into the murky water that flowed downstream.

Dwight began to cry uncontrollably. "Oh my God! Son, I'm sorry. I'm sorry. I'm so sorry," Dwight cried out as he wrapped his arms around Kyle.

Kyle stood stiff with his arms at his sides unable to reciprocate the affection. He was in too much shock. All he wanted was to get home and as far away from Dwight as possible.

It was like a switch went off in Dwight's mind. One minute he was funny and loving, and the next he was a demon straight from the pits of hell.

One thing was for sure, Kyle was going to beg his mom to never require him to be with Dwight again. Dwight was crazy. He had truly lost his mind. No kid should ever have to live like this.

Not a word was spoken between them as Dwight took the long way home. Kyle exited the car without saying goodbye. Dwight knew better than to push his luck.

Anna greeted Kyle at the door. "Get in here big boy! I've got your favorite goulash simmering on the stove," Anna said with the sweetest voice.

Kyle gave his mom the biggest, longest hug.

"Are you okay, honey?" Anna asked.

"Yes, ma'am. I guess I just really missed you."

Anna looked into Kyle's face, trying to decide what she saw in his eyes. But then she noticed the gun in his hand and stepped back.

"What in the world are you carrying?"

"It's a long story. Dad bought me a shotgun and taught me how to kill beer cans," Kyle said, walking straight to the table as the smell of his mama's cooking drew him there..

As Anna sat down to hear highlights from the weekend, she could sense something in Kyle. Something different. When she pressed him about it, he just shook his head and said, "I'm okay, Momma. I just don't want to go back to Daddy's again."

Kyle finished two bowls of goulash, and Anna presented him with his favorite dessert, chocolate cake with vanilla icing, complete with strawberry banana Jell-O. It was the perfect antidote for what he had just experienced. Such a welcoming feast was quite a change of scenery from the terror he had just lived through hours ago.

The thought of never having the opportunity to enjoy this moment passed through Kyle's mind as he said, "I love you, Momma. You are a good momma. You always make me feel loved. Not to mention you are the best cook ever!"

Kyle was exhausted by all that he had been through. He made his way to the bedroom that he shared with Timmy. Timmy was still sick in bed as Kyle showed him the new shotgun.

Timmy sat up in bed. "I missed you, Bubba. I wish I could have gone to see Daddy with you," Timmy said.

"You didn't miss much." Kyle said as he climbed into his bed. "Goodnight."

Kyle slid the 12-gauge shotgun under his bed where he knew it would be if he ever needed it. He had squared off with death, face-to-face. Maybe it wasn't the lesson his Daddy thought he was teaching him when he gave him that gun, but Kyle had learned he would do what he had to when it came to protecting his family from his dad.

CHAPTER 20

Despite Kyle's warning, Timmy insisted that he be allowed to spend the next weekend with his dad. Kyle couldn't help but think Timmy was fixated on the possibility of receiving a gift of his own.

Anna tried her best to encourage him to postpone a weekend away as well.

Timmy packed a small duffel bag, kissed his momma on the cheek, and gave his big brother a side hug.

"See you guys soon," he announced as he skipped his way to Dwight's car.

Anna and Kyle stood at the door holding hands and looking through the darkened screen door. They weren't visible from the road, but they could see clearly as the innocent little lamb was being prepared for slaughter.

Kyle had eventually told his momma the harrowing story of what transpired between him and his daddy down at the riverbank. Anna had immediately called the sheriff, but the man assured Anna it would be Dwight's word against Kyle's.

"I won't sleep until he is back home," Anna said as she watched Timmy ride off with Dwight. "It is all I can do to let him go. Dwight is a sick man, but my hands are tied. It just makes me want to run away and take you, boys, with me."

Kyle shared her perspective. Something was wrong in a society where a man could beat his wife, drink and drive, and threaten the lives of his children. Couldn't anyone see where this was heading? Couldn't anyone see the signs? This was a real-life horror movie playing out before their very eyes.

True to her word, Anna didn't sleep all night. She paced the floors of her tiny house wringing her hands in worry. This was her baby.

"The courts and the law are supposed to protect victims of domestic abuse, not force them into the dungeons of their captors," Anna railed at no one. She recalled what the sheriff had said to her.

"Anna, that sounds terrible, but there is really nothing we can do until he does something illegal."

Anna wasn't going to wait until he did something illegal. She was finished playing Dwight's game. With her mind made up, she went to her nightstand and removed the small .22 caliber revolver she had purchased for her personal protection. She slid the pistol into her purse and stormed out the front door.

"I'll be back in about an hour," she yelled out to Kyle. "If I'm not back with your brother by then, call the police, and send them to your dad's house."

Kyle had no idea what was going through his mom's head, but he could see the resolve on her face. He looked at the clock, then flipped on the television, hoping to catch the last of the Saturday morning cartoons. They served as a much-needed distraction as he sat and waited, keeping an eye on the hands of the family's grandfather clock. The large, pointed hands of the clock slowly made their way past each of the Roman numbers that adorned the bronze embossed face of the clock.

The grandfather clock was purchased when he was much younger. It had to be more than one hundred years old and had certainly survived the test of time. It was from Germany and showed signs of the struggles of two world wars. The top of the clock had been repaired and refinished due to a house fire that nearly killed it prematurely.

Kyle's attention shifted from the television and was now set on the tick-tock, tick-tock of the pendulum that swung back and forth behind the beveled glass door of the tall wooden mechanized work of art.

There had been no sign of his mother. As the clock hit noon, the sound of the clock's chimes made him jump. His jaw became tight as the tension of the next few minutes slowly passed. If his mother and brother didn't show up soon, he could only assume the worst. He might, in fact, be the sole survivor.

Anna parked her car under a shade tree near a park just far enough away to keep an eye on Dwight's house. She sat in the car with the window partially rolled down to gain relief from the scorching heat. She thought through what might happen next. She would knock on the door. Insist that Timmy come with her. If Dwight refused, she would pull out the gun and shoot him between the eyes.

She had simply had enough. She would rather Dwight be dead and she, herself, rotting on death row, than live with the thought of Dwight hurting one of her boys.

As she exited the car, the sound of children playing at the park caught her attention. There was a group of kids playing chase and taking turns spinning on the merry-go-round.

Smack dab in the middle of the action was Timmy. He was laughing and playing with all his new friends. Dwight sat on a park bench smoking a cigarette and as usual, drinking a beer. She leaned up against her car and sat there watching in awe as life stood still and felt normal for this small window of time.

How sweet it could be. The thought of a family spending a day at the park, laughing, playing, and enjoying each other's company made her sad. It was an opportunity lost. Something they had never experienced and something they never would.

The sound of a passing car shook Anna from her daydream. She glanced at her watch. She had lost track of time, and it was two minutes past the hour. If Kyle had done as expected, the police would soon be on their way. She jumped in her car and rushed to the nearest payphone knowing she could never make it back to the house in time.

She frantically dialed the number. A busy signal throbbed in her ear. She hung up and called back again. Kyle answered.

"Hello?" Kyle said softly. "Mom?"

"Don't call the police! Don't call them, Kyle. It's all okay!" Anna said in a panic. "Have you called them?"

"Well, I started to. I picked up the phone to call but had to pee!" Sorry, Mom, I just had to go really bad!" Kyle said with a bit of a giggle.

"Whew, it's okay. I'll be home in a bit," she said with relief. "Want to go grab a slaw dog for lunch?"

"Yes!" Kyle exclaimed as he sat down the receiver. Slaw dogs were one of his favorites. It was a local phenomenon. He hadn't seen or tried one anywhere else on earth. Slaw dogs were a combo of a hot dog covered in chili, cheese, diced onions, and the most amazing mustard-based slaw found anywhere on the planet.

Kyle's mouth watered as he waited with anticipation for his mom to arrive. He was feeling great relief when her car pulled into the drive. The rest of the evening was spent with some quality one-on-one time between mother and son.

Kyle felt special, like a modern-day knight as he held his mom's hand walking down the sidewalk of Main Street. As they approached the town square Anna challenged Kyle to a foot race.

"The last one to the car is a monkey's uncle," she declared as they both took off in a scurry.

Kyle quickly took the lead and arrived more than one hundred feet ahead of his mother. Anna gave up early and leaned on an old oak tree that stood tall on the grassy lawn. As Kyle turned, his strawberry blonde hair caught a ray of sunshine. Anna grinned and caught her breath.

"Aren't you a handsome devil and quick on your feet as well," she said as he kissed him on the forehead. "I'm going to have to send a note to school making sure they quarantine you from all the pretty girls."

Kyle blushed and said with a long whine, "Mom…. stop it. You are embarrassing me."

"Hey, it's true. You are a good-looking young man," she said as the thought of her little boy transitioning into manhood was starting to become a reality before her very eyes.

The phone was ringing as they walked into the house. Kyle ran to the phone and immediately recognized the caller. It was Dwight, and he was talking with slurred speech.

"It's Dad. He wants to talk to you," Kyle said as he reluctantly handed the telephone to his mother.

"He's gone," Dwight said, his voice low.

"What do you mean, Dwight?" Anna questioned with intensity. "The little bastard is gone. And it's your damn fault," Dwight said as he hung up the phone.

Anna immediately tried to call Dwight back, but he didn't pick up. She tried again.

"Hello," Dwight mumbled through the telephone.

"Dwight, let me talk to Timmy," she said in a forceful tone. "Right now! Or I'm calling the police!"

"Listen bitch, you can call the cops, but that ain't gonna help. He can't talk. He is gone I tell you. Let that soak in. You may have divorced my ass after all I've done for you, but you own this one. It's your fault. You will have to live with yourself for the rest of your life knowing you caused all of this."

And with that, the phone line went dead. Her heart sank. Anna nearly fainted, but she regained her composure and called the police. By the time she and Kyle arrived at Dwight's, SWAT teams and patrol cars had surrounded Dwight's house.

A loudspeaker blared a public announcement throughout the neighborhood, "Dwight, the house is surrounded. Send the boy out and come out with your hands up."

A helicopter with a spotlight appeared on the scene, illuminating whatever dark places remained around the house.

Dwight appeared in an upstairs window in nothing but his underwear and a butcher knife. Blood dripped down his forearm as a cigarette hung from his lower lip.

"The boy is gone I tell you. Get the hell out and leave me alone," Dwight yelled from the raised window.

"Hold your fire," came the command over the police radio. "Hold your fire. We can't risk any further loss of life here tonight."

As the police discussed knocking down the front door, a familiar figure appeared from the darkness. It was John, Dwight's older brother.

Apparently, a neighbor had tipped John off about what was going on. When he heard the news, he rushed to the crime scene.

"Let me try and talk to him," John said to the officer in charge. "I think he will listen to me."

This wasn't the first time John had been called on to try and talk sense into Dwight. He had done it many times over the years. Hopefully, tonight wouldn't be any different.

"Dwight, this is John," came the announcement over the loudspeaker. "Dwight, I'm coming alone. I just want to talk. Nothing else. Just open the door and let me in."

After a few minutes, the front door creaked open, and John was allowed inside.

For what seemed like a lifetime, quiet fell over the darkness of night. Nothing but the sounds of car engines could be heard as an ambulance arrived on the scene.

"I'm giving him five more minutes. If he doesn't come out, we're going in and taking control of this situation," came the instructions over the police radio.

Five minutes passed and then another five minutes as the police force practiced patience.

The commander cleared his throat over the loudspeaker and spoke clearly, "Dwight and John you have 60 seconds to walk out with your hands up. If you don't, we are coming in after you."

The front door started to open.

"On ready everyone," came the command from the lead officer. "Nobody fires unless I say so."

A man's boot pried open the bottom of the door. It was John, and he was holding what appeared to be a little boy in a wrapped sheet.

Everyone gasped as John walked softly down the steps.

Timmy's head raised from beneath the cover as he pulled his arm out from the restraint.

He had been crying and was clearly traumatized but other than being scared to death, he was alive!

Anna ran to her son and held him in her arms as she cried uncontrollably.

"Good job, John," the commander said as John walked quietly back to the SWAT truck and debriefed the officers on what waited for them inside.

"My brother needs help. He is a sick man. Apparently, he did all this to try and get back at his ex-wife for their divorce," John explained. "He wrapped Timmy up in a sheet and made him stand at attention while he threw knives at him. He then crammed him between the wall and the bed and insisted that Timmy not move or say a word. I guess Dwight cut himself messing with the knives. He's bleeding pretty bad. He might need medical attention."

"Is he armed?" asked the SWAT team leader.

"I don't think so," John clarified. "When I left, he thanked me for stopping by as nothing had ever happened. I told him I was taking Timmy with me. Dwight pulled back the bedspread and laid down to go to sleep."

"So, you are telling me, he is up there asleep?" asked the officer with a puzzled look.

"That's how I left him," John explained. "He's been drinking, and I think he has finally passed out."

The officers secured a battering ram and charged into the house with guns raised and ready.

They found Dwight fast asleep in a sea of beer cans, whiskey bottles, and butcher knives. The bed was covered in blood. And as suspected, Dwight had accidentally punctured his forearm.

He was handcuffed and escorted to the county jail where he spent the rest of the night.

Amazingly, no charges were filed the following morning as it was seen as an extension of a domestic dispute.

Since no one had actually been hurt, it was seen as a private matter that required no outside intervention.

Once again, the law had failed Anna and her sons.

CHAPTER 21

The last two weekends had left Kyle on edge, especially knowing that his dad was free to roam about. It seemed so senseless. Unthinkable really. Every night he laid awake in bed staring at the ceiling of the yellow house, headlights of passing cars dancing a rhythm across the dark.

Kyle watched intently to make sure none of the headlights turned into their driveway. There would only be one reason and one person who would show up that late at night, and if he did, Kyle was ready.

By two o'clock in the morning, the bars had closed and if there had been no activity within the subsequent 30 minutes, Kyle felt comfortable enough to step down from his guard post. Every night he went to sleep with his shotgun well within reach should he need it.

A few weeks had passed since the barrage of all police activity. Unlike a lot of boys his age, Kyle actually liked the police. More than once they had stopped him on the street to ask how he was doing. Yeah, they handed out tickets to hot rods and could be intimidating at times, but they also had guts and grit. They operated with an honor code. They looked out for kids like Kyle and Timmy. The men in blue were heroes in his book. More than once they had been there when his momma needed them. And for that, Kyle would be forever grateful.

One sunny afternoon, Anna and the boys were pulling weeds in the backyard flower garden that ran along the neighbor's property line. Anna had turned the vegetable garden into a huge bed of wildflowers after Dwight had left the house. The houses in the neighborhood may have been small, but the yards were huge and without fences. It was a great place to play hide and go seek with the neighbor kids.

As Kyle bent down to pull a massive dandelion weed from its roots, he heard the sound of a car racing down the street. Partly out of curiosity and half by instinct, he looked up to locate the source of the commotion.

It was as he feared. Dwight was speeding down the road and heading to their house. "Run, everybody! Dad is coming! Head to the house," Kyle screamed as everyone bolted for the back door.

Dwight saw them scatter. His vehicle jumped the curb and attempted to cut them off at the pass and run them over. The bumper of Dwight's car grazed the outside of Kyle's shin, drawing blood as he jumped to avoid being smashed under the grill of the out-of-control vehicle. Missing his targets, Dwight spun the car around in the backyard throwing dirt from his tires over into the neighbor's yard.

He floored the accelerator and took a second aim at his would-be victims. Timmy lagged behind and for some reason went the opposite direction as everyone else.

Anna and Kyle rushed through the back door and bolted the lock. Anna ran to the back bedroom to call the police, and

Kyle ran straight to his bedroom. As he reached for the 12-gauge shotgun that had been loaded with turkey shot, he heard an enormous and powerful boom as Dwight's car crashed into the back of the yellow house.

Kyle's heart sank as he imagined that Timmy didn't make it in time, and Dwight had plowed his car into the stone exterior of the house, crushing Timmy and pinning him to the wall.

The engine revved and a second boom followed as Dwight had backed his car through the front of the hair salon.

Suddenly, things were quiet. Kyle listened for signs that his brother might still be alive. He heard a car door screech open, followed by the sound of one door to the house being knocked down. Kyle continued to hear one door after another being kicked down.

As the sound got closer, Kyle raised his shotgun to his shoulder. Tears streamed down his face as he pumped a shotgun shell into the chamber and prepared to pull the trigger, putting an end to the madman who no one but Kyle seemed prepared to exterminate.

If Dwight was armed with a gun or a knife, the choice would be clear. Blow his head off. If he was unarmed but refused to halt, blow a hole through his chest. Kyle had played this scene over and over again in his mind. He wasn't a killer, but if he had to protect his family, the choice was obvious.

His brother was likely dead or nearly dead and broken into pieces in the backyard. His mother was on the telephone with the police and Dwight was blowing through the house like the big bad wolf. Unfortunately for Dwight, this little pig was ready to blow a hole through the big bad wolf's rampage.

Dwight kicked the door down and was met with the barrel of the 12-gauge shotgun placed right between his eyes. He wasn't armed so he avoided what would have otherwise immediately ended his life.

Kyle stepped back and pointed the shotgun at the center of Dwight's chest. Dwight froze and looked Kyle straight in the eyes.

"Make one more move and I will blow a hole clean through you," Kyle said with unwavering determination. "Don't test me. I'll do it. Not one move."

Sirens screamed in the distance and in a matter of seconds, police officers entered the house in tactical gear, wielding assault weapons and semi-automatic handguns, locked and loaded.

"Freeze! Everybody Freeze! Put the gun down! Now! Put the gun down now! The officer insisted with a commanding and powerful voice.

Anna stepped out from the hallway and said, "It's not my son's fault. It's him!" She pointed at Dwight in desperation.

"Step back lady! Nobody move," the officer commanded yet again. "Nobody move! Set the gun down son!"

Dwight was very calm. His hands were in the air, and he said, "Look fellas. Y'all know me. I'm a volunteer firefighter. This kid is just out of control, and I'm trying to settle him down."

"Don't believe him! He is trying to kill us," Kyle yelled, shaking from the adrenaline rush that had overwhelmed his body.

Dwight remained silent, his hands in the air. One of the officers grabbed Dwight by the shoulders and pushed him to the ground. "Stay down," he commanded.

The other two officers held their guns on Kyle.

An older officer stepped forward and spoke up. "Kyle, it's Officer Stephens. You know you can trust me. We are here now. It's going to be okay. Hand me the shotgun, son."

Kyle recognized the voice as one of the officers who had checked on him from time to time over the years. Officer Stephen's soothing voice continued to encourage Kyle to put down the gun as the seasoned officer reached forward and placed his hand on the barrel of the shotgun, gently pushing it toward the ground.

The moment Kyle relinquished the gun, Dwight lunged for Kyle. "I'll kick your ass you little son-of-a-bitch. You're not the man of this house, and you never will be."

Two of the officers tackled Dwight, one quickly cuffing him.

Kyle buried his head into Officer Stephens Kevlar vest. Officer Stephens handed off the shotgun to another officer and held Kyle in his arms as the boy began to weep uncontrollably.

Tears welled in Officer Stephens' eyes as he spoke softly to Kyle, "It's going to be okay buddy. It's going to be okay. You are safe now."

"Get your hands off my boy, you sorry piece of pig shit," Dwight barked at Officer Stephens. "I'm gonna beat your ass next!"

"Not today, Dwight," came the immediate reply from the six-foot-five rookie cop who had paid a visit to this same address many times before. "Give me a reason, and I'll gladly haul your ass out of here on a stretcher."

Dwight was snatched up to his feet and walked out through what was left of the front of the house, then he was shoved into the back of the rookie officer's cruiser.

It was the last time Kyle would see his dad for many years to come.

Anna stepped into the living room panicking and asking if anyone had seen Timmy.

Just then, Mr. and Mrs. Brown came walking carefully through the rubble that was scattered throughout the house. Dwight hadn't wasted anytime destroying anything that stood in his way. The floors were covered in shattered glass, broken furniture and dirt from potted plants that had tumbled on end, a demolished door holding onto its frame by a single hinge.

"Are you talking about this ornery little toot?" Mrs. Brown said with a smile on her face. "He made a beeline for our house as soon as Dwight lost sight of him.

Mr. Brown added, "I'm just thankful everyone is okay, and Timmy knew right where to go."

"You guys are incredible," Anna said as she grabbed Timmy into her arms and held him tight. "My sweet baby. Thank God you weren't killed."

In the coming days, Dwight stood before the same county judge who had been dealing with his case for months. The judge stripped Dwight of his parental rights and then offered Dwight a deal: leave the state for five years, and he would give him a suspended sentence of two years' probation. Otherwise, Dwight would be facing some serious time for the destruction and violence he had wreaked upon his family.

Dwight agreed to the sentencing, took the offer, and disappeared to California to start a new life.

CHAPTER 22

Life without Dwight was a lot like the tornado they had survived. After they'd surveyed the damage, their house in ruins, they were just grateful they'd made it through.

When it came to their childhood, the boys would say they had no good memories of Dwight. It was sad but true. As hard as they tried to recall a time when they had fun or laughed with him, they simply couldn't do it.

Kyle did have one memory that was tinged with happiness, but in the end, it had been colored with heartache like most of his memories of Dwight.

Kyle had been fascinated with aviation for years. One of his hopes was to be an airplane pilot. Those dreams were crushed when he discovered he was colorblind and wouldn't be able to qualify as a pilot. Nonetheless, he took an interest in remote control model airplanes and set his mind to saving his allowance to buy a kit to build his very own control line model airplane.

Control line model airplanes looked like real airplanes, had real engines, and flew at the end of a small cable string. Once powered up, the operator could fly the model airplane in a circular pattern until it ran out of fuel and glided to a halt, or the operator simply landed the plane at any given point during the flight.

On his tenth birthday, Kyle received the exact model airplane he had hoped for from his grandparents. He couldn't believe his eyes when he pulled the U-Control Junior Aviator Aircraft from the packaging. It was truly one of the happiest moments of his life.

Seeing the thrill on Kyle's face, Dwight grabbed the airplane from Kyle's hands, fueled the small engine, and walked with Kyle to an open field at the local park.

Excitement filled the air as Kyle anxiously waited to send his dream come true into the clouds. But his heart sank when Dwight said Kyle had to wait his turn because Dwight was going to fly the airplane first.

Dwight fired up the engine and Kyle started to jump up and down with great anticipation. Holding the cable handle in hand, Dwight pulled back, sending the model airplane into the air as a normal plane might do.

Sadly, Kyle's turn never came.

As the airplane was making its first round, Dwight stumbled and fell, sending the airplane into the sky at a 90-degree angle from the ground.

As per usual, he overreacted, yanked on the guiding cord, and drove the nose of the airplane flat into the ground. The fuselage crumbled, the wings broke free, and the propeller split into three separate pieces.

"Well, that's a bitch. I can't believe your grandparents bought you such a cheap piece of junk," Dwight said, as if the airplane construction was the problem.

Kyle's shoulders dropped. His eyes teared up, and he stood in bewilderment as Dwight walked away dragging the airplane like a dead dog at the end of a leash.

When they arrived home, Dwight raised the lid on the trash can and dumped the remains of the model airplane in the garbage.

Nothing else was said. The airplane was never replaced, and Kyle never forgot the sadness that overcame his heart as he watched his dad literally drive his dream into the dirt.

These were the kinds of days that Kyle and Timmy were looking forward to putting behind them.

CHAPTER 23

"Shh, be quiet. You guys are going to blow our cover if you aren't careful," came the cautious advice from Randall. He was the funniest of the band of brothers Kyle called friends. The group of boys, while kind and well-mannered, had a knack for crazy pranks that nearly got them thrown into jail on more than one occasion.

On this particular night, the goal was to TP a cute cheerleader's house. The goal was to cover every tree from top to bottom by throwing perfectly good toilet paper to the highest point possible in the tree.

If the launcher was lucky, the paper would snag at the top as the weighted roll of toilet paper fell through lower branches in a zig-zagged fashion throughout the rest of the tree.

The laughing and chuckling of eight teenage boys nearly blew their cover more than once. The trees in the front lawn looked like they had survived a blizzard. If the green grassy lawn was ignored, it would have been easy to assume that the cheerleader lived in a winter wonderland.

Nothing was worse than waking up to trees filled with toilet paper. The only thing that could have been worse was if the morning dew was heavy or a light sprinkling rain dusted the trees overnight. If such was the case, the toilet paper would stick to the branches and remain intact for months on end.

As much as parents hated it, high school girls loved the attention that having their trees covered in toilet paper brought. It was a sign of popularity. It meant the boys had taken notice of them and would do anything to gain attention for their antics, short of getting caught.

"We are almost finished. You guys head to the car, and we'll ring the doorbell and catch up with you," Randall whispered as he directed the secret operation to its conclusion.

The last roll of toilet paper was launched at the moon. Unfortunately, it was overthrown and landed on the roof of the house, the impact much louder than expected.

Everyone froze in a sea of toilet paper as the front porch light was switched on.

In a flash, the cheerleader's dad shot out the front door and demanded that everyone stop in their tracks. Despite his grandest ambitions, not one boy stopped to wave, say hello, or confess to their crime.

When the dad ran into the yard in his robe and slippers, an ash fell from his cigarette and landed in a pile of expended toilet paper. As he walked to the edge of his yard in an attempt to get a better look at the get-away car, a bright glow from a large elm tree caught his attention.

The cigarette ash had caught the toilet paper pile on fire and ascended up a large tree like a fuse on dynamite. The top of the tree exploded into flames but burned out as fast as it had started.

If the trees had been covered in fall foliage, it was possible the entire house may have burnt to the ground. Fortunately, the leaves were green and less likely to combust and ignite into an inferno. Several of the boys didn't make it to the car and remained hidden in the neighbor's shrubs long after the lights and flames from the cheerleader's house had gone out.

"That was a close one," Randall said to Kyle. "I've never seen anything like that in all my life."

"Yeah, that tree was nearly as hot as Susie," one of the other boys said as he laughed in reference to the cheerleader whose yard they had just invaded.

"Are you guys ready for the next trick?" Phil asked the little tribe of bandits.

Phil was one of Kyle's childhood friends. They had been together since kindergarten. Phil stayed close to Kyle and Timmy even in the crazy days when Dwight was drunk and banging on the doors at night during a sleepover.

If things got too wild, Phil would sneak out the back door and walk home to his house a few blocks away. Phil was a loyal friend and would remain so for many years to come.

"I'm all in," Kyle said, as all eight of the boys piled into the car that had looped back around to pick up the stragglers.

"What are we going to do next?" Timmy asked.

"You won't believe it until you see it," Phil said with a grin. "Let's just say it really stinks!"

"What in the world are you doing?" Timmy asked as he observed Phil 's pants at his ankles and a paper grocery sack covering his butt.

"What does it look like I'm doing? I'm taking a dump in a sack! Phil explained, using what was left of the toilet paper.

"What? Why are you crapping in a paper sack?" Kyle inquired. "What exactly are you planning on doing with that bag of crap?"

"Watch this boys," Phil whispered as he pulled up his pants and started toward the front porch of their high school principal's house. "Mr. Cramer is about to do a little dance for us. Just wait and see."

Fourteen sets of eyes gave their full attention to their comrade as he navigated landscaping, yard art, and bird feeders to make his way to Mr. Cramer's porch.

Once there, Phil pulled out a Zippo lighter and produced a small flame that he then touched to the tip of the paper sack full of what had to be a pound of poo.

In a matter of seconds, the sack was engulfed in flames.

Phil rang the doorbell and knocked heavily on the front door. He then leaped over the bird feeders and joined his friends on the edge of darkness.

The front porch light came on. A sleepy-looking Mr. Cramer saw the flames on his porch steps, and despite it being two o'clock in the morning, became fully engaged by stomping out the fire that illuminated the night.

It was instinct more than actual thought of getting burned that led him to pound that sack with his bare feet.

And then it dawned on him; he had been pranked. The smell of the contents awoke his senses as he shook his fist in the air and made his way to a nearby garden hose. Stepping in dog poop was awful enough. But the rancid smell of lumpy human excrement that stuck between his toes was violating. The smoky smell of dung would linger in his nostrils for days.

The boys did everything they could not to burst out in laughter. They knew that getting caught could cost them dearly, but the reward far outweighed the risk.

When school started later that fall, it was hard to see Mr. Cramer in the hallways of school without busting out laughing as they reflected on the principal standing in a pile of Phil's charcoaled dung, stomping out flames like grapes in a winepress.

CHAPTER 24

T he boys had survived most of the summer without getting caught. Their pranks were becoming more and more routine, so they turned to more clever endeavors to up the thrill of their escapades. This time it involved a series of automobile adventures.

Like most outlaws, the boys had developed a certain pattern to their style of mischief.

For the most part, it was essential that no laws were broken, no property was damaged, and everything was done in such a way that, while the pranks might be inconvenient for the victim, it still brought on a reluctant grin when all was said and done.

The boys grew up in a time when few people locked their doors at night let alone their vehicles. This proved to be especially convenient for pranks that involved automobiles.

"Hand me the flashlight. It is darker than a dungeon under this hood," Kyle said as his head was buried in the engine compartment of his favorite high school teacher's 1975 Chevy Impala.

Educators tended to be a prime target for the boys. If you fell victim to one of their pranks, it was more of a sign of affection and affinity than of malice or revenge.

"Forget it. I need both of my hands to make this work. Here, you hold the light and shine it on the back of the headlight while I attach this wire to the connector," Kyle insisted, as he strained to rig a jumper wire from the headlights to the car's horn. His summers at his grandparent's and cousins' farms had taught him a lot about machinery.

"That should do it," he said as he shut the hood and wiped his greasy hands on the front of his old blue jeans. "Next time Miss Hatcher turns on her headlights, her horn is going to honk. She won't notice until later tonight!"

Like clockwork the boys perched across the street from Miss Hatcher's house playing basketball at their buddy's house.

As night fell, the boys sat on the hoods of their cars while they cooled off, drinking sodas, and making predictions on what time Miss Hatcher might leave to attend the local PTA meeting.

Just after 7:30 p.m., Miss Hatcher made her way down the sidewalk to her car. She waved and smiled at the boys as she opened the car door and started the vehicle.

As expected, she turned on her headlights but much to her surprise, her car horn began to blast.

She shut off the headlights and the horn stopped. She turned on the headlights and the horn honked. Again, and again she went through the scenario. Eventually, she gave in to her frustration, backed out of the driveway with her lights shining and her horn blaring.

The boys rolled in the grass with laughter as they eventually heard the horn fading in the distance.

About two hours later, the horn could be heard coming back down the street. To no one's surprise, it was Miss Hatcher ashamedly announcing her presence to the entire block.

As she pulled into the driveway the boys rushed to her aid.

"Everything okay, Miss Hatcher?" Kyle asked the teacher whom he proudly admitted to having a crush on.

She rolled down the window of the car and said, "Hi Kyle. I'm not sure what is going on, but every time I turn on my headlights, my horn honks."

"Do you mind if I take a look under the hood?" Kyle asked with a handsome grin. "Pull the latch, and I will see what I can do."

The boys elbowed each other in the ribs as Kyle tinkered under the hood of the vehicle pretending to work as a master mechanic.

"Oh, I think I see the problem," he said as he turned his head, applied a little engine grease to his cheek, and winked at his buddies. "Pull the light switch now."

"You fixed it!" Miss Hatcher said with excitement. "Thank you so much, Kyle. That was the weirdest thing."

Miss Hatcher exited her car, walked up to Kyle, gave him a slight hug and a peck on the cheek. "You are such a sweet boy. Thank you so much."

Kyle's eyes bulged as he looked over her shoulder during the hug and winked at his accomplices in crime.

As Miss Hatcher walked away, the smell of her perfume lingered as he watched the wind blow her dress around her calves. She may have been a few years his senior, but this was one prank that was well worth the effort. He would do it again and again, in a heartbeat, if it meant he would be guaranteed a kiss and a hug from the prettiest teacher in all the school.

He wasn't certain, but he thought he might be in love.

While the night was young the boys made a tour of the neighborhood, finding classmate's vehicles that were left unlocked. When they did find an unsecured car, they placed a precisely fitted stick between the driver's seat and the car horn.

At just the right time, they released their grip on the stick allowing the pressure of the stick, between the horn and the seat, to sound the car's horn indefinitely until a reluctant resident would wander to the curbside in an effort to identify the source of the honking.

They pulled the same trick over and over again throughout the night, their howls of laughter rising like coyotes at a full moon.

CHAPTER 25

"Did you see that Mr. Jenkins put his old Rambler up for sale?" Kyle asked Phil as they drove down a side street. "I wonder how much he would take for that old car."

Kyle stopped and knocked on Mr. Jenkins' front door. "Hi Mr. Jenkins," Kyle said as he shook the elderly man's hand. "I wanted to stop and ask what price you were asking for that beautiful 1967 AMC Rambler."

"So, you'd like to buy my old Rambler?" Mr. Jenkins asked. "I'll tell you what I'll do. If you will take it off my hands today, I'm not sure what you will think about the price, but if you get it out of my sight by sundown, I'll let it go for one dollar."

"You are joking!" Kyle said.

"One dollar and it's yours. I'm tired of messing with it," came the serious reply.

"Done!" Kyle said, pulling a crisp one-dollar bill from his wallet. The Rambler fired right up with the first turn of the ignition key. The gas gauge showed just over half of a tank.

Kyle hollered for Phil to meet him at the parking lot of the local supermarket. "What are you going to do with this old car?"

Phil asked with a puzzled look. "You sure aren't going to get any dates cruising around in this blue beast."

"I've got a crazy idea," Kyle said.

"I've seen that look before man, and it usually means trouble," Phil said.

"Don't you love watching those crash derby races on TV?" Kyle asked.

"Those are a blast!" Phil said with interest.

"What do you say we take this tank out to your family's farm and drive the guts out of it and have a little crash derby of our own?" Kyle said with excitement.

The boys made the 10-mile drive to the outskirts of town. Phil lifted the gate on the farm's entrance. The farm was made up of 320 acres of hilly pasture, complete with rows and rows of irrigation terraces that helped preserve the precious topsoil from the effects of heavy rainfall.

Phil jumped in the passenger seat of the Rambler, and they were off.

If the Rambler would have had wings, they would have been flying around the tops of the prairie grass, given the reading on the speedometer. Kyle backed the Rambler up to a fence line, and then floored the accelerator.

Without hesitation, he plowed the Rambler over the tops of the hills and terrace. The Rambler was airborne about as much as it was on the ground.

After a while, the jumps were becoming old hat, so the boys started doing donuts at high rates of speed. The goal was to see if they could get the Rambler up on two wheels without tipping the car over on its top.

Kyle and Phil were stirring up a manmade dust devil about the time the centrifugal force laid the Rambler over on its passenger side. Had Phil not been buckled in, he would have likely been thrown from the car and crushed beneath the weight of the Rambler.

As dirt and debris floated and they settled in the cab of the car, the boys wiped their eyes clean, stared at each other in amazement, and simultaneously screamed at the top of their lungs with excitement.

"Unbelievable man! Are you okay?" Kyle asked.

"Dude, I'm fine, but I think your car might have seen better days," Phil replied.

Kyle climbed through the driver's side window and then stood on top of the driver's side of the Rambler. Phil soon followed as they gave each other a high five and jumped to the ground.

"I wonder if we can tip it back flat on the ground?" Kyle asked.

"There is only one way to find out," Phil quickly replied.

For about 10 more minutes the boys pushed with all their might, but the old Rambler just wouldn't give.

"I've got an idea. Wait here," Phil instructed. "I'll be right back." Fifteen minutes later, Phil came riding over the top of a terrace on a Shetland pony.

"What are you thinking, man?" Kyle asked Phil with a look of incredulity.

"This here is Ol' Clyde. As in Clydesdale. Yeah, I know he doesn't look like much, but this stud is as strong as an ox," Phil said with confidence. "Ol' Clyde is gonna show the old Rambler who's the boss."

Phil took a calf rope and attached one end to the side of the Rambler and the other end of the rope to the horn of the saddle. As the rope drew tight, Phil gave the command, "On the count of three, you give the Rambler a push, and I'm going to spur Ol' Clyde. Fifty bucks says that Rambler comes tumbling on the first try."

Much to Kyle's surprise, the idea worked, but only after Ol' Clyde raised up on his back feet and then landed back on all four hooves. With one mighty tug, Ol' Clyde brought the Rambler upright.

"Now that was crazy!" Kyle exclaimed. "What a day, and what a horse!"

Kyle jumped back in the driver's seat, turned the ignition key and the Rambler fired back up ready for more action.

Phil rode Ol' Clyde up to Kyle's car window. "Want to race back to the barn?" Phil asked.

"Game on cowboy! When I honk my horn, let her rip!" Kyle said as he laid into the car's horn and buried his foot on top of the car's gas pedal.

The horn scared Ol' Clyde into a buck as the tires of the Rambler spun out and threw dirt 12 feet behind the car's tailpipe.

Phil leaned his head down by Ol' Clyde's ear and said, "Let's git, boy!"

At first, it looked as though the Rambler would be the clear winner, but the terraces proved to be a major hindrance as Kyle had to slow down at each rise in the ground in order not to bury the bumper of the car in a mound of earth.

Ol' Clyde was kicking up plenty of prairie grass about the time he got to the wire gate that was strung between two fence posts.

In all the excitement, Phil had failed to remember that he had latched the gate shut.

In an uncanny series of events, the saddle began to slide to the left side of the horse as Phil hung on for dear life. At about the same time, Phil drove Ol' Clyde straight into the wire gate.

The horse flipped, sending Phil 10 feet in the air as the saddle migrated to the belly of the Shetland pony.

Phil landed on his chest and slid facedown for 15 feet like a baseball player sliding into home plate. The only difference was that the rider was safe, smack dab in the middle of a fresh cow patty, not home plate.

Amazingly, nobody had been hurt. Not even Ol' Clyde.

As Phil struggled to get up, Kyle pulled up next to him in the Rambler, then howled with laughter as Phil stood up and started digging cow manure from the inside of his shirt.

"Phil! Are you all right?" How did that happen? I saw the saddle sliding off, and the next thing I knew, you and the pony were flying over the top of fence posts," Kyle said as he exited the vehicle and checked on the well-being of his friend and sidekick.

"Other than a shirt full of cow crap, I think I'm going to be okay," Phil said as he caught his breath and gave out a laugh.

"The only thing that could come close to topping today would be last winter when we drove your Honda Civic through those one-story snowdrifts on the country roads," Kyle said with a big grin. "I still can't believe we crammed all eight of us into that little car."

Phil responded with a tired sigh, "We would have gotten stuck if all those guys weren't there to help push us through the snowdrifts. It was crazy blowing through that snow surrounded by nothing but white walls on every side. We are lucky we didn't slam into a car that was buried beneath the snow."

The guys dusted off, jumped in the Rambler, and headed back to town.

Kyle parked the car at a busy intersection and put a for sale sign in the front windshield. The sign read: Runs great. Priced to sell. $250. The Rambler sold within 24 hours. Kyle split the profits with Phil. After all they had been through, he felt certain Phil had earned his fair share of the take.

CHAPTER 26

Dwight had always told Kyle he had no business playing basketball. Timmy was the natural-born athlete. Kyle would need to find something more suited for his talents. Basketball wasn't one of them. But Kyle was determined to prove his dad wrong. Trouble was, Dwight was right. Kyle was built for football and baseball. Basketball really wasn't his sport; but that didn't stop him from trying.

When he was a sophomore, he played on the high school basketball team. Because of his size, more his weight than his height, Coach Wilson would often use Kyle during practice to guard the A-team starters. Not one of them was under 6' 2." The coach knew Kyle was tough and wasn't intimidated by anyone, a trait Kyle had learned from his dad.

"Get in there, Kyle, and push those big boys around. Make them work for it, Kyle," the coach would say as he lined Kyle up at the baseline against guys six to 10 inches taller than him.

It was brutal work. The seniors would elbow Kyle, push him down, pinch him, and do all they could to try and get him to cut them slack during practice.

It never worked. Kyle never relented, and he stood his ground in an attempt to toughen up his teammates and get them ready for fierce competitors. The coach's strategy worked. While Kyle didn't make the traveling team, he watched from the bleachers as his team won the state high school basketball championship. It was a glorious day. Kyle may not have been on the court when the nets were cut, but he knew he played a role in making sure his team could win it all and win it all they did.

Being a B-teamer meant he occasionally got to travel with the A-team. B-teamers might not ever see any action, but they did get to sit closer to the cheerleaders. For that reason alone, Kyle was fine sitting at the end of the bench. Every B-teamer knew that to see the hardwood, the team had to either be ahead or behind by at least 30 points in the fourth quarter.

During one particular away game, Kyle had the opportunity to ride the pine near the water bottles. He served as more of a towel coordinator than a contributing player. By the fourth quarter, every player had played except one, Kyle. The gap in the score continued to grow, and Kyle knew what that meant, there was a high probability that the coach would be calling his name.

As the time clock clicked down to under 20 seconds Kyle did his best to disappear. He leaned as far back on the bench as possible and prayed the coach wouldn't call his name. Kyle was the only player that remained in his warm-up suit, and at this point in the game, who cared if he played? It would be a joke and an embarrassment to get in the game with such little time left to play. It wasn't like Kyle's arrival on the court was going to be a game-changer. "Sanderson!" came the cry from the other end of the bench. "Sanderson, come here. Get your butt in the game."

It was at this point that the next few moments became a blur. It was as if Kyle's life shifted into slow motion. Kyle ripped his warm-ups from his body and stepped onto the court. His teammate immediately threw him an inbound pass. He was in the game!

Normally an inbound pass would not have been a problem for most players, but Kyle was a B-teamer making his first appearance in an A-team game as a forward, not a guard. He wasn't known for his ball-handling abilities. He had more of a reputation as a terminator. Jump in the game. Aggravate the opposing team's big man by drawing four fouls, and then take a seat back on the bench.

Kyle felt as though he was in a trance as he turned and began to dribble the ball toward the basketball goal. The lights were bright, the crowd was huge, and the cheerleaders were shaking more than their pom-poms. It seemed as if time stood still, and the entire auditorium was focused on him.

As the clock neared the zero-mark, Kyle crossed the half-court line and found himself living his greatest nightmare.

Just as he crossed midway, the ball left his left hand but rather than bounce on the basketball court, the ball landed on the end of his basketball shoes. Kyle then kicked the ball skyward toward the basketball goal, the buzzer sounded, and the crowd roared in laughter.

Kyle stood at half court in absolute astonishment. What had just happened? Was this a dream?

As his teammates swarmed him to poke fun and join in on the laughter, Kyle turned and ran toward the locker room. On his way down the stairs, he hit his head on a water pipe causing a huge goose egg sized knot on his forehead. The locker room erupted into chaos and pandemonium as Kyle became the brunt of every joke.

"Come on Kyle! Tell me you did that on purpose?" the team captain asked as he rubbed in the embarrassment. "I thought there for a minute you were kicking a field goal, and you were about to earn us an extra point."

The locker room exploded into uncontrollable laughter as the entire team gave credence to the captain's comments. Kyle gathered his things, lowered his head, and took the longest bus ride of his life back to the team's home court.

All Kyle could think about was what his dad had told him. He wasn't good enough to play basketball. By the looks of it, he should have taken his dad's advice.

A few days later, the team participated in a late evening practice in preparation for a big tournament the following day. Kyle had made it a habit to help the coach make sure everything was orderly and in place before the gymnasium was secured for the night. As Kyle stood with the coach locking the doors, Coach Wilson turned to Kyle and placed a fatherly hand on Kyle's shoulder.

"You know Kyle, it's fair to say that you and I both know it's not very likely that you will ever start on the A-team," Coach Wilson said with tenderness and absolute sincerity. "But let me tell you this. You keep your work ethic and your attitude, and you are going to be something someday."

It was a powerful lesson—one he knew he'd carry with him forever. Everyone has the ability to uplift someone else. A simple smile, a nod of encouragement, a pat on the back, or a few kind words could shift a person's perspective in their hardest moments.

A little positivity didn't just brighten a moment—it had the power to change a life.

Kyle had spent his lifetime desperately in need of affirmation, and his coach had provided encouragement and inspiration in a way that would alter Kyle's life.

CHAPTER 27

Basketball impacted Kyle's life in more ways than one. Being on the team was not just about winning ball games and flirting with cheerleaders; it was about a sense of belonging. There was one group of guys in particular who had gained Kyle's interest. They were outgoing, genuinely good guys who were fun and inclusive. They didn't seem to care where Kyle was from, who his dad was, or what all the other kids at school had to say about his family.

One day in particular, they invited Kyle to a huddle. The name sounded cool, and based on the fact that it was called a huddle, he assumed it would involve other athletes. As it turned out, it was a place where jocks talked about personal challenges and shared struggles they were dealing with. They also talked about things they were learning from a devotional book they had all been reading. At the end of the meeting, the guys prayed together and hung around to help each other with homework.

These guys were different. Not different in a weird way, but in a real and authentic way. They weren't pushy or selling any particular brand of religion. They basically hung out, included anyone, athletic or otherwise, who wanted to have fun together without being vulgar, rude, or obnoxious. Kyle couldn't quite put his finger on it, but he liked the way these guys rolled, and he wanted to know more. He continued to attend huddles and even found himself sharing a few challenges of his own during the meetings.

One Saturday afternoon, Lynn, one of the guys from the group, invited the huddle members over to his house to grill hamburgers and eat homemade ice cream. Kyle was welcomed at the door by Lynn's dad who was wearing a leather apron and holding a spatula in his hand.

"Come on in, my name's Mike. I'm Lynn's dad. Lynn is out back with the rest of the guys," he said, showing Kyle to the backyard where the smell of charcoaled burgers and toasted hamburger buns made everyone's stomach growl.

Lynn's mother was busy preparing homemade ice cream, but immediately relinquished her duties and came over to greet Kyle.

"You must be Kyle. Lynn told me about you. We are glad you are here! I'm Lynn's mom, Mary," she said with a warm smile.

The burgers were great and the ice cream even better. Unlike most teenage parties Kyle had been to, Lynn's parents hung out with the guys, laughing, telling stories, and poking fun.

Kyle had never seen a family be so welcoming and interested in each other and their guests. The hospitality was genuine and from the heart. The house was filled with an atmosphere of peace and acceptance. It was like nothing he'd ever known.

As the boys said their goodbyes and thanked Lynn's parents for dinner, Mike used his forearm to wipe his mouth free of excess ice cream and said, "I'll see you guys in the morning."

The next day was Sunday and Kyle was left to conclude Lynn's dad must have scheduled an early tee time at the country club.

"You guys golf?" Kyle asked the guys as they made their way to their cars.

"No not really, we are more into fishing than golf," Steve replied. He was one of the managers for the football team.

"Oh," Kyle said. "I just assumed you had a golf game going on in the morning."

"Not tomorrow, man," Steve explained. "Tomorrow we are going to church. I thought someone had already invited you. Sorry, man. You are welcome to come. I think you would really enjoy hearing from Pastor Catt."

The following morning Kyle found himself sitting on a church pew with a group of guys who had made him feel right at home. Kyle had been anything but a regular at church. He really wasn't too familiar with how it all worked, but he couldn't help but think this was where he belonged.

These guys weren't super-spiritual, religious nuts, or weirdos, all words he'd heard his dad use to describe church people They just liked hanging out together and encouraging one another in their faith.

For the next several months, Kyle found himself running with a group of guys who would become lifelong friends. They never pushed their faith on him. They simply accepted him and included him in all that they did. It only seemed natural that he would find faith among friends like these.

Faith was something that had been missing from Kyle's life, and once he found it, he never let it go. Thanks to his buddies and Pastor Catt, Kyle discovered a whole new way of living, a completely different way of looking at life and relating to family and friends.

Some would say he found Jesus. He was okay with that, but Kyle preferred to say that he had found the Father of the fatherless. It wasn't religion; it was an intimate relationship with the Creator of the universe.

The next Sunday, Kyle was baptized. The water in the baptistry felt like it was nearly at boiling point. As Kyle stepped into the water, the hair on his legs stood up. Later, he told his momma that the water was so hot that he thought the preacher was trying to baptize the hell out of him.

Anna saw the humor in the joke and reminded Kyle that based on his family tree that might be the very thing he needed!

CHAPTER 28

People at school, and everywhere else, started noticing a difference in Kyle. He smiled more, laughed more, and seemed to be at peace. He had never been a bad boy, but his Bible reading, churchgoing, and huddle meetings were turning him into the kind of man he had hoped someday to be.

With Dwight gone, Kyle began to take on more responsibility at home. He wasn't asked to, but it just seemed like the right thing to do.

Knowing his mom was working long hours, Kyle and Timmy did laundry, cleaned the house, and even made breakfast for dinner on occasion.

One night, Kyle was cleaning up the kitchen, and he noticed a really bad smell. He assumed it was the trash, and even though it was his least favorite chore, he pulled the weighted bag out of the bin, tied it up, and headed out to the big can outside.

It wasn't the garbage duty in and of itself that was the problem, it was the neighbor lady's cats. She must have had 25 that she had to keep fed regularly. But when the cat lady's cat food ran low, the cats would fan out in search of leftovers at all of the other neighbors' trash cans.

As Kyle flipped on the porch light, he saw what felt like a hundred pair of eyes glowing at him. When he pulled the lid off the can, four cats sprang out of the can, screaming and flying at him, claws out. Kyle had really grown to hate cats.

After he took the trash out, Kyle still noticed the weird smell. For several days Kyle, along with Timmy and Anna, searched for the source of the terrible smell, but to no avail.

"Kyle, I think we have a serious problem," Anna said with a worried look. "I think there might be a dead cat under the house."

"What do you want me to do about it?" came Kyle's horrified reply.

She looked at him matter-of-factly and said, "I need you to go get it out. Pretty please. If you don't, that smell is going to be in our entire house.

Kyle was fine learning how to become the de facto man of the house but the thought of crawling under the house in pursuit of a dead cat made him nauseous. However, aiming to please, Kyle made his way outside and stuck his head into the hole of the house's crawl space.

The verdict was clear. The rancid and rotten fumes of a dead animal were coming from somewhere deep in a claustrophobia inducing tunnel that ran the length of the house.

To make matters even more terrifying, dozens of feral cats were running wildly in every direction as the sunlight from the pulled cover of the crawl space cast a thin beam of light beneath the narrow dungeon packed with a colony of feral felines.

Kyle pulled his head out rapidly from the hole as goosebumps erupted on every inch of his body. There was a reason they called it a crawl space. There was no way to maneuver under the house other than like a snake on its belly.

What if the cats decide to attack him and scratch his eyes out as they sank their pointed fangs into his neck. Kyle shivered at the thought of it.

There had to be a safe way to survive the wild-eyed cats and remove the rotten corpse from the darkness.

Kyle got an idea. What if he put on extra clothes, wore gloves, and an overcoat, as well as his old motorcycle helmet that included a face shield. This could provide him the protection he might need should he come under attack.

He didn't realize it at the time, but days and decisions like these were developing him as a leader. He had learned that leaders woke up asking how they could help. Leaders had to make tough decisions and take action in the face of adversity. Most of all, leaders served those they loved.

He felt certain that dragging a dead cat out from underneath his mother's house had to qualify as leadership training for sure.

Kyle suited up like a makeshift astronaut taking his first step on the moon. As he stuck his head back through the hole in the crawl space, he shined his flashlight into the black hole before him. Cats went crazy! Dust went flying and cats exploded into a frenzy. They rushed past, over and around Kyle like pop bottle rockets sent skyward on Independence Day. Luckily, not one cat dared to confront the intruder. Everyone wanted out, including Kyle.

After a few minutes, the dust settled, and an eerie quietness fell over the dank underbelly of his house. The dead body was nowhere to be found, but the smell of death was stronger than ever. Kyle crawled for what felt like 100 miles searching every corner under the house. As he reached through a small hole that separated one side of the house from the other, Kyle heard a squishing sound as his hand pressed down to pull him through to the other side.

He had found the source of his quest, and it was mushy. The remains of an old cat lay on its side with maggots having a feast. It was worse than he had ever imagined.

Kyle grabbed the cat's tail and did his best to navigate in reverse, full speed. If ever there was a scene from hell, surely this was it. Once outside, Kyle took a shovel from the shed and buried the dead cat near the neighbor lady's property line. He was hoping every cat in the neighborhood was watching and realizing that if they ever came near his house again, they would soon be joining their friend in the kitty cat cemetery.

CHAPTER 29

Kyle had developed an entrepreneurial spirit early on. When he was younger, he set up a picnic table on the family's front lawn and sold fresh produce from their garden. And while most kids had rabbits as pets, Kyle and Timmy raised rabbits to sell for food. People loved it. The yard sign read: FRYER RABBITS $1. The boys couldn't keep up with demand.

Eventually, they expanded their enterprise and started mowing lawns in the neighborhood. On one particularly hot summer afternoon, Kyle rode his motorcycle to check on a lawn that Timmy was mowing a good distance from their house. As Timmy wrapped up the work, Kyle came up with the idea of tying the lawnmower handle to the back of the motorcycle to make it easier and quicker to get home.

It seemed like a fun idea, especially when Timmy jumped on top of the lawnmower's engine, hugging that lawnmower like a cowboy hugging a bucking bronco.

Things started off pretty good, but as the motorcycle picked up speed, the lawnmower began to fishtail wildly, leaving Timmy hanging on for dear life.

About the time Kyle was about to lose control of the rig, the flashing lights of a patrol car pulled up behind the haphazard towing operation, commanding Kyle to pull over.

Kyle looked down into his side mirror and hoped for the best as he recognized the officer who approached him shaking his head.

"Boys, what in the world are you thinking? Are you trying to get yourselves killed, or are you just practicing for a new circus act?" the officer asked as he did his best to suppress a grin.

"Hello, Officer Bullard," Kyle said with humility. "I suppose this isn't one of my better ideas?"

"Well, considering your brother was hanging on with a terrified look on his face, and this motorcycle didn't come equipped with a trailer hitch, I think you might do better-selling vegetables and slaughtering those cute little bunnies you guys are known for," the officer said with a stern voice.

"I tell you what. If you unstrap that lawnmower and push your motorcycle the rest of the way home, I won't impound your motorcycle, and I won't give you a ticket."

"Yes sir," Kyle said hurriedly as he swung his leg over the back of the motorcycle and Timmy joined him to assist in untying the lawnmower. "Not a problem at all, sir. Thank you very much."

"All right then. You boys keep up the hard work but stay out of trouble and use your heads. My goodness!" the officer said as he turned and walked back to his patrol car.

The officer grabbed the mic to his radio as he regained his seat in the patrol car. "Unit 39 to base," he said as he connected with the police dispatcher.

"Go ahead unit 39," came the reply.

"The motorcycle lawnmowing crew has been taken off the street. No harm. No foul. They have been advised to walk the rest of their route home. Over," the officer said as he updated headquarters on his traffic stop.

"Roger that, those boys are a mess, Officer Bullard," the dispatcher chuckled

"Good kids for sure. Especially given their home life," Officer Bullard said as he made one final comment. "Going offline for about 30 minutes. I am making a pitstop to pick up some fresh produce and a couple of fryer rabbits."

"Roger that. I know just the place. Over and out," came the sign-off from the dispatcher.

It was clear by the sound of her voice, that she was smiling from ear to ear. She knew those boys well. The whole police department did. They had been protecting and pulling for these kids for years.

Later that Fall, Kyle secured a part-time job as a parts runner for a local electrical company. One afternoon, Kyle was making a delivery to a job site when the operator of an underground boring machine asked if Kyle would mind helping him break the joints in the drilling rig that was running under a road where a high voltage electrical wire would soon be laid. Kyle jumped out of the delivery truck, slid a long cheater bar over a large pipe wrench, and laid it on the ground for leverage.

As he stood with his legs apart directly facing the pipe wrench and cheater bar, he gave the signal for the operator to spin the drill in reverse.

Confused by the control panel, the operator mistakenly sent the drill in the opposite direction.

The pipe wrench and cheater bar spun rapidly in the wrong direction and slammed Kyle in the face. The force knocked him backward and on his back. Blood erupted from his face. He was immediately surrounded by the work crew who did their best to come to his aid.

"Oh my God, call an ambulance. His face is crushed. I think I killed him," the operator screamed in panic.

Kyle slipped in and out of consciousness and eventually fell into shock as medical personnel arrived on the scene and tried to stop the loss of blood. Blood covered Kyle's chest and filled his eye sockets as the extent of his injuries was assessed.

The last thing he remembered was the face of Officer Bullard as he gripped Kyle's hand and told him to hang on. "You're a fighter son. I've seen you fight off worse than this. You're going to be alright."

Kyle woke up in the hospital following emergency surgery. Officer Bullard was seated next to his hospital bed with Anna. He was still in his bloody uniform. He hadn't left Kyle's side throughout the night.

Kyle tried to speak, but his face was too swollen, and his mouth was wired shut.

The doctor walked in, and Kyle overheard the conversation between his mother and the medical team.

"He is lucky to be alive. If he had been a centimeter closer to the boring machine, it would have driven his nose into his brain. A little to the left or right and he would have lost his vision. If it had hit his chin, it would have shattered his jaw. It hit him right under the nose," the doctor explained. "If it was going to happen, it landed in the perfect place."

The doctor continued, "Due to the extent of the injuries to his upper lip and teeth, we had to wire his mouth shut. Luckily, there was a plastic surgeon in the hospital at the time Kyle arrived at the ER. The surgeon assisted us with stitching him back up. It's a very ugly gap. It split his lip in half, all the way up to under his nose."

Anna broke down and cried as Officer Bullard consoled her aching heart. It seemed so much of her life was wrapped in tragedy and near-death experiences. This one had come too close. She could have lost Kyle before he was born. She nearly lost him at birth. He had nearly lost his life at the hands of an insane father. The thought of losing him now was unthinkable. He was a true survivor.

Kyle was soon out of the hospital and feeding himself smoothies through a straw. The hardest part was trying not to laugh when friends stopped by to check on him. He had to squeeze his upper lip together with his hand so the stitches wouldn't pull apart when he laughed.

His friends had a field day teasing him about his mangled face.

"Come on guys," Kyle said, "don't you know girls love a man with scars. Makes him look rugged."

"Yeah man," they teased, "You'll be lucky if you even get a girl to look at you."

Kyle threw his pillow at them. He was lucky alright, lucky to be alive. It wasn't the first time in his life he'd felt that way. He looked around at the friends who surrounded him and knew he was lucky in many ways.

CHAPTER 30

Kyle started back to school with a zipper in his lip. Not literally, but it looked as such. It made for great conversation and surprisingly, served as a chick magnet. The girls at school had already found him to be handsome and endearing, but now they had an opportunity to express their sympathies and admire his toughness.

"You should run for student council," one of the cute girls suggested as she looked at Kyle, batting her eyelashes .

"Me? Nah, nobody would vote for me. I'm just a working-class kid that lives next to the railroad tracks," Kyle said, brushing off the suggestion.

"I'm serious," she said, and she was. "I'm nominating you and making your campaign signs."

The election took place the following week and Kyle won. It was a huge self-esteem booster. It strengthened Kyle's confidence and began laying the foundation for leadership roles that he would play throughout the rest of his life.

His senior year he was encouraged to run for Student Council President against a very popular opponent among the more affluent kids in school. Much to Kyle's surprise, he won hands down.

"You won because people feel like you are one of them. You know everybody, and they know you. You accept them for who they are, and you don't run in clicks," came the comments from his original campaign manager. "You're a tough guy who found Jesus, but you are the real deal, and people get it."

Kyle was genuinely humbled by her comments. All he ever knew was to be himself. He understood rejection and what it was like not to be accepted in the so-called, "in crowd."

Kyle had spent the better part of his early life crushed by a man who didn't know how to love anyone. Kyle had made it his goal a long time ago, to wake up every morning looking for "the one" to love that day. He rarely missed an opportunity to fulfill his ambition. Somedays it was the cashier behind the counter at the convenience store who needed to know she was loved. At other times it was the cafeteria lady who dished out mashed potatoes. It might be the janitor who was working two jobs to make ends meet or even a fellow classmate, teacher, or coach who needed to feel the love. Regardless of who it was, Kyle went about his day looking for ways to lift people up and help them recognize their lives mattered no matter what their role in life might be.

* * *

Kyle's leadership skills eventually led to an opportunity to accept a scholarship at a state university. College was something Kyle had thought about occasionally, but he never gave too much thought to it because he wasn't sure how he would ever afford it. His leadership scholarship opened doors he never thought would be open for him. Needless to say, he accepted the scholarship and became one of the first in his entire family to ever attend college. The scholarship provided the open door to college, but staying there would also require Kyle to be part of a work-study program.

Kyle was fine with working hard for what he wanted. At one point in his college career, he held down four different jobs to make it through. There was one semester where he was lucky to get four hours of sleep before having to attend class.

College exposed Kyle to a whole new world. There were so many different types of people from all around the globe. He wanted to meet them all and learn about life where they came from. His interest in people led him to be elected to the university student body senate and to become a resident adviser to the international dormitory. This international exposure gave Kyle a strong desire to see what life looked like beyond the southern plains of the United States. He quickly learned that cultural norms weren't wrong per se, they were just different, and being different is what brought spice to life.

Something else Kyle learned about himself was that despite how much trauma he had experienced in his life, and how that life had matured him in many ways, he lacked a lot of information about everyday life. One such piece of information was how in the world the college boys got their shirts so stiff. As hard as he tried, he could never get his ironed shirts to look so crisp and clean.

One day in class he leaned over and asked a fellow classmate what the trick was to getting shirts so well pressed. The classmate laughed and said, "It's all about the starch, man. Haven't you ever heard of a dry cleaners?"

Kyle raised his eyebrows and gave the comment some thought. He recalled seeing a business in his hometown with that title, but he never knew what the business was about. Thinking he had figured out the solution. Kyle purchased a can of spray starch, read the instructions, and laid on the spray. Unfortunately, as hard as he worked at ironing the shirts and applying the starch, he could never get his shirts to the level of stiffness that he desired.

At the risk of looking the part of a fool, Kyle confessed his dilemma to that same classmate. "Hey, I bought some starch and applied it during my ironing, but I must be doing something wrong. My shirts still aren't as stiff as yours."

"Dude, you are killing me!" came the reply. "Take your shirts to the dry cleaners and ask them for heavy starch. Trust me you will be walking at attention for the rest of your life."

The next day, Kyle gathered his shirts and made his way to the dry cleaners. He wasn't sure what to say but the lady behind the counter took control.

"How many you got, sweetie, and how do you like your starch?" she asked as she began to scribble on a ticket.

"Uhm…. six," came Kyle's reply. "Six, heavy starch."

"When do you need them by?" she asked without looking up.

"Need them by? Kyle asked.

"Baby, have you ever been to a dry cleaners?" the lady asked.

"No ma'am," Kyle replied.

"Let me help you out. Come back in two days and I'll have these shirts on hangers for you ready to go," she said with a smile.

"Excuse me," Kyle inserted. "Do hangers cost extra? I already have hangers."

"No, honey they don't, and let me give you a hint. If you want your shirts to stand stiff like those fraternity boys . . . you aren't in a fraternity are you?" she said with a pause.

"No ma'am. I am not," Kyle replied with interest.

"Didn't think so. Anyway, if you want your shirts to be like theirs, you need to buy 100% cotton shirts. Starch will work on polyester shirts, but it really loves cotton. Make sense?" she asked.

"Yes, ma'am and thank you," Kyle said as he walked away with a wealth of laundry knowledge.

His family had always bought polyester shirts. The cotton shirts cost a whole lot more. Besides, you couldn't just throw cotton shirts in the dryer like you could a polyester shirt. If you did, they would come out as wrinkled as a bulldog's face.

In a few days, Kyle found himself prancing around campus like a toy soldier freshly unpacked from a bandbox. He did his best to straighten his posture. His newly starched shirts gave little choice to do otherwise.

CHAPTER 31

Summer break came, and that meant more time with friends and plenty of time for parties, cookouts, and opportunities to catch up on life since high school.

There had been eight guys that Kyle had grown close to over the years. Based on their ages, some were in college and others were still in high school. Several of the guys were brothers, so the overlap kept them close but also at different stages of schooling. One thing they did have in common was a love for attending the largest youth encampment in the world, Falls Creek.

Falls Creek was host to thousands of young people each summer. The gathering was so large that the camp even had its own post office and grew to the size of most county seat towns overnight. Growing in your faith was the purpose of the camp, but someone would have to be a fool not to recognize the potential to meet someone cute during walks between camp meetings and recreational activities.

ICEE dates were the perfect opportunity to get to know someone better. The summer heat had couples standing in long lines for the fruity crushed ice treat that had more the consistency of a smoothie than a traditional snow cone. The lines didn't seem to bother anyone, so long as they had the opportunity to meet a cute guy or girl as they endured the dry heat and dusty breezes.

If campers weren't at the ICEE stand on a date, they found themselves cheering on a volleyball team, playing softball, swimming at the Olympic-size pool, or hiking on the miles of trails that lined the foothills of the Arbuckle Mountains.

Following the nightly service, there was about an hour of free time when groups of teenagers would roam the streets of the camp, basically cruising pedestrian style as their parents did on public streets in their hotrods in the 1950s. On one particular evening, Kyle and his group of friends were making the rounds. Pretty girls were as plentiful as stars in the sky and scattered everywhere you looked.

It wasn't always easy to gain the attention of the opposite sex without looking like a goon or coming off as too forward. Kyle and the guys came up with an idea. It was borderline goofy but in their minds, pure genius. The idea was for Kyle and Gregory to act as if Gregory had lost his contact lenses and crawl around on the ground as they tried to locate them. The rest of the guys were to circle around Kyle and Gregory and ask onlookers to please stand back, so as to not step on the valuable corrective lenses.

Kyle placed a small bottle of eyewash in his hands, knelt down on his knees, squirted liquid in both eyes, and did the same for Gregory. Once the props were in place the bad actors began to crawl around pretending to be crying and searching for Gregory's lost contact lenses. They asked for assistance from anyone who passed them by.

It was pitiful in every way, but it worked! Guys who passed by saw right through the antics, but girls on the other hand, either out of sympathy, naivety, or seeing the opportunity to meet a group of guys, stopped and offered to help in any way possible.

Seeing their time for milking the deception was quickly coming to an end, Gregory miraculously pretended to find his contact lenses. The boys may have looked silly and desperate, but as a result, they were surrounded by pretty girls. Who could have asked for a better outcome?

One girl, in particular, caught Kyle's eyes. His heart raced when he looked into her eyes. Her smile was like something out of a Hollywood movie and when she spoke, it was all he could do not to just look at her in an absolute stare.

"Hi, my name is Kyle. Thanks for helping us find Gregory's contact lenses," Kyle tried to say convincingly. "What's your name?"

She gave her name, but Kyle's mind had entered into another orbit. She was the most beautiful girl he had ever seen. Everything around him disappeared, and all he could do was look into her eyes and daydream. When he noticed her lips weren't moving, which provided a whole other level of distraction, Kyle awoke from the trance that she appeared to hold on him.

"I'm sorry, forgive me. What did you say your name was?" Kyle asked as he stepped closer to her and picked up on the smell of her perfume.

"My name is Christine," she said with an adorable smile. "You really don't think we bought into your whole sideshow, do you?"

"What do you mean?" Kyle retorted with a bit of a giggle and a slight sigh of exasperation. "He totally has contacts."

"I never said he didn't have contacts. You know what I mean," she said as she walked away joining the rest of the girls she had come with.

Kyle couldn't help but watch her, mesmerized by every part of her as she walked away. He stood frozen in what had to be the beginnings of love.

"Hey, did anybody get any of those girls' names or phone numbers?" Kyle announced to the group of guys.

I got you covered," Lynn said as he held up not one, not two, but three sets of digits. "I may not be good with words, but I'm good with numbers!"

"Are the numbers from near here?" Kyle asked.

"It appears so my friend," Lynn continued. "The good news is that they all live just on the other side of the lake from us. But there is some bad news."

"I'm listening, "Kyle said inquisitively.

"None of them have boyfriends, except for one," Lynn explained. "Care to guess?"

"Don't tell me. Christine," Kyle said with a disappointed voice.

"You got it, big boy! Sorry to break the bad news. She was the cutest one for sure but, hey, were those other girls not sweet?" Lynn said as he motioned for everyone to move along.

Kyle knew Christine was special. In fact, he believed she was "the one." He couldn't help but think that God had orchestrated all of what just happened so they would meet.

She may be gone, and she might be taken, but as far as Kyle was concerned, all that was temporary.

"Oh, hey, Kyle. Did I mention she's fourteen?" Lynn asked. "Get your head out of the clouds old man. She's jailbait for a college guy like you."

"That can't be possible. She looked so much older. She acted so mature." *She was so beautiful*, Kyle thought to himself. "I may have lost my mind, but I'm not giving up just yet. I'll wait for as long as I need to," he said to his friend.

It turned out that the girls did live close, and they were just as nice as the guys had hoped. In an unpredictable way, the guys and girls became good friends as much as anything else. Kyle would show up at parties from time to time and Christine would be there. He tried his best to simply speak to her, like he did all the other girls, keeping it cool, keeping it appropriate, but his heart just kept drawing him back to her.

He realized the age difference, and he knew she was seeing someone else, but none of that mattered if she was the one.

The age difference would mean less over time, and based on what he was hearing through the grapevine, the guy she was seeing wasn't that great of a catch. Kyle decided to take a bold step and had a little chat with her closest friend, Carla.

"Carla," Kyle said as he stood by an ice chest near the swimming pool at a friend's party.

"Yes, Kyle," Carla replied.

Carla was a beautiful young lady as well. She had long blonde hair, a great smile, and an awesome personality. Everyone loved her. Like Kyle, she was often the life of the party.

"Carla, I wanted to tell you something that I hope can stay between us," Kyle said with a whisper.

"Certainly," she said as she bit the end off of a carrot stick and gave Kyle a wink. "I'm listening."

"Carla, I know that Christine is dating another guy, and I know I'm one of the older guys in the group, but," Kyle paused and looked Carla directly in the eyes.

"But, what?" she said with a smile.

"Well, if anything ever changes in their relationship, would you mind letting me know?" he asked almost inaudibly.

"Mr. Kyle, I've got you covered," she said with a smile as she stepped into his personal space. "Not only do I have you covered, but I like the way you think."

She bumped him with her hip, smiled, and walked away.

Kyle stood there wondering what Carla was trying to communicate. Had he stepped over the line? Did Carla know something he didn't? Was she trying to play matchmaker? Did she think Christine and Kyle were a match made in heaven? He sure hoped so! Whatever it was, it would have to wait. Kyle had to be at work early the next morning, so he had to leave before the party ended. He said his goodbyes and headed home.

Little did he know, for some in the group there, it would be their last goodbye.

CHAPTER 32

The telephone rang in the middle of the night. Kyle heard his mother answer the phone and immediately heard the concern in his mother's voice as she spoke softly to the caller.

Anna hung up the telephone and began to cry as she walked in and sat at Kyle's bedside.

"What's wrong, Mom. Everything okay?" Kyle asked as he sat up in bed.

"There has been a terrible accident and some of your friends have been killed in a car wreck," she said as she wept uncontrollably. "Some of the parents wanted to make sure you knew and felt you would want to be at the hospital. There is concern that some of the others might not make it through the night."

Anna didn't say who had been killed, their lives cut short way too soon. No matter who it was, the loss to Kyle would be the same. His love for his friends was no respecter of persons. He loved them equally. The news would not be easy regardless of who it was.

The emergency room lobby was packed tight with parents doing the best they could to comfort their children. Everyone was in tears. Some knelt in circles praying. Others wrapped their arms around friends and wept uncontrollably, unable to speak. Nearly everyone was still in their bathing suits or had beach towels wrapped around their waists to stay warm.

Lynn's dad, Mike, saw Kyle from across the room and lumbered his way through a sea of mourners to share the terrible news of what had happened.

"Kyle, I'm so sorry. It is just terrible. It is tragic in every way," Mike said, before he was abruptly interrupted by Lynn before he could finish his explanation.

Lynn barreled into Kyle and buried his head in Kyle's chest and wept uncontrollably. He tried to speak but the words would not pass through his lips. His throat was locked tight, his eyes were bloodshot and bursting with pools of tears. Snot ran freely from his nose. His mouth was dry as foam gathered at the corners of his mouth.

"They are gone. I can't believe it. They are gone," Lynn said as he forced the words from his mouth. Every word was laced with the impact of gut-wrenching pain.

Kyle looked deep in the eyes of Lynn desperate to gain clarity in the midst of the jarring chaos. "Who is gone? What happened? Who was killed?" Kyle asked as he swallowed panic, breaking free from Lyle's tortured embrace. Gripping Lynn's shoulders he asked again, "WHO?"

"Carla and Rick. They didn't make it. Gregory is in surgery, and they think he might either die or be a vegetable if he lives," Lynn said as he struggled to stand. He leaned into Kyle and held him tight as he sought relief from the trauma that weighed heavy on the hearts of family and friends.

Not believing what he was hearing, Kyle sat solemnly among his friends, piecing the story together. He felt as if he were walking through a war zone where shellshocked survivors tried to gather their senses and process the scene before them.

From what he gathered, shortly after he had left, a few other friends left the party early as well. Carla and Christine had ridden to the party together, but when Christine had to leave early, Gregory offered to give Carla a ride home.

Gregory had just bought a Ford Mustang convertible. It was fully loaded with a high-fidelity stereo system, leather seats, and plenty of power. Brian and his little brother, Rick, jumped in the car with Gregory and Carla, and together, they sped off to try to get Carla home by her midnight curfew.

Gregory and Brian sat in the front seat, and Carla and Rick sat in the back seat as Carla's long blonde hair danced across the trunk of the convertible.

The stereo was at full volume as the friends danced in their seats and pretended to be performers in an air band. If it had been a karaoke competition, they would have been the clear winners.

As they sang carefree, the cool night air blowing across their skin, Gregory became distracted as he tried to advance to the next song on his mix tape.

The highway was pitch black, and a curve in the road was quickly upon them. Unmarked road construction caused the passenger wheels of the Mustang to drop off a one-foot unguarded shoulder of the road.

Gregory panicked and did his best to keep the vehicle from sliding off the edge of the highway. He rammed through road signs, wooden barriers, safety cones, and yellow warning tape. In his attempt to avoid colliding with a massive road grader, he yanked the steering wheel of the car to the left.

He overcompensated, and the vehicle was soon out of his control. The car plunged into a grass covered culvert that separated opposing traffic. Spinning in circles and heading toward oncoming traffic, the vehicle exited the culvert, became airborne, and flew recklessly through the air.

A family of four was making their way home down the highway and never knew what hit them as the front grill of the Mustang slammed into the driver's side window of the oncoming car.

The impact flipped the Mustang end over end as Carla and Rick's heads were crushed beneath the weight of the car during ejection.

Brian was trapped in the vehicle and nearly bled to death as his back was cut open from being dragged beneath the front windshield of the car.

Gregory had been thrown clear during the collision but sustained massive head injuries as his head was slammed against the roof of the opposing vehicle.

Reports confirmed that no one in the other car had survived the accident. A total of six people had lost their lives in just a matter of minutes. And now, Gregory was battling to stay alive, and Brian was in excruciating pain and would require multiple surgeries and months of rehabilitation before he would even be able to walk without assistance.

Denying his own emotions, Kyle made his way from friend to friend, comforting them and listening as they released their anguish and pain. Inside he was heartbroken, devastated, and crushed. But, just as he had done as a young boy, for his mother and brother, the protector and warrior in him rose to the mission at hand. Somehow he found a way to draw from his inner strength and leaned on the faith that had gotten him through tragedy so many times before.

As the morning sun began to shine through the glass of the automatic doors of the emergency room, a doctor and medical team entered the lobby to provide a long-awaited update.

"First we want you to know that we did everything we could to save Carla and Rick. Their injuries were just too severe, and there was nothing we could do. I'm terribly sorry," the surgeon shared with a heavy heart.

"It is still touch and go for Gregory. He has suffered a severe brain injury. We have been able to stop the bleeding and are doing our best to keep his brain from swelling. If he pulls through, he will have a long road ahead. Truthfully, he might never be the same."

"Brian has had more than 1,000 stitches and has had to have multiple skin grafts. He is sedated. Infection is our greatest concern. It took hours to clear his wounds of glass and gravel. I expect he will make a full recovery, but it will be months before life will ever be close to normal for him."

"Finally, please know that our thoughts and prayers are with you. I have never seen such a caring and loving group of family and friends. You are fortunate to have each other. Hold each other tight as you do your best to recover from this terrible loss."

The medical team exited the lobby quietly as a painful silence held for several minutes in the room.

Exhaustion finally started to take its toll on everyone. Slowly and reluctantly the friends began to leave the hospital.

The night's events were a sober reminder that no one ever knows when they might breathe their last breath. It was a reminder never to take for granted the privilege of friendship. It was certainly a reminder to hug a little longer, forgive a little faster, and express love and appreciation every chance you got.

CHAPTER 33

The parking lot of the church was packed beyond capacity as police officers on motorcycles did their best to direct traffic and get everyone inside before the funeral began. Extra seats had to be brought in to accommodate the crowd. It was as if the entire community had come out to mourn the loss of a beautiful soul who had left way too soon. Carla had been one of those people who made everyone smile. She lit up the room when she walked in. Everyone loved her.

As Kyle sat in a row directly behind Christine, he couldn't help but think of the last conversation he had had with Carla. Did she make Christine aware of his affection for her, or was it a secret that she would take to her grave? Kyle knew it was far from what mattered at that moment. The heartbreak that filled this somber event had captured the minds of everyone present. It was so senseless, tragic, and unfair.

Tears were not enough. Hugs were not enough. Kind words fell short. Carla's friends walked about in silence. Sadness covered their faces. They had lost the heart of their friend group. How would life go on without the sunshine Carla brought to each and every person she touched. The casket sat starkly at the front of the auditorium. Organ music played, and while it was meant to be beautiful, it felt more haunting than angelic as it filtered over hearts deadened by grief.

Rows and rows of colorful flowers made it difficult to see the platform. Word on the street was that it took the efforts of three florists from two separate counties to accommodate the needs for Carla's funeral. No one was surprised. If there had been more time and enough inventory, there wouldn't have been enough flowers in the entire state to help heal the hurt that penetrated so deeply into the hearts of the onlookers.

The minister's words seemed appropriate, but no one really remembered a word he said. All they could think about was that sweet Carla was at rest under the lid of the beautiful walnut box that should have otherwise contained the lifeless body of a senior citizen, not a high school senior and former beauty queen.

No one looked up. Heads turned downward as tears stained the small paper obituary that somehow hoped to encapsulate all that Carla's life had represented. Words were worthless in this setting. There was no way to summarize a life so well-lived, a life beautiful in every way. If ever there was someone who was beautiful inside and out, it was Carla.

The funeral service was nearing its end when the moment everyone dreaded was about to take place. No one had taken it harder than Christine. It was all she could do to keep from collapsing as the reality of the moment overwhelmed her. Kyle couldn't help but notice the lack of empathy and concern Christine's boyfriend expressed throughout the service. Her boyfriend sat there stiffly beside her. Not one tear so much as pooled in his eye. He never put his arm around Christine. While the heads of others bowed from the weight of their loss, he gazed around the room and kept pushing back his shirt sleeve looking at his watch.

Kyle felt a surge of anger rise from deep within. It was all he could do to keep from slapping the idiot boyfriend in the back of the head. What an insensitive, selfish jerk. Kyle leaned forward and placed his hand on Christine's shoulder. He whispered in her ear, "She loved you. You were her best friend."

Christine bent her arm at the elbow, continued looking forward but placed her hand on top of Kyle's and gently patted the top of his hand.

Kyle's heart sank as he felt a certain part of her pain transferring to his shoulders. These types of burdens were meant to be shared. No one should ever have to face such a great loss alone, certainly not among a sea of friends.

The director of the funeral home approached the casket and gingerly removed an array of magnificent pink roses from the top of the casket. Tension took hold of every onlooker in the room. No one wanted to experience what would happen next, but everyone knew this moment was needed to bring closure.

Kyle would have been satisfied to hold his last memory of Carla from the party in his mind forever. She had been so charming, playful, and supportive. The thought of that being their last encounter broke his heart.

As the lid to the casket was pushed back, a somber hush and palpable gasp fell across every spirit present. The funeral director stepped away, and there she lay, her motionless, dead body adorned in a beautiful pink dress.

Lines began to form as the procession to view the body was underway. A quiet hush fell across the mourners. As Kyle neared her body, it was all he could do to move forward. It was her, but it looked nothing like her. Her beautiful face was swollen beyond recognition. The powdery makeup concealed deep dark bruises. Her lips lacked the smile that she was known for as they were sealed with some sort of undertaker glue that had dried to a fine crust between her lips.

And then, what he saw next nearly brought him to his knees. Christine slowly and calmly approached the casket. Her mental resolve and strength were stoic as she looked upon the face of her friend, and then ever-so-gently, she kissed Carla's cold and clammy forehead and held her hand for one last time. How she had made it through her visit to the casket was beyond him.

Christine wept quietly, but deeply as she stroked Carla's hair. The injury had been primarily to the back of her head. The pillow that supported her helped hide where surgeons had to shave her golden locks away as they had tried their best to bring her back to life. The doctor's efforts had failed, and the life that was so alive and full of joy was crushed and destroyed in an instance. Her body was there, but Carla wasn't.

Kyle had a deep sense of understanding that life was more than just the physical. There was another dimension to life, that while not visible, it existed in a realm where Carla's soul now resided. He couldn't help but think that they would someday meet again in a new and different way.

Along with Carla's other male friends, Kyle placed his hands around the rails that ran down the sides of Carla's casket. They did their best to hold their heads high as they tried to honor

Carla with valor. Tears streamed down their cheeks as they slid the heavy wooden box into the back of the hearse.

The funeral procession was more than a mile long. Motorcycle cops blocked off intersection after intersection as the long row of black vehicles slowly made their way to the cemetery. The wind blew gently as a thunderstorm began to form in the western sky. Clouds brought much-needed relief from the summer heat.

Once the young men placed Carla's casket in its final resting place, they stepped aside allowing Carla's family and her best girlfriend space to say their final farewells. As Christine stood alone weeping, Kyle could take it no longer. He stepped past her boyfriend and took her into his arms. Together they cried and comforted one another as they embraced tightly with deep concern and pain. Kyle placed his hand on the back of Christine's neck and softly whispered in her ear," I'm so sorry. I know she was everything to you. I'm here for you. You don't have to go through this alone. I love you." Kyle wiped a tear from Christine's cheek and gently touched his lips to her forehead as he kissed her and stepped away.

Other than attending Rick's funeral, the group didn't see each other again. The friends couldn't bring themselves to gather without Carla's presence. It was their way of mourning her loss. None of them were ever the same again.

As the years past, graduation came for many of them and their focus shifted to becoming active college students. Kyle had been a patient gentleman, waiting for Christine just as he had always known he would.

They had spent some time together before she arrived on the university campus, but Kyle felt the need to make his feelings clear and their relationship official before he left to take a job at the United States Senate in Washington D.C. Long-distance relationships were never easy, but how could he deny that this girl had captured his heart?

He wondered how a person could ever know if they had found true love. All he knew was that he couldn't imagine spending the rest of his life without her. They would be apart, but his heart would be with her no matter how much distance came between them.

They had gotten close and had even kissed. It was up for debate who had kissed whom first. They had been together for more than a month before his lips touched hers. He would swear for years to come that she leaned in and laid one on him. She would deny it forever. He knew how he remembered it, it was beyond his wildest dreams, either way.

Before he left for the nation's capital, Kyle saw an opportunity to express the overflow of his heart. As they sat on the fireplace of her sorority house, he looked her in the eyes, held her hands, and softly said, "I love you."

There was no reply. Nothing. Christine surrendered a small smile, patted him on the tops of his thighs, hugged him, and encouraged him to write letters while he was away.

He wouldn't learn until a holiday break that she had felt the same but was simply too overwhelmed to express her feelings. At the time, Kyle was slightly crushed by her response but was determined not to give up on the girl of his dreams.

CHAPTER 34

Professor Bennett had taken a job in Washington D.C., and when he saw a job opening at the United States Senate, he thought of Kyle.

Based on his leadership connections, Kyle received excellent referrals from one of his state's U.S. Senators, the president of a local TV station, and Professor Bennett.

Kyle's arrival to Washington D.C. was truly monumental. He was taken aback by the majestic buildings, beautiful cherry blossoms, and the number of world leaders he was meeting face-to-face. Not only that, these leaders here were commonplace on the nightly network evening news, and he was there with them walking the halls of the United States Capitol.

He had come a long way since he had been a kid who lived next to the railroad tracks, whose dad was a dock worker who beat his momma, whose momma had become a beautician and raised two young boys on her own.

He had survived nearly being killed at least three times in his life, now wore starched shirts, a suit, and wing-tipped dress shoes. He had a beautiful girl in his life, and now he was literally working alongside world leaders. Could this really be true? Was this really his life?

Professor Bennett offered Kyle a place to stay, and Kyle seized the opportunity to live with such a loving and caring young family. There was something very special about the professor and his wife, "Ollie and Nita" as they'd instructed Kyle to call them. They weren't perfect, but they demonstrated a commitment to each other, their family, and their faith, that Kyle had never experienced before. They were living examples of how to love your spouse, raise your kids and live out your faith in a practical nonreligious way.

It was not enough to say he was grateful for the experience; it was more like a miracle to him.

Life with the Bennetts was like an incubator for life that filled in all the missing cracks from his upbringing. It was an opportunity to unlearn and relearn what it meant to be a man who truly loved and cared for his family.

Working at the United States Senate was amazing enough but living under the same roof with the Bennett family changed Kyle's perspective on manhood, fatherhood, and what it meant to be a loving husband.

Kyle kept his promise to send letters to Christine. He missed her severely. He had discovered what it meant to be lovesick. He thought of Christine constantly and wondered if she thought of him as much as he thought of her. Her birthday was coming soon and as much as he hated it, he wouldn't be there to celebrate with her. Never short on creativity though, Kyle devised an idea that nearly got him into serious trouble. If he couldn't be there to cut the cake and blow out the candles, why not send her a cake of his own making?

Hostess cupcakes provided the perfect baseline for what he called: The Compact Cake Kit. Kyle packaged the cupcakes neatly into a shipping box along with candles, a card, a small butane lighter, and meticulously hand-written assembly instructions. He thought nothing of it as he innocently passed the Compact Cake Kit through the X-ray machine and dreamed of Christine's reaction as it moved down the conveyor belt at the Capitol security checkpoint on his way to the Capitol post office.

As soon as the box made it through the X-ray machine, the hallway was suddenly lit up with flashing lights, alarms sounding, and Capitol policemen at full attention.

"What's in the box?" the stern Capitol police officer asked as he approached Kyle with his hand on his holstered firearm.

"It's a Compact Cake Kit," Kyle said immediately, wide-eyed with an anxious look of concern.

"A what?" came the reply. "Based on what I am seeing, we are going to have to call in the bomb squad if you don't make yourself clearer. Looks like explosives to me."

"Officer let me explain," Kyle said rapidly as he did his best to clarify the contents of his special delivery. "My girlfriend's birthday is this weekend, and I am sending her cupcakes and a lighter, along with everything she needs to make a compact cake kit. Make sense?"

"You can't be serious? You are attempting to send flammable materials not only through security at the U.S. Capitol but through the postal service as well?" grilled the exasperated officer. "You do realize this is a federal offense, and you could go to prison?"

"Oh my! No, I didn't, officer. Please forgive my stupidity," Kyle said with embarrassment. "May I open the box and show you? I am happy to remove the lighter."

"Step on through. I'm going to cut you some slack. I recognize you, and for that you are lucky. Open the box, give me the lighter, and then get to work," the officer commanded.

Kyle stepped through security, removed the obvious hazardous materials, and gladly handed them over to the Capitol police.

"Well, this is a first," the officer commented. "I'll give you this much, you are creative. Seems like your girl might have herself a pretty nice guy. Get your butt out of here and get that thing mailed before you miss your deadline."

"Thank you, sir! I'll make you proud," Kyle said as he smiled and rushed to the post office.

There was hardly a time that Kyle didn't pass through Capitol security without the officers teasing him. They would say, "Here comes lover boy," or "You got a light?" It was all in fun and reminded Kyle of the relationships he had made with law enforcement growing up as a kid.

Life at the United States Capitol was full of excitement. Kyle had earned a spot as a member of the Senate radio and TV team. The Senate Recording Studio, as it was called, served the broadcasting needs of every United States Senator as well as the Vice President of the United States, since he also held the title of President of the Senate. Interacting with these world leaders regularly caused Kyle to realize that everyone was vulnerable and had insecurities.

More than once, a head of state had asked for Kyle's perspective or advice on their appearance before going live to the nation on network television and radio.

Many notable people had made their way to the Senate Recording Studio, though none was more notable than John Glenn, the former astronaut, and current United States Senator.

Senator Glenn was a kind man with a shiny bald head. He was always polite and straightforward. When it was suggested that he might need to apply a bit of makeup to his head to minimize the glare, it was clear he wasn't exactly excited about the idea. He was eventually persuaded and agreed to submit to the professionals regarding how to put his best head forward.

The idea was solid but how it was to be implemented lacked foresight and finesse. Normally, a makeup artist would have been available to meet the needs of the Senator, but unfortunately, she was out on maternity leave, and this left young cameramen to do the deed. No one wanted the job. After all, they had never worn makeup, and who were they to practice their powder-puffing on, of all people, a national hero and a United States Senator.

With just minutes before airtime, the TV director ordered one of the cameramen to step forward and apply a bit of powder to the top of the Senator's head. Kyle watched with great anticipation as the cameraman removed a powder-filled pillow from the makeup container. The cameraman looked at the powder puff and then at the Senator's head. He looked at Kyle, shrugged his shoulders, and tapped the top of the Senator's head with the powder puff releasing what became a small mountain of powder in the center of baldness. The studio became deathly quiet.

"Is there a problem?" the Senator asked.

"Uhm… no sir, things are looking great," replied the cameraman.

And without hesitation, the cameraman covered the Senator's face with one hand and blew the excess powder into the air. It produced an immediate dust storm. Powder particles were sent floating into the bright studio lights and beyond.

"We are live in two minutes! Someone, anyone, get a blow dryer in there and blow off the Senator's dark blue blazer!" came the command over the headset. "This is an emergency. If this Senator can survive outer space, he is for sure going to survive live television in our studio. Get it together, people!"

The countdown from 10 seconds began as the Senator sat stoically awaiting his cue. "Hello everyone, I'm Senator John Glenn, and the news I'm about to share is no powder puff," the Senator said without a flinch. He may have been the serious type, but he didn't lack for a sense of humor.

As the live feed ended and his lapel microphone was removed from his tie, Senator Glenn stood up, winked, and said with a smile, "You boys had better stick to running cameras and leave the makeup to the girls. There is a reason they say bald is beautiful. Next time, I think I'll just let mine shine."

He shook everyone's hands and without further comment made his way to the Senate floor for a roll call vote.

Kyle couldn't help but be impressed with how a real leader responded under crisis. He didn't panic or lose faith in his comrades. He remained calm and trusted them to do what they were called upon to do while he fulfilled his role to lead.

Senator Glenn demonstrated real leadership under pressure. Circumstances in the studio weren't the end of the world, but how the little things were handled, by a big-time leader, stuck in Kyle's mind as an example of true leadership no matter what the circumstances. He couldn't wait to share this experience with Christine as he looked to make a bit of news himself in the coming days.

CHAPTER 35

It had been five years since they had first met, and Kyle could wait no more. It was true, distance had made his heart grow fonder. During Christine's sophomore year of college, he asked for her hand in marriage. The big wedding day was to take place in June.

He had a great job and loved living in Washington D.C., but other than the clothes on his back, Kyle had few worldly possessions. The chorus to Danny's Song, a popular country and western tune from the 1970s, often came to his mind, reminding him that they might not have money, but they had love, and that was more than enough. He wondered if a young man in love could ever have enough money to marry the beauty who had captivated his heart.

Despite a shortage of funds, they were full of love, and he was committed to doing whatever it took to provide for his family, even if it required extra effort and plenty of ingenuity. Kyle had done the math and the best he could figure, the cost to rent a moving truck would be approximately $1,500.

Seeing the cost, Kyle set his mind on beating the system. Based on his estimates, he could purchase a pickup for nearly the same price as a rental truck and then resell the pickup and basically move for free. Kyle flew home over Spring Break and went to work searching for the perfect deal. With one day left, before he had to fly back to work, his brilliant idea was failing. He must have looked at 15 pickups and not one was what he was hoping for.

And then, a classified advertisement caught his eye. The price was right but would the 1972 Ford pickup, priced at $250, make it all the way from Oklahoma to Washington D.C.? After pinpointing the address on a street map, Kyle and Timmy headed down a long driveway to a ram shackled wooden garage that looked as if it hadn't been attended to for more than a decade. An elderly man in a pair of bibbed overalls soon appear from beside an outbuilding.

"She's parked in the garage. You know what they say about not judging a book by its cover? Right? Well, she's not a looker, but she runs great," said the kind, gray-haired man who led Kyle and Timmy down the long driveway to an old wooden garage that looked as if it hadn't been attended to for well over a decade.

Creaking a loud protest at being moved, the worn out springs slowly lifted the dilapidated garage door to an off-center position. Sunlight shined in from a dirty side window and cast light on the four-wheeled relic that had to have been covered in at least a quarter inch of dust.

"Here is the key. Jump in and crank her up. I'll bet you my first gold tooth she fires off with the turn of the key," the old man said with a smile as a pair of gold teeth revealed his bet was covered.

Kyle looked at Timmy, took a deep breath, pushed his thumb into the button of the heavy steel door handle and took a look at what remained of a bench seat.

It was clear the truck had seen better days, but Kyle sensed the truck might still have a few more miles left to roll.

"Was this your truck?" Kyle asked the old man.

"I'm afraid not. It belonged to my boy. He was a carpenter, and this was his work truck," the old man explained as he pulled a red bandana from his pocket and wiped tears from his eyes.

"Johnny was paralyzed when he fell from scaffolding. He lived in a nursing home for 15 years until he died last month. His birthday was last week. I finally decided it was time to let his truck go since he wouldn't be coming back home to get it."

"I'm sorry to hear of your loss. I bet Johnny was a great carpenter," Kyle said as he paused to express sympathy to the old man.

"You know, he had at least two fingers left on each hand when he died," the old man said as he snickered and busted out into laughter. "I'm kidding. Johnny liked a good joke. He did make me proud. He wouldn't want us moping around, fretting over his memory. Jump in there and go take her for a spin."

Kyle was wearing gym shorts and took care sitting his butt on top of the exposed cushion springs that barely had one thread left to their name.

"Here goes," Kyle said as he turned the ignition key.

The old truck roared to life. The old man was right. One turn and the truck was up and running like a formula one race car on pit row. Kyle turned on the windshield wipers and slung dust into the face of Timmy and the old man. They coughed and waved their hands trying to catch their breaths.

Kyle put the pickup in gear, then pushed on the accelerator pedal as the dual exhaust pipes made it clear that it was far past time to hit the road. There was so much dust on the truck that it looked as if it was engulfed in flames as dust rolled off the hood and out through the tailgate. "I'll take it!" Kyle said following his test drive, and as he left the motor running at the curbside.

"You'll take it?" Timmy asked with a look of amazement.

"Sold!" the old man said with excitement and a smile.

"Yes, sir. This is just the truck I've been looking for," Kyle said as he handed the old man $250 in cash.

Pulling away, Kyle looked in the rearview mirror as Johnny's daddy stood in the center of the street until the old pickup was well out of sight.

Kyle wondered what it must have been like to have a father and son relationship like the one Johnny had with his dad. There was no missing the love and wonderful memories the old man and his son had once shared. Theirs was the kind of relationship Kyle wanted with his kids someday.

Kyle had learned how to drive "three on the tree" from his grandpa. Pushing the clutch and working through the column shifter from first to third gear flooded Kyle's mind with memories of Liam. Kyle had learned to drive his grandpa's pickup down dusty country roads. Those were the best of times.

As Kyle made his way onto the interstate, he decided to open things up and blow out any cogs that might be holding Johnny's old pickup from reaching its full potential.

The speedometer showed 55 mph and then 60 mph. Somewhere between 65 and 70, as the 1972 Ford pickup was just hitting its stride, the hood of the pickup blew off its hinges and went flying into the air.

Kyle gripped the steering wheel with all his might, ducked instinctively, and then immediately looked in the rearview mirror fearing the hood of the pickup would be crashing into the windshield of Timmy's car as he followed close behind.

Luckily, the hood landed on its top, and then slid for at least 100 yards spraying sparks in all directions as cars wove in and out of traffic to avoid running over the hood or crashing into each other.

Timmy's eyes were as big as silver dollars as the hood came to a stop on the shoulder right in front of the grill of his car. Without missing a beat, the boys jumped out of their vehicles, grabbed the hood, and placed it in the bed of the pickup. They gave each other a high five and were then up and running again as if nothing had ever happened.

Excited about his purchase, and with little concern for how a hoodless pickup might look pulling up outside a sorority house, Kyle parked the pickup just outside Christine's room and revved the engine as the pipes of the dual exhaust made Kyle's powerful but hoodless presence known.

Girls from the sorority house recognized Kyle and ran in to inform Christine that Prince Charming had arrived in his chariot. Christine sheepishly appeared on the lawn of the sorority house.

"If you weren't so cute, I might just call the cops and have you arrested for disturbing the peace," Christine announced as she smiled and leaned in from the passenger's side window of the truck.

"Get yourself out of here before I decide not to run away and get married to you!"

Kyle knew better than to push his luck. He honked the horn of the hoodless pickup as he drove away and blew Christine kisses with a smile on his face.

She had been a good sport, and he had probably made her want to run and hide. Nonetheless, she knew his heart, and even then, she was fully aware that she would follow him to the ends of the earth, even if it was in the cab of an old beat-up hoodless 1972 Ford.

CHAPTER 36

The wedding was huge. It was a community-wide celebration. So many family and friends attended that the church was packed to capacity. The wedding party alone had more than 25 participants. Clearly, the beautiful young couple was adored.

Christine's white wedding dress was majestically crafted by a master seamstress. The details were flawless. Highlighted with pearls, sequins, and dainty lace accents, it was elegant, graceful, and enchanting. Her veil covered the innocence of her soft and rosy cheeks, as her beautiful seductive green eyes hid faintly behind the translucent thin lace. A subtle hint of her ivory white teeth appeared between her luscious red lips. The curvature of her body was outlined by the fitted seams as her magnificent train extended down nearly the entire aisle.

Her daddy's blessing and 30 feet were all that stood between her and the man of her dreams.

When Christine made her entrance, it was as if Princess Diana had entered the room. Every wedding guest stood to their feet in awe as she gracefully glided to the front of the church.

Kyle's heart immediately dropped at the sight of her. Her beauty was beyond comparison. His vision narrowed, and the room disappeared as his eyes met hers. This was his bride, and he would soon be holding her in his arms. Love was in full bloom. He felt the power of passion overwhelm his mind and body. He was lost in a trance as he fought back tears and could do nothing more than smile. She was truly captivating. And she was his. He felt as if he was marrying an angel, and it had been a miracle no less. He was an emotional mess as his future father-in-law offered her hand in marriage. He was smitten and had fallen deeply for this women.

In addition to the traditional wedding ceremony, which included the exchanging of vows, rings, and communion, Kyle had prepared a special letter to be read aloud for Christine as a surprise on their wedding day.

My dearest Christine,

I have longed for this day since the first time I laid eyes on you in the Arbuckle Mountains at summer youth camp. It was your smile, your eyes, and the sound of your voice that stole my heart that day.

It is true, at my age I could have been one of the camp counselors, but how was I to know that I was more than five years your senior? Nonetheless, I packed away my passions and determined to wait, and I watched you grow into the woman you are today.

You proved to be quite a challenge as you were much more mature for your age. You were distracted by other interests, but I have never had a reputation as one to give up easily. I waited, and I won.

It was tragedy that brought us back together. So much of both of our lives have been built on hardship and loss. I wonder at times if this isn't, at least in part, what has drawn us to each other. With you I feel safe. I am able to be who I am without reservation. You encourage me, inspire me, and challenge me to be the man I only hope to be.

We found faith separately, and it is faith that is at the very center of who we are. The two shall become one today, but we know all too well that it is the Lord who holds us together and will continue to do so, no matter what might come our way.

I will never forget the day that I realized you were the one for me. The thought of not spending the rest of my life with you became unbearable. It was then that I knew, God willing, we would someday be together forever.

As we stand here today before family, friends, and the Lord Himself, please know that I am captivated by you in every way, deeply committed to you, and promise, with every fiber of my being to love and cherish you all the days of my life.

I love you Christine. No man has ever been prouder to call a woman his wife. Today, that dream comes true. Today is the day that life truly begins for me, anew. From this day forward, I will be with you, forever!

Love Kyle.

A deep hush fell across the ceremony as men and women alike wiped tears from their eyes. If ever true love was to be witnessed, surely this was it.

The ceremony was simply a blur for Kyle and Christine as well-wishers participated in the wholehearted celebration of love. They were simply too caught up in the moment to immediately retain its significance.

"You may kiss your bride," the minister proclaimed as Kyle began to come back to reality. He slowly lifted the veil from her face and placed his hand ever so gently behind her ear. The softness of her neck invited him to draw closer as he felt the energy between them intensifying. It was if he was looking into her soul as his lips touched hers and their eyes closed only to enhance the power of the moment. Her lips were like honey, soft and far more than desirable, they were heavenly.

He had kissed Christine many times before, and she continued to debate who kissed who first, but this kiss, their first as husband and wife, brought excitement to his soul like no other. This kiss was with the woman of his dreams, the woman who had stolen his heart, captured his very being, and would bear their children, God willing.

Christine was overcome with joy and was elated to hold him close as Kyle placed both hands on her face, touching his lips ever so gently to hers. It was happening, they were becoming man and wife, and she felt certain no bride could have ever felt more in love with the handsome young man that whisked her off her feet and into his forever arms.

It was more than a fairy tale. It was heavenly, inspiring, and pure. Those who looked on were witnesses to true and everlasting love budding before their very eyes. They were a beautiful couple who adored, respected, and cherished one another. It was clear they were deeply in love and were a match made in heaven.

The wedding reception was alive and active as guests celebrated the newlyweds with excitement. The cake was cut, and toasts were being made when suddenly Kyle's group of friends pulled him aside and insisted that he reveal where the limousine for the grand departure had been parked. Kyle knew these friends too well and was not about to submit to their requests. Together, the lot of them had spent their lives pulling pranks and teasing disaster as they danced on the edge of lawlessness. They weren't outlaws, but they had come close, more than once. Surely today, on such a special and sanctimonious day, they would lay down their antics and rise to the dignity of the occasion. Such was not to be the case.

They insisted with their demands. Kyle refused to give in. They threatened to make him regret his silence, and he doubled down with resistance. As one of their leaders, the posse expected nothing less of him and soon had him manhandled and swept away from the reception.

They offered him one last chance before they promised to unleash unforgivable embarrassment. Kyle would not relent so his closest friends lost their better judgment and stripped him down to his underwear and dress socks.

With the ease of experienced hoodlums, they then tied his hands behind his back, blindfolded him, and secured his ankles to the legs of the chair with duct tape.

"This is your last chance," Nolen grunted through gritted teeth. "Tell us where the car is, or you will forever regret it."

"Never!" came Kyle's reply as sweat dripped from his determined brow.

The posse immediately responded with action and proceeded to carry Kyle, in the chair, on their shoulders to the parking lot. As they placed him in the parking slot, wedding guests gathered and looked on with shock and awe. If this was meant to be a harmless prank, it had utterly failed. If it was meant to cause heartbreak, it had certainly succeeded.

No one knew whether to laugh or cry. It was simply atrocious that such stupidity would rise to such a level at the wedding of a lifetime. About the time everyone assumed the torture was about to end, it only got worse.

The group had come prepared, and they each opened up a bottle of pancake syrup and took turns pouring the contents over Kyle's head and entire body. So as not to appear to have given any mercy, they busted open bags of powdered sugar and emptied the fine white sugar over every inch of Kyle's body.

Amazingly, no one came to Kyle's aid. No one could believe their eyes. This was like tar and feathering without the tar and feathers. People were too sad to cry and too shellshocked to intercede. There was no mistake about it, his buddies has stepped over the line. They had done the unthinkable. It was borderline criminal and something they would come to regret for years to come.

It was as if the struggles of the past were doing all they could to prevent Kyle and Christine from moving beyond their troubled upbringings. But as he had done many times before, Kyle stood on his own, stiffened his back, and refused to give in to the evil that often pursued him. Today would be a turning point in their lives in more ways than one. What his so-called friends didn't realize was that there was no limousine. Kyle and Christine had decided to honor her grandparents by driving away in their brand-new Cadillac.

There was no way Kyle was going to jeopardize Christine's grandparents' vehicle. He resolved to remain silent, and despite the price he paid, he was proud to have preserved his secret.

Kyle was finally cut free from the chair. He did his best to wipe the thick maple syrup from his eye sockets. The crowd gasped as he stood upright, covered from head to toe in syrup and powdered sugar. As he took his first step away from the carnage, he heard the sweet sound of Christine's voice and the welcoming rumble of the getaway car.

"Sweetie. Come here. I'm over here," called Christine's tender voice from the driver's seat of her grandparents' Cadillac. The passenger's door was opened as a caring bystander managed to cover the bench seat with a blanket. Kyle did his best to blindly make his way to the car. No one dared to stand in his way. They knew he had had enough. The band of brothers had gone too far; no one was laughing at their ill-timed caper, and it was time to leave well enough alone.

Christine leaned toward Kyle in her wedding gown and kissed him firmly on the lips. The crowd went wild as the car sped away into the setting sun.

"I am so sorry, babe. I can't believe these idiots have ruined this for you," Kyle said with obvious disdain. "What were they thinking?"

"It doesn't matter now. We're married, and nothing is going to change the fact that I love you even though you look like you fell into a bowl of pancake batter," Christine said as she licked her finger clean of pancake syrup.

"We can't check into the hotel like this," Kyle said. "This is terrible."

"Let's go to my house, and I'll hose you down," Christine said. "I grabbed your tuxedo. It will be like nothing ever happened.

They pulled into Christine's house. She pulled her wedding dress up as high as she could and pulled the water hose to the driveway.

Kyle located an abandoned dishwasher box that had been left behind by a delivery man earlier that day. He stood in the center of the box butt naked as Christine approached him with the water hose flowing full force.

Christine walked to the edge of the makeshift shower stall, looked Kyle in the eyes, smiled, and peeked over the top of the box.

"Well, lookie there. It appears my husband might need a little assistance clearing powdered sugar and syrup off his manhood," Christine said with one eyebrow raised. "Do you mind if I help? I'm just sorry I didn't bring any hand soap!"

They both laughed as she stood there holding the water hose and watching him in all his glory. This was certainly not the way he imagined his wife seeing him naked for the first time, but he had to admit, it probably relaxed a little of the attention they both felt about it.

"I have to admit, I like what I see," she said as she reached across the cardboard, handed him his clothes, and laid a big wet kiss on him as she squeezed his bare bottom.

"Sorry, I forgot your socks and those underwear have seen better days. Looks like you are going commando big fella!"

Despite the awkwardness of the setting and the chill in the air, Kyle was starting to show visible signs that he knew quite well what would soon be happening. The need for underwear was the last thing on his mind. Love was in the air and the lovebirds weren't going to let a little savory toppings spoil their big day. The night was young, and a horse-drawn carriage awaited their arrival at the honeymoon suite.

As the driver of the carriage issued the command for the horses to giddy up, Kyle crossed his legs revealing his bare ankle to all who cared to notice. No one did except for the beautiful young lady at his side. She placed her fingers on his ankle and gently rubbed the soft spot just behind his ankle bone. Kyle could tell by the twinkle in Christine's eyes that the carriage ride could end none too soon. They had waited for this night for all their lives. It was the night that the two would become one.

CHAPTER 37

The honeymooners escaped to the tropics and spent a week playing in the ocean, walking the beach hand-in-hand at sunset, and exploring the wonders of love. The world had become a better place. Life was carefree, without worry and regret. They had each other and a wonderland to explore.

The intimacy they shared was more than romantic, it was beyond description. Sensual, tantalizing, passionate, and full of pleasure. It was far more than a physical experience. It was deeply emotional, spiritual, and enticing in every way.

Their senses were fully alive, and their hearts, souls, and minds were igniting like never before as the heat between their nude bodies drew them closer and closer in ways they had never dreamed.

For Kyle, the mystery of knowing a woman was becoming more and more inviting all while revealing there was so much more to explore and to be known.

Christine was deeply comforted by the masculinity she experienced in the safe harbor of Kyle's arms. To be with him was to encounter more than a boy who had become a man, it was to give herself away without hesitancy or fear. To be with him took her to a life in another realm.

Life in paradise was beyond expectation until unexpectantly, Christine became deathly ill. Upon arrival back in the United States, she had to be rushed to the hospital emergency room. It was soon discovered that she had contracted Montezuma's Revenge and was severely dehydrated to the point of needing several rounds of IV therapy.

As Christine recuperated, the medical necessity left little time to spare as Kyle was required to be back to work soon. He faced the grim reality of having to transport the love if his life and all of their belongings across country in a few short days. The journey would take them close to three days if they drove at a relaxed pace. Such would be required given Christine's weakened state.

The resurrected old Ford pickup had been practically restored and was ready for the challenge of the open road.

Much to Kyle's surprise, additional space was needed to accommodate all of Christine's belongings. Her shoe collection not being the least of which. Kyle added plywood sideboards to the pickup. Despite his best intentions, even more space was needed to meet the payload.

Using his small-town connections, he was able to locate a Chevy pickup bed for sale that had been converted into a make-shift trailer. It would look awkward being pulled behind a Ford pickup, but it would get the job done just the same. He bought it.

The trailer would make the trip possible, but only if additional plywood sideboards were secured into place. There were no other options, especially if everything was to be transported in one trip. Success was finally achieved as blue tarps were tucked around the contents and a total of three used spare tires were strapped to the top of the heap. All three used spare tires were cheaper than buying one new spare tire, so Kyle took the risk and went for the trio!

The pickup and trailer idea had worked even though the temporary vagabonds looked like they had just driven straight off the set of the hit Hollywood TV series, *The Beverly Hillbillies*. All that was missing was a rocking chair and a granny.

Christine's dad wished them well and watched with concern as his little girl set out on her life's journey with an ambitious young man full of promise and with a crazy idea of trusting an old worn-out pickup to bring them safely into harbor.

Optimism would indeed be the fuel that was needed to survive the cross-country adventure. He knew Kyle had what it would take. Christine's dad would later admit to resisting the urge to follow them from a distance just to make sure they got there alright.

Instead, he didn't sleep a wink as he waited by the telephone all night, anticipating a collect telephone call that would request his assistance. The call never came, and he was glad.

However, the lack of a telephone call didn't mean that there weren't challenges along the way. The sojourners had gotten no further than five miles outside of town when the gear shifter on the old Ford locked up. Never one to back away from a challenge and guided by sheer determination, Kyle raised the hood and crawled in on top of the engine. Christine watched from the driver's seat wondering if they would make it, but she was confident Kyle would find a way.

Kyle glanced back at Christine. He suspected she might be second guessing his better judgement. But the look on her face reassured him that she believed in her man, and he would find a way. After a few bangs of a hammer and a bit of southern ingenuity, Kyle made the needed adjustments, and they were on their way again but not before Kyle ran back and grabbed a kiss from Christine, even with the grease and sweat on his brow. She never hesitated to return the gesture. She simply adored him and knew they made a great team.

Together they would learn they could conquer nearly anything that came their way. It was a lifelong principle and philosophy that ultimately typified their marriage. *Better together than we would ever be alone*, became their credo. It represented their belief in what it meant to be happily married to a lifelong partner.

For sure they were different. He came from a working-class family and she, a family full of successful business entrepreneurs. He was a small-town boy. She was from the big city. He wore cowboy boots, and she wore designer shoes. He was ambitious, energetic, assertive, and impatient. She was intentional, calm, caring, and extremely patient. But through those differences, they would grew stronger and came to appreciate what they could learn from each other. Most of all, their values were rooted in their shared beliefs. They believed their weaknesses would be made strong as they yielded to the guidance of the Creator.

"Here comes another one!" Christine announced to Kyle over the citizen band radio as they traveled down the open road. "The station wagon is packed full of a family on vacation. Don't let them down! This is your moment to shine!"

Throughout the trip, passersby simply couldn't believe what they were seeing. Was it a pack of gypsies? Lost carnival workers? Hillbillies on the run from the law? The intrigue of the overloaded Ford and the wobbly Chevy pickup bed trailer attracted gawkers of all sorts.

Their fellow travelers lost all sense of manners and politeness as nearly each and every vehicle decelerated in order for passengers to take in a full view. As the station wagon full of vacationers pulled up alongside Kyle's rig, he slipped into character and pumped up the theatrics. Everything went into slow motion as the audience pointed, covering their mouths and falling into belly rolls. Kyle did his part by leaning out the driver's side window, crossed his eyes, raised one side of his upper lip, and with careful precision, pushed the index finger of his left hand as far up his nose as he possibly could.

Following a deep breath, he proceeded to blow snot out of his right nostril stringing stretchy mucus across the white striped lines of the highway. The sinus cavity projectile kissed the windshield of the onlookers, like a frog's tongue licking a fly off a lily pad.

Kyle was elated with his Academy Award winning performance. The audience was horrified, and Christine was in tears with laughter, making it difficult to see the road at times. No doubt motorists would be sharing scenes from this unusual family vacation during dinner conversations for years.

More than once a vehicle swerved to the shoulder of the highway as it tried to avoid the boogery bazooka blast in an attempt to wipe the unwanted mucus bomb from the vehicle's windshield. If they were lucky, they would regain alignment and speed away to clearer skies.

"How was that one babe?" Kyle said as he tried to control his laughter over the CB radio.

"I hope we don't see them at the next rest stop," Christine replied. "If we do, I'm avoiding you like the plague. I do have to admit, you deserve a standing ovation."

Kyle was pleased to hear that his number one fan was pleased with his performance.

As the traveling circus pushed on toward the nation's capital, Kyle took a swig of his favorite traveling concoction, an ice-cold bottle of Pepsi, filled to the brim with salted peanuts. It was something his Grandpa Liam had shared with him each time Kyle visited for summer vacation. It was one of Kyle's fondest memories. Sharing a tractor seat with his grandpa under the hot summer sun as a makeshift umbrella did its best to prevent a farmer's tan was a rite of passage of sorts. It was hot, sweaty, and dusty work, but somehow a Pepsi, filled with salted peanuts made the day more manageable and memorable.

Liam taught Kyle what it meant to be a man. He taught him that tenderness didn't mean you weren't tough. That being a family man meant doing what it took to provide for your family and that hard work didn't have to require you to sacrifice the ones you love most. Somehow Kyle sensed his grandpa was with him as he dialed in a country and western tune on the pickup's AM radio.

He was somewhere between the hills of Tennessee and Virginia. They would have to make one last stop on the road, but they would be pulling into their little one-room studio apartment by early the following afternoon.

They had left a world of hurt behind. Dwight hadn't been heard from in years. The distance helped ease the threat that was always in the back of Kyle's mind. Would Dwight leave them alone? Would he hunt them down and attempt to destroy their new beginning? Dwight was out of sight, but he was never out of mind.

CHAPTER 38

The journey to Washington D.C. hadn't been without challenges, but nothing made them feel more at home than a porch full of new friends standing ready to help them unload. With all the extra crew on hand, unpacking didn't take long at all. Kyle knew it would make Christine uncomfortable, but as he had done since he was a teenager, he slept with the loaded 12-gauge shotgun under his bed. He would rather be safe than sorry. Dwight, and others like him, would always be a threat. But Kyle would be ready for whatever came his way.

They only had one closet but that didn't mean Christine didn't have two closets worth of shoes. The sight of them all made Kyle laugh. Christine was known for her fashion. Shoes were at the center of her wardrobe. It was one thing about her that would never change. Shoes were essential.

Christine was quick to make the little bungalow home. Kyle loved coming home to her savory home-cooked meals. She was an excellent cook and homemaker in addition to holding down a full-time job. They eventually bought a couch that in all honesty, looked a lot like lawn furniture, but they were happy as larks because it was theirs. Everything, that is, except a table they had borrowed from the Bennetts.

Making good on his financial strategy, Kyle ran a classified advertisement putting the traveling rig up for sale. He left work early one day to show his first prospective buyer the complete package that included the pickup, trailer, sideboards, tarps, and three spare tires.

"She runs great! We made it all the way from Oklahoma without a hitch in our giddy-up, and we didn't even have to use one of those spare tires," Kyle said with pride as he walked about the exterior of the rig.

"We don't get many trucks like this out this way. Most are rusted out. This truck looks solid," the potential customer shared as he went to talk it over with his wife.

After a few minutes, the man returned with a defeated look on his face. "She won't let me buy it. She thinks it looks a little too 'Appalachian' for her taste," the man said. "I hate that I had you take off work early. Here is $50 for your time. Best of luck, man."

Kyle was surprised that the pickup didn't sell, but he had another opportunity to show another potential buyer the truck on Saturday morning.

"I'll take it! It is perfect!" proclaimed customer number two. "I only have one request. Will you hold it for me if I spot you five hundred bucks? I'm good for the thousand I owe you by next Saturday. What do you think?"

"Well, I suppose that will work," Kyle said with a bit of reluctance. "I'll hold 'er for you."

A week came and no sign of customer number two. Another week and still no sign of the would-be buyer. Eventually, the customer showed but failed to have the $1,000 he owed.

"I'm sorry I'm not going to be able to make the deal. I know I promised, and the money is yours to keep," the man confessed.

"I tell you what. I would be lying if I didn't tell you I could have sold it by now, but I respect that you came back to tell me," Kyle said with grace. "How about we split the difference? Here is $250 back, and I'll keep the other half for my trouble."

"Are you serious? You aren't from around here, are you? Nobody does this. Thanks, man!" Customer number two shook Kyle's hand and got in the car of a friend and drove off.

Kyle hadn't sold the traveling rig, but he had already made $300 back on his investment.

The pickup cost him $250, repairs another $250, the trailer, spare tires, tarps, and sideboards had cost him another $500. In total, he was out $1,000. And now he was only $700 from breaking even!

Customer number three showed up the following day with cash in hand. He operated a landscape business, and the rig was tailormade for his crew. He offered Kyle $1,200, and Kyle didn't flinch or even attempt to negotiate.

As the old Ford rolled away pulling the Chevy pickup bed trailer, a big grin crossed Kyle's face. He had just closed the deal on a $1,500 transaction that netted him $500 in profit. That was even better than the profit he had made on the Rambler he sold in high school.

"I added it all up. Including the rig, gas, hotels, and food, we spent close to $1,450 to get your pretty face out here," Kyle said with a beaming look of accomplishment. "That means I get to take you on a $50 date to celebrate!"

This would not be the last time they felt they had been blessed by putting their faith into action. It wasn't magic, but it sure wasn't fate.

As they prayed over dinner that evening, they thanked the Creator for the adventure they were on and the thrill of knowing they were in it together.

CHAPTER 39

Kyle excelled at his job in the U.S. Senate. His work ethic was second to none, and he was chosen for several special projects including one with Vice President Bush. He often found himself working on programs associated with network television and notable people from around the world. It wasn't unusual to have movie stars, astronauts, public figures, Wall Street moguls, and many powerful politicians in the studio.

It was during this time that Kyle became aware that no matter how recognizable a person was or how successful they were in the eyes of the world, everyone was vulnerable and insecure in some way.

Despite an invisible tough outer shell, which for many served as a protective personal barrier, even the most famous, wealthy, popular, and prosperous leaders had a need to know they mattered. Seeing these needs in the lives of prominent people gave Kyle a sense of confidence. He knew that apart from fate and circumstance, these leaders were no different than him. Yes, he was a young man from a small town in Oklahoma who grew up in a dysfunctional family, but he also had a tremendous amount of potential.

While weekdays were spent catering to the high-profile needs of others, weekends were spent relaxing and doing life with the Bennett family. After Sunday lunch, they played a game of Pictionary for entertainment. As much as they practiced to improve their drawing skills, practice never made perfect. Kyle and Christine could never quite find a way to win. Kyle had always been a competitor and losing week after week was getting to him.

When they got home, Kyle pulled out a piece of paper and drew a picture, showing it to Christine far closer to her face than needed.

"Look, this is a stick man, if I add a hat and a pitchfork, what does that make him?" Kyle said to Christine with obvious frustration.

"I'm not stupid, Kyle. "You are taking this way too seriously," Christine retorted as the temperature of the conversation started to rise.

"I just don't get it. It seems everyone else knows what I'm drawing but you. Are you doing this on purpose?" Kyle said as he was losing perspective.

"I'll tell you who doesn't get it. You!" Christine said as she exited the conversation and presented Kyle with a cold shoulder.

"Seriously? You think it's me? Give me a break!" Kyle said unbridled in a frenzy. "I'm the only reason we ever come close to winning." Kyle's desire to be right had eclipsed his need to be kind.

"Fine, Mr. Picasso!" Christine said with renewed fervor. "I'm done. You will have to find someone else to interpret your chicken scratch."

It wasn't their first fight, but it was a doozy. Kyle leaned into a good fight. He had learned how to fight from the best. In Dwight's house, if you wanted to make your point, you raised your voice. If you really wanted to make your point, you threw something or hit someone. It was ugly.

Although Kyle would never resort to physical force with family, he did have plenty of room for growth when it came to his tact, timing, and tone of voice.

Christine had grown up with a different approach to dealing with conflict. If you got mad, it was easy. Walk away and say nothing. Ignore the issue long enough and theoretically, it would simply go away. Or so it seemed.

They were learning to fight, but if they didn't make a course correction, they wouldn't learn to fight fair through healthy confrontation. Over time, they learned how to listen better, to empathize, and to see things from the other's perspective. It was okay to honestly critique ideas and methods but never right to criticize identities or motives. It didn't mean they always agreed. But they did agree never to go to bed angry. It seemed easy enough, but keeping the commitment to communicate often led to plenty of late-night discussions. Compromise was often the key to success. Remembering they were on the same team brought little victories that helped them win as a couple.

Occasionally, somebody ended up on the couch for the night. And usually that somebody was Kyle.

Such was the case on this occasion. They had talked it through, but the aggravation simply wouldn't subside. Kyle fumed as he squeezed himself onto the love-seat sized couch. He tossed and turned until he finally fell asleep.

Around 3:30 A.M., Kyle woke up to the familiar smell of Christine's perfume and the gentle touch of her hand rubbing his forearm. She came in close and rubbed her nose up against his.

"You should come to bed. This is silly. Do I need to draw you a map of how to get there? Maybe we'd win next Sunday if I did," she said as she offered a graceful and lighthearted truce to the tiff.

"I've been an idiot. It's not you. I have been convicted in my spirit about my whole approach," Kyle confessed. "I really don't get it, do I?"

His time alone on the couch caused him to reflect on his mindset towards games. He remembered a time when he was a boy when his Uncle Gene came by his parents' house for a visit. A poker game soon broke out with plenty of beer and smokes to boot. Somewhere about midway through the game, an argument ensued and the next thing the families knew, Dwight and Gene were in a knock-down-drag-out in the living room over a stupid card game.

Plants went tumbling, furniture got broken into pieces, lips were busted open, and eyes were blackened as two grown men locked horns in a bullfight. Why? All because Kyle's dad and uncle had missed the point of the game.

The goal of games wasn't to win at any cost or to annihilate your opponent. The purpose was to be together, share memories, foster conversation, and grow deeper in relationships. Winning isn't everything. Winning a board game at the sacrifice of relationships with others was ultimately losing in the game of life.

Kyle realized that his attitude was toxic and unproductive. He had become a spoiler, but due to his wife's unyielding love and patience, he came to realize there was a better way to engage with others during games. In the early morning hours, Kyle found his way back into the welcoming arms of Christine. Like a lot of couples, they found a way to kiss and make up that made it almost worth all the fuss. If only they could play Pictionary with the same level of skill!

The Christmas holidays were approaching and provided a much-needed break from Pictionary. It was going to be their first Christmas away from family, and the thought of missing it was becoming more than they could bear.

Gatherings at Christine's family farm were like something out of a Norman Rockwell painting. Five generations of family would gather to feast on juicy farm-fed ham, homemade dumplings, noodles, bacon wrapped green beans, fresh baked rolls, and a wild turkey that had been harvested from the land. The aroma from the apple and pecan pies welcomed everyone home as they walked into the farmhouse. Laughter and warm hugs were plentiful. Football was on the big screen, horse rides were active in the arena, and special Christmas gifts were ready to be opened under the Christmas tree.

Kyle could faintly remember Christmas with his dad's side of the family. Once the divorce was final and Dwight disappeared, Kyle lost touch with so many that he loved. No one ever knew when Dwight might reappear to stir things up, so eventually, big Sanderson family gatherings just stopped happening.

As Christmas Day grew closer and closer, they decided to go for it! They were heading home! No one would be expecting them, and the surprise would be a gift in and of itself. If they drove straight through the night, they could be with family within 24 hours. It would be worth it!

They packed an ice chest full of food, mapped out the fastest route, and pointed Christine's Toyota Celica in the direction of the Southern Plains.

CHAPTER 40

They were making great time. Before they knew it, they were back in the hills of Tennessee surrounded by absolute darkness. The highway was pitch black as their headlights pushed through the depths of the night.

Suddenly, without warning, the Toyota lost power. The engine died, and they were coasting off of the engine's momentum. The car eventually rolled to a complete stop in the absolute middle of nowhere. They were alone and extremely vulnerable. There were no signs of other travelers. No headlights and no city lights. Nothing but a crescent moon and thousands of stars accompanied them.

"This isn't good. The engine won't crank," Kyle said as Christine sensed a bit of panic in his voice.

He stepped out of the car and used a small flashlight to examine where the smoke was coming from.

"I think we may have cracked a head or blown the motor. We haven't given the motor any rest, and we have kept the pedal to the metal," Kyle said as he shared the bad news with Christine.

"What are we going to do?" Christine asked with fear in her voice.

"Not much we can do right now. We will have to wait until daybreak," Kyle explained. "Let's lock the doors and try to get some rest until we can assess the problem in a few hours."

They settled in holding hands and eventually faded off into a cat nap hoping the sunrise would bring much needed insight into their dilemma. Without warning, hurricane-style winds began to shake the vehicle immensely. Torrential rains beat down on the car as lightning erupted and thunder lit up the night's sky.

Then, as if straight out of a horror movie, the silhouette of a stranger appeared and began tapping on Kyle's window. The wind and rain, combined with the darkness, prevented Kyle from getting a good look at the unwanted visitor. Lightning hit a nearby tree and was immediately set ablaze.

Kyle's heart beat wildly as he whispered softly to Christine, "Don't move." He reached for the pistol he had tucked beside his seat. Sheer terror had taken over as he prepared to protect all that he held dear.

He whispered softly again, "If he tries to break into the car, I might have to fire a warning shot. I don't think he knows we are here. He thinks the car is abandoned."

Almost as if the ghostly man could hear the soft conversation from within the car, he suddenly disappeared in the same way that he had come. His shadowy figure faded into the night.

It was more than a creepy experience. It was frightening, dangerous, and weird.

At the first sign of daylight, Kyle cautiously opened his car door and looked to see if anyone was lingering around. Confident they were alone, he took another look at the car's engine. With the pistol tucked in his waistband, he knelt down and saw what appeared to be a pool of motor oil or was it blood?

He returned to the driver's seat and turned the ignition key. The engine struggled a bit but actually started. It sputtered, growled, paused, backfired, and then came to a grinding halt.

The momentum from the wounded engine was enough to get them on the other side of a mountain. With luck, they picked up enough speed to coast to a filling station that came into view at the bottom of the hill.

The engine was dead, but the Toyota was rolling on its own. Unbelievably, they made it to the gas pumps.

The filling station was closed. They weren't sure if it was closed for the holiday or just until their regular business hours came into play.

At around 6:30 A.M., a scruffy older gentleman showed up in a pickup with the name of the filling station, Raw's, painted on his truck doors.

"We might be in luck," Kyle said.

"What in the world are you kids doing here so early?" he asked as he began to unlock the front door to the station.

He walked inside, flipped on the lights, and put on a pot of coffee. Kyle walked in behind the man and waited for him to settle in. When the older gentleman turned around, he did so with fear in his eyes.

"You here to rob me?" he said with a nervous twitch. "There are a few hundred bucks in the register. It's yours just take it. Just don't plug me." "Excuse me?" Kyle said with a look of bewilderment. "Shoot you? Why on earth would you think I want to shoot you?"

"Why else you got that there gun tucked away in your britches," the older man asked sheepishly.

"Oh, my word! I am so sorry! We broke down on the interstate, and I just had the gun handy for our safety. Please forgive me," Kyle said apologetically.

"Well, if you ain't gonna shoot me, would you care for a cup of truck stop coffee?" the old fellow said with a sense of relief.

Kyle took him up on his offer as the two of them popped the hood on the Toyota and discovered that the engine was definitely blown.

"There ain't nobody who could touch this until after Christmas. And besides, it's another 100 miles before we could even begin to think about parts," came the news that Kyle regretted to hear.

"It would be at least a week, maybe two, before we could even hope to have you fixed up."

The severity of the problem was really starting to set in. Kyle walked away to a pay telephone as he fought back tears. He had pushed his luck this time, and he found himself stranded at the mercy of strangers.

He picked up the telephone and made a regrettable collect telephone call to his mother.

"Mom, it's Kyle. I'm okay but I'm in a bit of trouble." His voice was heavy with sadness as he explained the situation.

"You kids sit right there. We will come and get you and load the car up on a trailer. We will get it repaired while you spend the week with family," Anna said with assurance.

Kyle and Christine spent the next 12 hours swapping stories with the owner of the gas station. Not one customer darkened the door of the station all day. They both knew they were lucky to have had a place to wait in safety, especially, with such a helpful and hospitable old gentleman at their side.

"Whereabouts did y'all break down? You know we had a small Tennessee twister come across the top of them there hills last night?" the old guy said with little concern.

"A tornado? Last night? We were right where you are talking about!" Kyle said with excitement.

"Sure was. Rumor has it that old man Rawlings redirected the storm away from his moonshine still that sits just off the interstate. They say he stood on the shoulder of the highway shaking his fist at God and the twister. You didn't see him out there did ya?"

Christine and Kyle locked eyes in astonishment. Could it have been the moonshiner tapping on their windshield in the middle of the night?

"I hate to admit it, but I think we slept right through all the excitement," Kyle said as he attempted not to go into much detail.

A familiar and welcoming Ford F-250 interrupted the conversation when it appeared pulling an empty car hauler. It was Anna and Kyle's stepdad, Reed.

Anna had gotten remarried a while back and Kyle really liked Reed. Reed adored Kyle's mother and took great care of her. He had come to rescue Kyle and Christine who were extremely grateful, although disappointed that their surprise wasn't exactly the way they had hoped it would be.

Anna hugged Kyle tight, then pulled Christine into their hug.

"Merry Christmas kids," said Reed. "You ready to get home?"

"YES!" exclaimed Kyle and Christine in unison.

"Then let's get going! We're burning daylight," Reed said.

Reed secured the Toyota on the trailer and circled his finger in the air, signifying it was time to load up. There wasn't enough seating in the truck, so Kyle and Christine climbed into her Toyota and rode in it atop the trailer. It was cold, but they snuggled into each other.

Christine laughed then looked up into Kyle's eyes. "It's not exactly a winter sleigh ride, the this is definitely an adventure we won't ever forget."

Kyle waved goodbye from the front seat of the Toyota as the old man walked out the front door of the filling station carrying what appeared to be a case of moonshine. That's when he noticed the sign above the filling station. *Rawling's Quick Stop, Open 24/7, come rain or moonshine.*

The realization of just who the old gentleman was brought a huge smile to Kyle's face. Raw's was old man Rawlings! That old moonshiner had been a guardian angel to a couple of overly ambitious kids trying to get home for Christmas. Shaking his head, Kyle said, "The Lord really does work in mysterious ways."

When they pulled into town, their family gathered around the truck and trailer, excited voices filling the air.

Their time together flew by, but soon it was time to return to D.C. The Toyota was scheduled to be overhauled just in time for them to hit the road and return back to the Capitol for the inauguration of George H. W. Bush as the next President of the United States. Everyone from the U.S. Senate who was on the inaugural team had been put on notice to be back to work on time or don't come back at all.

With just 36 hours before the deadline to report to work, Kyle was standing at the mechanic's garage looking at the underside of the Toyota, still on the rack as it underwent final repairs.

"How much longer?" Kyle asked the mechanic, trying to be diplomatic with his inquiry.

"It will probably be at least another four hours. Maybe five," came the mechanic's reply.

"Whoo, man, that's cutting it close. It will take me 24 hours to get back to D.C., even if I drive straight through. That is what got me in this trouble in the first place," Kyle explained with urgency. "This is really cutting it close. If I don't make it back in time, I'll lose my job."

The mechanic shrugged his shoulders and said, "I get it man. I'll do my best." He worked for another five hours, and then an hour more. He lowered the Toyota off the rack, started it up, and indicated he was going to take it for a test drive.

"There isn't time for that. I have to go now, and I mean now," Kyle said insistently.

And with that, he paid the mechanic and headed back out onto the open road. Just east of Little Rock, Arkansas, the check engine light turned bright red on the dashboard of the Toyota. Kyle decided there wasn't much he could do about it at this point, so he kept driving and threw up a little prayer. He was determined he was going to get to the Capitol in time for the inauguration, even if he had to hitchhike, though Christine reminded him that was not a viable option.

More than once he thought about whether or not the old 1972 Ford pickup would have given him any trouble. For now, his hope was in the newly repaired Toyota with the shiny check engine light glowing with intensity.

They made it to Washington D.C. with four hours to spare. Kyle had driven 24 hours straight on his own. He was too amped up to sleep, so he gave that privilege to Christine. He grabbed three hours of sleep back at the apartment, showered, and headed downtown to the Capitol for his assigned duties.

The coming days were a blur as the nation celebrated its new president, a man Kyle couldn't believe he had met and served in person and the man whose official inaugural documentary Kyle would be chosen to help produce.

Kyle had to admit, he was proud of his work that honored the President of the United States. Given all that he and Christine had survived to make it happen, car trouble, ghostly encounters, lightning strikes, tornadoes, time with loved ones, and the bleary-eyed and grueling 24-hour cross-country drive to get back to work in order to maintain his integrity with his team, had left him exhausted. But he had pushed through, a trait he'd learned early in life, and one that continued to serve him well.

CHAPTER 41

The job at the U.S. Senate had been great for Kyle in so many ways, but one; he needed to make more money if he and Christine were to start a family. They agreed to make the potential career change a matter of prayer.

An increase in salary was needed for the family to grow. The goal was to have enough income in order to move from the studio apartment into a townhouse down the street.

It wasn't always the case in their lives, but their prayer was answered for the exact amount they needed to make the change. Kyle accepted a lucrative offer to become a TV and radio producer for a national advertising agency.

Seeing the new career opportunity as a green light, they felt the freedom to unlock the door to the baby department. Within two weeks of accepting the new job, Christine was pregnant. They thought for certain it would take a few months, but they had acquired new nicknames from friends, Fertile and Myrtle.

Kyle was proud to know he had what it took to be a daddy. "That family recipe is proof our secret sauce is the best in the land," Kyle bragged as he shared the news with his grandpa over the telephone.

Liam laughed and praised his grandson for all that he was becoming. Liam had always found a way to express the fatherly love that Kyle had so desired from Dwight. With one child of his own on the way, Kyle hoped to model the affirming approach of his grandpa.

Kyle and Christine soon moved into their new townhouse as their little one continued to grow safely tucked away in his mother's belly. Christine complained about getting big as a barn, but Kyle assured her that he thought she looked hotter than ever. He wasn't lying. Christine had a natural beauty about her, but the glow from the pregnancy made her all the more enchanting.

As many young couples did, they attended Lamaze pregnancy classes in an effort to do everything just right. Kyle became an expert comforter as he practiced rubbing a watermelon in a figure-eight pattern. He even helped Christine practice her breathing techniques.

Christine continued her prenatal care up until 40 weeks. She looked more like a duck when she walked than the cute pep club member she was in high school.

"I'm huge!" she expressed to the doctor. "Is this baby ever going to come?"

She referred to their unborn child as "the baby" because Kyle and Christine had put into place a tradition that they would retain through all of their pregnancies, Kyle would announce the gender of the baby at birth as he cut the umbilical cord.

"I am concerned that you may be at high risk if we don't induce your labor," the doctor said with concern. But, Christine was determined to have the baby on her own. She remained active and tried any home remedy that might induce her labor.

Anticipating the baby's arrival, both their mothers were in town. To keep everyone entertained, they decided to go on a tour of the Capitol. Long marble hallways and numerous stairs eventually brought the tour to an end in the Capitol Rotunda.

As she looked up into the majestic dome that topped the historic building, Christine felt a sharp pain. She waited a bit and then came another. Her water hadn't broken, but one thing was clear, she was going into labor, and it felt like if they didn't get moving pretty quick, the Capitol police might be delivering the baby!

The contractions were regular but still far enough apart that it was too soon to be admitted to the hospital. Around midnight, Christine tapped Kyle on the arm and softly whispered in Kyle's ear, "It's time. We have to go. These labor pains are getting ."

Kyle jumped into action having slept in his clothes. "Today is the day. We are going to have a baby!" Kyle said as he loaded her suitcase into their new Volvo.

Kyle had hoped the baby would come on his birthday. They were 10 days ahead of his own date of birth, but he was okay with it, so long as the baby was delivered safely.

Christine was prepped for delivery. Five hours passed with no signs of a baby. Ten hours passed. Fifteen hours passed, and at the 20 hour mark, Christine looked as if she had run more than one marathon.

She was exhausted and doing all she could to breathe through contractions, but there were few signs that the baby would be delivered any time soon.

"If things don't start to change, we will need to deliver the baby by C-section," the doctor explained. "This is becoming life-threatening for you and the baby."

Kyle and Christine leaned on their faith and trusted the baby would come naturally, but also with a little assistance of Pitocin.

Within the next two hours, Kyle made the announcement, "It's a girl!" He was absolutely giddy, so much so that the doctor and nurses couldn't contain their laughter as they did their best to attend to Christine and the new baby.

The couple named the beautiful baby girl, Lori-Ellen. It was a hyphenated name. It was to be spoken together. It was in keeping with their southern roots, and they simply loved the way it sounded.

Kyle looked Lori-Ellen over from head to toe. She was so tiny and petite. One thing about her did capture Kyle's attention. He pulled the doctor aside and inquired about his concern.

"I'm not sure if you noticed, and I'm not sure if there is a reason for concern, but is it me or does the baby appear to have a bit of a conehead?" Kyle asked with all sincerity.

The doctor produced a huge smile and said, "She has been trying to make her way into this world for nearly 24 hours. Don't worry. She will be as pretty as her mother in a few days."

Kyle sighed with relief and said, "Whew, I think she is beautiful now, but the thought of her wearing a top hat for the rest of her life did enter my mind."

Christine overheard the comment and responded, "Oh my word! She is perfect. Bring her to me. I want to hold her before my milk comes in, and I need a dairy farmer's milking machine for assistance!"

The little family was soon home, and life had never been better. Kyle loved his new job, but it was demanding. He left home before sunrise and arrived at sundown.

With Lori-Ellen, it was as the old adage says, "The days go by slowly, but the years fly by." She grew so quickly. Seeing her watch for her daddy to come home through the front window of the townhouse was nearly all he could stand.

As work ramped up, it felt like Kyle saw her at dinner, played with her for a short while, and then tucked her into bed. It wasn't enough time with her, and it was killing him.

Seeing his TV commercials air across a metropolitan area with over five million viewers was exciting, but as a young producer, the recognition meant less to him than his family.

Kyle knew he needed to make a change for his family's sake, but he didn't know how it would happen. In an unexpected turn of events, Kyle was at a client meeting with the owner of the advertising agency when all of a sudden the owner collapsed with a grand mal seizure.

Kyle immediately began administering CPR, which saved the owner's life, but the long-term health complications of the owner forced the agency to have to close.

"I have some bad news," Kyle said as he sat down for dinner with Christine one night. "They are closing the ad agency. We have about a month before we are out of a job."

"Hmm," Christine replied. "I guess this is as good of a time as any to give you some news."

Kyle looked up from his plate with a look of concern and replied, "Yes?"

"We are pregnant." She reached across the table and grabbed his hand.

The timing of it all brought on a mixture of happiness and sadness. The weight of providing for his family kept Kyle awake that night. Staring at the ceiling, he wrestled with uncertainty, wondering what the future might hold.

"I think we should move home," Kyle shared through a mouth full of toothpaste foam as he stood in the bathroom brushing his teeth the following morning. "Our lease is up. There is no guarantee we will find a job anytime soon. And let's face it, do we want our kids to know their grandparents as a UPS box of gifts? They will hardly know our parents' names at this rate. Who wants to raise kids in a city this big? It's a concrete jungle!"

Christine put her hand on his forearm and said, "Hey. Take a deep breath. I'm with you."

There was not a word of debate. Within a matter of weeks, Kyle flew Christine home with Lori-Ellen, and he stayed behind to pack up their belongings and their life. This chapter of their life was closed.

He loaded down the moving truck, and with his father-in-law at his side as copilot, Kyle made the one-way trip back to where he belonged, life at home with the Prairie people.

CHAPTER 42

It was good to be back home. The big city was exciting, but life in a flyover state had much more appeal than some people would ever come to realize. Nothing rivaled the beauty of an Oklahoma sunset. Each evening, the sky transformed into a masterpiece, with vibrant colors and shifting shapes painted effortlessly across the vast, open horizon.

Kyle had missed the smell of rain showers as they sprinkled across the dusty roads and the waving wheat fields. The damp air carried an earthy freshness, bringing a sense of renewal and revitalization. The rains were often accompanied by massive thunderhead clouds that billowed as high as the eye could see. The shapes and sizes of the clouds were beyond description and provided opportunities to imagine the forms of bears, dinosaurs, Disney characters, and other abstract works of art. It was simply breathtaking and peaceful. It was home.

As nice as it was to be among familiar people and places, Kyle needed to relaunch his career. He picked up a few consulting jobs until eventually he landed a position as the head of communications for a large regional financial institution. For the next 10 years, his career blossomed to the point that the board of directors approached him about becoming the next president of the multi-million-dollar financial institution. Kyle gave it serious consideration as he reflected on the fact that his grandfather, Riff, had been in banking. He wondered if perhaps the legacy should live on through his generation.

Ultimately, he turned down the opportunity and instead took a position as the Editor-in-Chief of the state's largest weekly news journal. It was a massive responsibility but a challenge he gladly accepted. The publication was struggling, but through Kyle's leadership, it regained national recognition and awards for its overhaul and reorganization.

In addition to the news journal, Kyle was asked to host a statewide radio broadcast and to serve as a public affairs spokesman for several public policy issues that were threatening the underserved in the state. It wasn't uncommon for Kyle to be seen on the evening news providing perspective on issues that were at odds with certain leaders in state government.

Life was exciting, busy, and fun. Especially with not two but six children now under their feet! At one point, Kyle and Christine had four children under four! Keeping the diaper sizes straight was one of the greatest challenges of all. Each of their kids had different personalities and brought unique stories and drama into the life of the growing family. One thing was for certain, children didn't come with an instruction manual.

Christine grew up in a large family where she took on motherly roles at an early age. Like Kyle, her parents had divorced, and as the oldest daughter, she was relied upon to fill the gap where her parents needed help.

As a couple, they were navigating the journey of parenthood, determined to shield their children from the dysfunction they had endured. They soon realized that raising a family required as much unlearning as learning. Surprisingly, their children became some of their greatest teachers.

Kyle and Christine also felt deeply grateful for Ollie and Nita Bennett, whose time together in Washington, D.C., left a lasting impact. Their Pictionary games were more than just fun—they quietly demonstrated what a loving, nurturing family looked like. The Bennetts never preached or claimed to have all the answers; they simply lived by example. Were they perfect? No, but they were committed to each other and constantly building upon the foundational principles that brought stability to their family.

It was a bit of a zoo at times in the Sanderson household, but Kyle and Christine loved the challenge of raising children. They never let their small tribe slow them down or hinder their activity. Wherever they went, the kids were often in tow.

The kids grew up with a sense of adventure and confidence as life at home was balanced with discipline and a whole lot of love. One thing was certain, over the years, Kyle and Christine had learned that when you lead with love, mercy and grace were certain to follow. This was the one thing they hoped the kids never doubted, they were loved and loved deeply, no matter what.

Home movies were a favorite pastime for all as Kyle organized full-day shoots with the children starring as actors and members of the set design and production crews. The mini-movies often took all day to produce. With titles like, Bazooka Butt Boy, Puppy Power, and Funny Fishing Tips, friends, extended family, and plenty of neighbors couldn't wait to see the latest Sanderson production. It was through these little productions that the children learned how to work as a team. Leadership skills, interpersonal communication, conflict resolution, and the ability to use critical thinking to problem solve, all while entertaining and being creative, made every scene worth the effort.

Discovering each of the children's unique gifts and talents made parenting more intriguing. Personalities, skills, and aptitudes were as diverse as there were kids. There could have never been any doubt that several of the children would go onto to produce programming for major TV networks, be involved with movie productions, and not only perform in the arts but win national awards as well. Some went on to be real estate developers and interior designers. The combination of creativity and an entrepreneurial spirit was evident in each of their lives.

Outdoor adventures were also the norm at the Sanderson house. One summer afternoon, Kyle filled clear trash bags with helium that had been left over from one of the bank events. The kids became the envy of the neighborhood as they pulled floating, makeshift balloons from the backs of their bicycles. The train of giggling kids parading around brought smiles to onlookers as the children waved and bragged about their dad's creativity.

Never at a loss for ingenuity, Kyle helped the boys convert an old riding lawnmower into a miniature customized driving machine that they affectionately referred to as Black Beauty. The boys and Kyle worked for hours using PVC pipe, zip ties, cardboard, tarps, and pieces of wood to shape Black Beauty into something even Henry Ford would have been proud to present as a prototype. The bonding between the father and his sons couldn't be missed. The time together produced memories that would last a lifetime. Kyle often wondered what it might have been like to have times such as these with his own dad.

Watching the reaction of neighborhood kids and parents as his sons, Ben and Ike, navigated the back streets and sidewalks of suburbia brought plenty of grins and admiration. The number 34 on the side door made the motorized contraption look more like a race car than a homemade bucket of bolts on wheels. Few knew that the number 34 represented the birth order the boys had in the family. Ben was number three. Ike was number four. Together, 34 was the number that represented the Sanderson manufacturing team and pit crew!

Baseball games and ballet recitals kept the family's minivan coming and going. It was hard to do at first, but Kyle and Christine eventually gave in and traded their beloved Volvo in for a fully-loaded minivan. Over the years, it would gain the nickname as the French Fry Mobile due to the guarantee of finding at least one stray petrified McDonald's French fry tucked away in some dark nook or cranny.

There were other times when each of the kids found a way to stand out from everyday life. Certainly, Lori-Ellen's entrance into the world established her as the leader of the pack. She was often found to be the one who served as the spokesperson for the troops. One such example occurred on a road trip during an extended family vacation.

"Daddy," Lori-Ellen said quietly from the back of the minivan. Based on the sudden loss of noise and the stillness that had overcome the vehicle, Kyle sensed something had gone awry.

"Yes?" Kyle responded in hopes that the mention of his name might be the predecessor to a request for a potty break.

"Daddy," Lori-Ellen said once again.

"Yes, Lori-Ellen?" Kyle said as he looked at her through the rearview mirror.

"Daddy, Amelia has a French fry stuck up her nose," Lori-Ellen reported.

Kyle looked at Christine and then back into the rearview mirror and said, "A what? Stuck where?"

"A French fry. She has a French fry stuck in her nose," Lori-Ellen said insistently.

It was true. Somewhere between the Golden Arches and their current location, in the middle of nowhere, Amelia had managed to push a French fry deep into her sinus cavity. Kyle calmly pulled the minivan off at an exit and proceeded to perform minor surgery on Amelia.

He held her upside down so he could fully see into her nose. Sitting there on the floorboard of the van's open side door, children surrounding him and looking over his shoulder, he said, "Christine, hand me my knife."

Amelia shot straight up and screamed as the remaining kids scattered to the back of the van. Eyes wide, she went into full panic mode, and it was all Kyle could do to contain her.

"It's a Swiss Army knife, baby. I'm just going to use the tweezers," Kyle said in an effort to calm his frazzled patient. Amelia squirmed and wiggled a bit as Kyle did his best to grab hold of the tip of the French fry that hid in the back of Amelia's nose.

The salt from the French fry was making Amelia's eyes water as Kyle prodded around trying to rescue the potato particle.

His efforts failed. In fact, they only made matters worse. Unfortunately, he had succeeded in driving the French fry deeper into her sinuses.

"Geez, what are we going to do," Kyle asked Christine as he tried not to laugh. "I guess this is life on the road with a bunch of kids. It's certainly an adventure."

Christine unfolded a paper road map and located a hospital about an hour away. Seeing the knife was put away, everyone calmed down and waited patiently as Kyle explained the predicament to the emergency room doctor.

"No worries. You can't imagine what I have pulled out of kids' noses. This won't be my last French fry," the doctor said with a smile.

"Next time, buy tater tots, they are larger and won't fit into her nose!" he advised.

The joke was well received, and in a matter of minutes, Amelia rejoined her siblings with a handful of lollipops that had been provided by a nurse in celebration of the properly pulled potato!

While Lori-Ellen was the leader, and Amelia the one with the knack for creating unexpected adventures, Ben was known as the sharpshooter. His eye-to-hand coordination was uncanny. He and his brother went on to play college baseball, but it was hard to decide what was more impressive, Ben's ability at sports or his marksmanship skills.

If a fly appeared on the ceiling or on a wall at the house, Ben was quick to bring the buzzing pest to sudden death. While most might pride themselves in using a flyswatter, all Ben needed was a rubber band. The distance was hardly a hindrance. He would simply pull back, take aim, and fire away.

"Do you see him, Dad?" Ben asked in a whisper, his eye on his target like a sniper under cover.

"See what, son?" Kyle asked.

"There on the tip of the ceiling fan blade. One big old horsefly looking for someone to bite. I have been stalking him for the last few minutes," Ben said with stern intent. "He is going down!"

And just like that, the fly's life came to a sudden end. Ben rarely missed, and he won plenty of bets proving his talents.

Ike was known in the family as the big little brother. He arrived in the world at 10 pounds and six ounces. The doctor joked that he came out smoking a cigar and wearing a baseball cap. Truth was, that if not for the fast-acting instincts of the delivery team, he would have died at his birth. "Christine, the baby's head is down and in place, and I am concerned that you haven't delivered at this point. I need you to push as hard as you can on your next contraction," the doctor said with a critical look of concern.

The contraction came and Christine pushed with all her might. The baby's head emerged but nothing else.

"Push Christine! Push!" the doctor yelled.

The baby's head had cleared the womb, but its face was turning purple. There was no cry, and the room became deathly silent. Dr. Chambers jumped into action wearing her favorite pink Converse tennis shoes. If something didn't change quick, both the mother and child would be in grave jeopardy. With the skill that only comes with years of experience, Dr. Chambers performed a last-ditch maneuver that pushed the baby's shoulder through Christine's tiny birth canal. Within seconds, baby Ike was born, and the entire room gave out a huge sigh of relief.

"Is the baby okay? Is the baby going to be okay?" Christine pushed out the words through exhaustion and concern. "Is it a boy or a girl?"

As Kyle snipped the umbilical cord he declared, "It's a boy, honey! He is going to be just fine! He is huge! I cannot believe you just gave birth to Goliath!" Kyle shouted with excitement and utter relief. "You are an amazing woman! I love you so much."

"I'm proud of you Christine," Dr. Chambers said with a smile. "If you hadn't pushed Ike out on that last contraction, I was going to have to push him back in and do an emergency C-Section. This is the perfect outcome. I can't tell you how relieved I am. The odds weren't very good otherwise."

Following an unforeseen miscarriage, Rosemary made her debut in the world. Among the kids, Rosemary was known as the 30-year-old. Of all the children she grew up fast, but it wasn't by choice.

When Rosemary was three years old, Kyle and Christine assumed she was suffering from a lingering bad case of the flu. She had lost a considerable amount of weight, was tired a lot, and seemed to constantly have to pee. But, when she became very lethargic, her parents made an emergency visit to the pediatrician. The doctor did a few quick tests in the office and came back with his diagnosis.

"I hate to tell you this, but based on the tests I ran, I believe your daughter has type 1 diabetes. I've already contacted the hospital to let them know she is headed that way. You have two options. I can call an ambulance and have her transported, or you can load her in your car and drive her the two miles down the road yourself. Either way, she needs to get to the hospital."

Kyle and Christine stood in shock by the exam table where their daughter rested motionlessly. Of all the things Kyle had been through in his life, this was by far the worst thing he'd ever experienced.

"This can't be! She's too little. Too beautiful. Too precious. He must have misdiagnosed her," Kyle said as tears flooded his eyes, and his world came crashing in all around him.

He looked at Christine, scooped Rosemary up in his arms, and they headed out to their cars.

"I'll meet you there," Christine said as she gave Rosemary a kiss atop her head.

When Kyle loaded Rosemary into the car she said, "Daddy, I'm hungry. Can I get an ice cream?" Rosemary asked in a weakened state.

How could he deny her? She was so sick. What could it hurt? Rosemary devoured the treat in an instant. Kyle didn't realize it at the time, but he was actually making matters much worse as Rosemary's body had lost the ability to turn glucose into energy. He was literally driving her blood sugar levels off the chart. If he didn't get her to the hospital soon and get insulin into her small little frame, she could quickly fall into a coma and die.

Upon her arrival to the hospital, the awaiting medical team strapped Rosemary to a gurney that was equipped with side planks. Her outstretched arms were tied down to the planks and without consideration for her age or pain, the hospital staff began stabbing needles, IV's, and other probes into her tiny arms.

"Daddy! Daddy! Make them stop! Daddy help me!" Rosemary screamed as the team did their work.

CHAPTER 42

Kyle broke down in tears, looking down into his little girl's eyes. There was nothing he could do but cry with her and assure her it would be over as soon as possible.

A tall, brown-eyed doctor entered the room and placed his hand on Kyle's shoulder. "Hang in there Dad; she is going to be okay. Minutes matter at this point, and the team is doing all they can to save her from a tragedy," Dr. Domek said with deep concern and empathy.

It was touch and go for a while, but Rosemary pulled through. The family learned there was no cure for type 1 diabetes. Without rigorous lifelong attention to sugar levels and frequent insulin injections, she could die. It was all so overwhelming to think about.

On the day Rosemary was released from the hospital, the phone rang. It was his good friend, Bill.

"Hey man," Bill said, "Sorry I missed your call. Just giving you a call back."

"I didn't call you," Kyle explained, somewhat confused.

"Really, that's weird. I swear I had a call from you. Oh, well, I just felt like I was supposed to call you. Everything okay?" the caller inquired.

"You wouldn't believe me if I told you. I just got home from the hospital with my little girl. She is three years old and was just diagnosed with diabetes," Kyle explained, choking back tears.

The phone went silent.

"Are you there?" Kyle asked.

"Yeah," came back the reply as Bill was obviously having trouble not crying himself. "I'm so sorry. She is such a pretty little girl. But I think I know why I called."

"Why is that?" Kyle asked.

"My daughter was diagnosed with type 1 diabetes when she was three. She is now on her way to college. It is tough. It sucks. But you guys can do this."

The timing of the call was anything but circumstantial. Kyle needed hope, and hope came from a random telephone call that could have only been prompted by angels or perhaps even a direct dial from the Lord Himself.

Rosemary continued to fight the disease throughout her life, but she never let it define her. She would often say that it made her stronger even though more than once she had come close to never waking up from a prolific low blood sugar incident.

Raelyn was the runt of the family. She was the life of the party and along with her brother Ike, and at Dad's encouragement, they kept the family in stitches. The older kids often complained that Raelyn never got a spanking.

"Aren't you glad I finally figured it out?" Kyle would tease as he came to her defense. "Not all my kids could be perfect!"

The children knew Kyle was kidding about Raelyn. As the baby of the family, she never lacked for love and affection from the other children.

Family movie night was a favorite among the children. On one particular evening the family made the decision to watch a movie that featured alien avatars.

Raelyn had a knack for the dramatic. She could play for hours on end all by herself as she made up stories and activities with dolls and stuffed animals. Kyle often joined in on the fun with her as he assumed various characters and traits with his aspiring little actress. In Raelyn's world, it was as if there was little difference between reality and the theatric. The smell of popcorn floated throughout the house as everyone snuggled up in their pajamas to watch the feature film on the family room big screen.

Everything was going along nicely until just after a major action scene. As the music and volume transitioned to the next panoramic, a hard thud sounded in the middle of the room.

Kyle rushed to flip on the light switch only to discover that Raelyn had fallen face first onto the floor. She was unconscious and nonresponsive.

"Raelyn! Raelyn! Talk to me. Talk to Daddy," Kyle shouted as he did his best to gain a response. "Call 9-1-1! Something isn't right. Her eyes have rolled back, I barely feel a pulse, and she doesn't appear to be breathing!"

The other children started to cry. The mood went from fun and exciting to panic and horror.

Ever so slowly, Raelyn started to regain consciousness. Her breathing became evident, but she stared straight ahead as if she was lost in another world.

"Momma! Momma! Where are you? I can't see you! Momma, Daddy what is going on? I can't see anyone! Help me," Raelyn screamed as she started to regain her faculties.

The paramedics soon arrived and began to check Raelyn's vitals. Within the next several minutes, she was back to being her normal silly self.

"What in the world is going on?" Kyle asked the team of first responders. "We were just enjoying a movie and the next thing we know she is out cold on the floor."

"We have seen this before. My guess is she got scared when she looked into the big eyes of the avatar, she simply held her breath until she fainted," the paramedic explained. "Keep your eye on her, but I think she is going to be just fine."

It was true, there was never a dull moment at the Sanderson house. No matter how crazy the day had been, Kyle always did his best to end the day in peace. He never wanted his children to lay awake at night in fear as he had done watching the headlights of automobiles pass outside his bedroom window as he feared one of the vehicles might be driven by his drunken father seeking to unpack rage and deliver abuse on the family.

In Kyle's mind, the fear of what Dwight might try to do lingered. It had rented space in the back of Kyle's brain for most of his life. Where was he? Had he slipped into insanity? Had alcohol finally taken its toll? Too much was unknown not to consider and be prepared for the worst.

The children had come to expect a nightly ritual that often comforted them and provided them with a sense of safety and peace. There was an intentional phrase they would hear as Kyle made his rounds during nightly bedside prayers.

"You know I love you. There is nothing you can ever do that will change that, right?" Kyle would say as part of his regular routine. As he walked out of the bedrooms and turned off the lights he would often pause, turn around and ask, "You know what?"

"Yup," would come the reply from any one of the kids.

"What?" Kyle would ask.

"You love me," would come the predictable response.

"I sure do. I love you," Kyle would say as the kids faded off to sleep with the assurance that everything was right in the world and come what may, their momma and daddy loved them, no matter what.

CHAPTER 43

Getting out in public with six children was always an adventure. The world was designed for a family of four. Most automobiles could handle a family of four with ease. When four was the number of guests, restaurant booths provided plenty of elbow room for dining. Double that number and life took on a whole new set of challenges. The car had to be larger and the wait time for combined seating at a favorite diner was always longer. Keeping up with a headcount was always top of mind for Kyle and Christine. Lose focus for a minute and a misplaced kid was sure to happen.

In an effort to wrangle the sheep, Kyle came up with a few techniques for bringing order to the chaos. His first strategy was a recognizable and unique family whistle. Even the best of plans could fall apart, so if one of the kids got lost in a rack of clothes at a department store, rather than scream or call 9-1-1, the family developed a customized family whistle.

Should one, two, or even three kids go adrift, the simple whistle was implemented, and the cows would come home. Follow the whistle, and you would be back in the herd in no time.

At other times, keeping the kids together required more of a military-style approach. Rather than roam about aisles in freeform as free agents, Kyle simply implemented the D.I.N.A.R. protocol. D.I.N.A.R. was short for DUCKS IN A ROW.

If things started looking like a train wreck, Kyle simply announced, "D.I.N.A.R." and the little ducks would line up from youngest to oldest in a flash.

D.I.N.A.R. became a game as much as it was a necessity. The kids enjoyed the excitement of finding their place and marching in place.

D.I.N.A.R. had its benefits, but it also had its drawbacks. On one occasion, Kyle saw the need to utilize the D.I.N.A.R. protocol.

"D.I.N.A.R.," he announced. And in an instance, the children were aligned in a stair-stepped row like little toy soldiers.

Kyle led the way and continued to navigate the troops without recourse, until, without thought, as he often did, he let loose a butt bomb or as Christine referred to them, a love puff, which blew straight into the face of the youngest of the six.

Much to Kyle's embarrassment, and without any opportunity to silence the reaction, Raelyn sent out the warning to her comrades, "Dad farted!" She didn't just mention it, she proclaimed it loud and clear. Like clockwork, the message was relayed down the chain of command with passion and commitment.

"Dad farted! Dad farted! Dad farted! Dad farted! Dad farted!" came the public service announcement from each and every child.

Kyle was mortified.

"I've been telling you to hold it," Christine said with little sympathy as onlookers watched and broke into laughter as if they had front row seats at a comedy club.

Needless to say, the troops had scattered upon notice, and Kyle was required to incorporate the family whistle into the comedy routine, much to the delight of the impromptu audience.

"I haven't had this much fun shopping in years," one mom said to another as she stood watching with a baby on her hip.

"I have to give the guy credit. My husband would have just fired away and left me to deal with his stink bomb," another shopper commented as the department store returned back to normal.

Following a full day of shopping, the family made the decision to enjoy brinner, short for breakfast for dinner, at their favorite restaurant.

Kyle settled in at an extra-large table designed for families their size. The table was just another reason why they liked dining out at Cracker Barrel.

Christine stepped away to wash up as Kyle placed the order with the waitress.

"The kids' pancake breakfast, all around, please," Kyle said as he gave instruction to the older gray-haired waitress whose kind eyes showed signs of a busy shift.

"How about you and the little lady? What are you folks going to have?" she asked with a sweet and genuine smile. "Your kids are so cute and well-behaved," she added.

"I don't know these kids. I just saw there was an extra seat and sat down," Kyle joked with the waitress. "We will have the special. Thank you, ma'am."

The kids were occupying their time by playing a game of tabletop paper football when Christine approached the table with a look of shock and fear.

"Are you okay? What's wrong?" Kyle asked with immediate concern.

Christine sat down beside him with tears in her eyes and was unable to speak. She presented her left arm to Kyle and pointed to her ring finger.

"I don't understand. Is something wrong?" Kyle asked.

"The diamond in my wedding ring. It's gone! I noticed it was missing when I washed my hands in the restroom!" Christine explained as she placed her head on her crossed arms on the table and wept.

"What's wrong, momma?" Ben asked. He had always been sensitive and intuitive to the needs of others. "Daddy, why is momma sad?"

"Momma has lost the diamond in her wedding ring," Christine explained as best she could as the thought of her loss overwhelmed her.

"Kyle, I have to go look for it."

"Where? We have been all over town today. Where would you begin? Besides, stores will be closing in the next 30 minutes," Kyle said as he tried to appeal to her with reason.

"I'm going back to Sam's Club. I just think it may have come out while we were shopping. I will ask the manager to wet mop the floor for me. Surely, they will have mercy on me," Christine said as the food arrived. "I'll take my car and drive back there, and you and the kids can all pile in your car when you're done. I'll meet you at home."

The ring meant the world to her. She had to at least try.

"Kids, momma needs a miracle. Let's pray for our food and ask God to help her find the diamond to her wedding ring," Kyle instructed as the little tribe bowed their heads out of respect and reverence for their mother's loss.

Kyle helped the kids cut up their pancakes and finish their dinner. He paid the waitress and gathered the kids for departure. With a baby on one hip and holding Ike's hand with his free hand, Kyle stepped out into the dark of the night. The parking lot was freshly tarred, and the lighting was especially dim from the scarce streetlights.

As Kyle stepped down off the sidewalk and Ike stepped in the opposite direction, Kyle stumbled in an attempt to remain balanced with the baby at his side.

When he stepped to gain his bearing, a twinkle in the black asphalt caught his eye. Kyle froze.

No way, he thought.

He knelt down and picked up the source of the sparkling light on the asphalt.

"It's a MIRACLE!" Kyle screamed at the top of his lungs. "It's a MIRACLE!"

"What Daddy? What is a miracle?" Lori-Ellen asked with curiosity.

"This is the diamond from your mother's wedding ring! God answered our prayer! Your mother is not going to believe this!" Kyle exclaimed as he carefully placed the precious stone in his pocket then gave the family whistle.

The troops reorganized as they loaded up and headed to Sam's Club to give Mom the news.

The doors were locked when they arrived, but the night guard understood the circumstances and let Kyle into the store.

Kyle located Christine on aisle 10 surrounded by employees carefully sorting through dust and dirt at the end of a large industrial floor mop. He could see their hope was fading fast with no sign of the diamond.

Christine continued to cry as she saw him approaching.

She stood up to give Kyle a hug, and as she did, he knelt down on one knee and said," I know it meant a lot to you when I gave it to you the first time. I hope it means as much the second."

He presented her with the diamond in the palm of his outstretched hand. Her mouth dropped open wide, and she screamed with joy. The employees cheered as everyone celebrated what could only be described as divine intervention.

"Looks like God is watching out for us," Christine said to Kyle hugging him fiercely.

"He always does," Kyle answered in return.

CHAPTER 44

For years, Kyle and Christine had lived off the grid of sorts. Their home telephone number was unlisted, and they never sent out the traditional Christmas card with a photo of how the family had changed throughout the year. No one knew for certain where Dwight was living. But in the back of his mind, Kyle was ever vigilant to keep a look out for any signs of trouble. Dwight was erratic and threatening.

Life was better than ever. And although there were occasional bumps in the night, anything that once seemed threatening now belonged to the past.

In retrospect, they should have probably considered the ongoing risk more thoroughly, but didn't give much thought to the level of public exposure Kyle received through the news journal, his statewide radio program, and his appearances on the evening news presenting regular perspectives on public policy.

Kyle's heart sank when he received his first disturbing letter at the office. It was from Dwight.

The tone in the letter was accusatory and belittling. While not exactly a vendetta, it placed blame on everyone except

Dwight. There was obvious hate for Anna, and Dwight accused Kyle of being part of the family's problems.

"Your mother ruined my life. I worked my ass off for her and what do I get? I'm left with nothing," came the lines from Dwight's letter.

"Someday, she will live to regret messing with me. You have taken her side, and you too will pay the price."

It was clear to Kyle that Dwight continued to suffer with mental health issues and alcohol abuse. He likely wrote that letter (as well as many others that would follow) while in a drunken state of mind.

But how did he know where Kyle was? How did he gain the information he needed to make contact? Was Dwight still in California? Surely he was out of range of the broadcast signal and the publication was only sent to subscribers. Was someone tipping Dwight off?

Kyle felt like he had forgiven his dad for the pain he had caused in his childhood. But he had struggled at times with what it meant to honor your parents. For him, he felt like he could honor his parents by restoring honor to the family name. But honoring his father didn't have to mean allowing him a place back in his life.

Kyle's thoughts immediately went to protecting his family. They were his priority. Old familiar defense mechanisms began to resurface as the idea of sleeping with a firearm reentered his mind.

Hearing from Dwight gave reason for concern. He informed Christine of the news. They agreed to be more vigilant about their privacy. The kids would play in the backyard, and they would, unfortunately, have to keep an eye out for Dwight. He was simply too unpredictable and dangerous.

Living in fear was not going to be an option. Kyle refused to be held prisoner by the past. He resolved to continue on with life as usual. His job provided the opportunity for him to travel to other countries, and although it was hard to leave Christine and all the kids, especially with what might be lingering in the shadows, he couldn't let Dwight hold him hostage to fear.

Christine shared his perspective and assured him they must carry on. "We have to live our lives, Kyle. We have to have faith and trust that our guardian angels are with us. You go. We will be just fine," Christine said with assurance and confidence.

Kyle struggled with the idea of leaving his family behind and alone. He reluctantly taught Christine how to use the pistol. They bought a guard dog, and Kyle asked his closest friends to take turns stopping by the house to check on how things were going with Christine and the children while he was away.

CHAPTER 45

Of all the places he had traveled, Africa held a special place in Kyle's heart. Africa was much more primitive than he had ever imagined. But the people were endearing and kind. The main cities provided a certain level of modern accommodation, but for the most part, it was like going back in time. Despite the lack of creature comforts, Kyle was amazed at the happiness that filled their lives.

On one particular assignment to Africa, Kyle visited a small island in the center of Lake Malawi. He stayed in a remote village that was absent of electricity and running water. His first night in the village, Kyle nestled into a small cinder block room with bars on the open windows.

A mosquito net hung from the ceiling and was draped across his bed. His flashlight served as his only source of light. He had been warned only to drink bottled water and that included the water used to brush his teeth.

As he lay in bed, he heard the creatures of the night loudly making their presence known. Monkeys, exotic birds, and other strange nocturnal sounds were just outside his window. He had spent his fair share of time sleeping by the light of the moon, but these sounds were different from anything he had ever heard before. He struggled to sleep, but eventually found rest due to sheer exhaustion from his hours of travel.

The next morning, he was surprised to learn his room came equipped with a gravity-fed shower. He hadn't noticed the setup the night before. It produced nothing but cold water, but it did the job well enough when a bar of soap was lathered to life.

He ate breakfast in an outdoor gazebo and the food was fit for a king. There may have been a shortage of electricity and running water, but the beans, rice, maze, and cabbages were plentiful. He later learned that eggs and other sources of protein were hard to come by. The eggs he received at breakfast had been reserved for special guests. He understood the privilege and felt a bit of guilt as he ate while others looked on, ready to attend to his needs.

Each morning at breakfast, Kyle noticed how local families walked past the gazebo on the shores of the beach. They were always accompanied by goats, cows, and various beasts of burden. He couldn't believe his eyes as bathing in the shallow water was a common practice. This wasn't as alarming as the fact that the bathing took place in the same waters where cows and other animals walked and relieved themselves regularly.

"Do they not realize they are bathing in the same water where the animals have crapped and taken a leak?" Kyle asked his tour guide.

"Yes, they do, but they know where and how to stand in order to make it work," the guide explained. "They take great pride in being clean. Trust me, they are fully aware of what they are doing."

"I just can't imagine bathing in that kind of water. You couldn't pay me to jump into that mess," Kyle said as his guide gave no reply except for a huge smile.

Kyle spent the week gathering photos and stories for his report. His only regret was that Christine wasn't there to enjoy it with him. They both loved to explore new places and discover new cultures together. She would have loved being with him.

On the final day of his journey, Kyle enjoyed another wonderful breakfast on the beach. And like every day before, the happy families paraded to and from the beach with their children and animals all doing their own thing.

As Kyle took one final sip of coffee, he noticed two local men digging in the sand at the water's edge. Eventually, the end of a PVC pipe appeared, and the men attached a portable motorized water pump to the end of the PVC pipe.

They tossed the suction line out into the water near the area where the cows were known to stand and relieve themselves.

The men fired up the pump's engine and started running toward the guests' rooms. They scurried up a bamboo ladder and stood beside the water tank just above Kyle's room.

In a matter of minutes, water was flowing into the tank as the men watched to determine when the fill line had been reached.

Kyle looked over at his guide who produced the same familiar grin from a few days before.

"You are kidding me, right?" Kyle said with disbelief. "The water source for my shower has been that lake water?"

The guide remained silent, nodding in agreement while holding his wide smile, his pearly white teeth gleaming against his deep, dark lips.

"Oh well, I am proof that the system works!" Kyle said as he and the guide busted out into laughter. "At least I figured out how to get warm water. The heat of the day warmed the tank by late afternoon. Evening showers were warm and a lot more enjoyable than those in the morning. Nobody likes a cold shower. I'm just glad I didn't sing in the shower with my mouth wide open!"

The men said their goodbyes as Kyle boarded the boat back to the mainland. But Kyle's surprises were far from over. The small little tugboat wasn't fast, but it was steady and comfortable. The captain and his team took good care of their passengers and related cargo.

About a mile offshore, the engine to the tugboat began to present signs of struggle. The captain killed the engine and went down below to assess the situation. The sounds of clanging and banging were the first signs that trouble lurked beneath their life above-board on the boat's deck.

The captain eventually emerged from the boat's belly with grease on his face and the engine's water pump in his hand.

"My friends," the captain started, "our boat is adrift, and we are currently at the mercy of the wind and the undercurrents."

The captain gave his first mate instructions and in a flash, the sailor dove headfirst into the clear blue water.

To Kyle, it seemed unthinkable, but then again, this was Africa. The sailor was swimming to shore for help!

In about an hour, the first mate could be seen on the horizon paddling a hollowed-out log that served as his canoe. He soon came up alongside the boat and presented the captain with a small silver tube. It was unclear what was happening, but what unfolded was simply ingenious.

Kyle learned that the sailor had swum to a small little bamboo kiosk that served as the island's general store. The island may have been remote, but its inhabitants had learned to take advantage of certain necessities from the outside world. Nothing proved to be more valuable on the island than Super Glue!

Africans may have been frozen in time, but they were anything but ignorant. They could fix anything because they had to in order to survive. Kyle knew that instinct well.

He watched with amazement as the captain tore small pieces of fabric from his shirt and applied layer after layer of glue and fabric over the crack on the inside of the engine's water pump.

"There is no way this is going to work," Kyle expressed to a fellow traveler. The captain overheard the comment, winked at Kyle, and made his way back below deck to test his theory.

To everyone's amazement, (everyone but the captain), the engine fired up, the pump repair held, and the little tugboat that could, brought everyone safely into harbor.

Nothing thrilled Kyle more than sharing stories from his travels with Christine and the kids. As he made friends worldwide, many visited and stayed with the family for weeks, exposing the children to new cultures, languages, and perspectives. Over time, each child joined him on adventures, planting seeds of curiosity that would later inspire their own explorations. Kyle believed great memories were far more valuable than material things, always choosing experiences over gadgets. He wanted to be the old man in a nursing home sharing incredible life stories, not an old man boasting about unspent money in a dusty bank account. Striking that balance wasn't easy, but to him, a life without risk wasn't a life at all.

Little did he know, risk was about to take on an entirely new meaning.

CHAPTER 46

"Did you see that?" Kyle asked Christine as he sat up in bed. It was the middle of the night and Christine was in deep sleep. Kyle, on the other hand, was now wide awake.

"What, baby? Go back to sleep. It's early," Christine said as she struggled to open her eyes. She touched Kyle's arm and tucked her head under her pillow.

Kyle knew what he saw, and it defied belief. He needed confirmation that the figure at the foot of his bed was not just a dream or vision but a vivid revelation of another dimension. He wasn't one to chase signs or dwell on the supernatural, yet this was anything but ordinary.

Awakened from a deep sleep, he found himself staring at a massive, majestic angel. Despite its towering presence and undeniable power, Kyle felt an overwhelming sense of peace and comfort. He wasn't an expert in such matters, but this had to be what some called an archangel—strong, mighty, yet strangely empathetic.

Whether real, a dream, or a hallucination, the experience was unforgettable. As the angel ascended toward the cathedral ceiling, Kyle's gaze locked onto its massive white wings, gently folded around a figure. Just before disappearing, the face of an elderly man emerged—Dwight, in what appeared to be the final moments of his life.

Kyle had an overwhelming feeling that his dad had died, and this was some sort of spiritual message that the end had come for Dwight and that Kyle could now live in peace knowing that his dad had come to rest. His lifelong nemesis would finally find defeat.

"I'm sorry, babe. I hate to wake you. But I think my dad may have died," Kyle said as he re-engaged with his sleepy wife.

Christine could sense the concern in Kyle's voice and turned on a lamp by their nightstand.

"I'm serious. Did you really not see anything in the last five minutes?" Kyle inquired with greater intensity. "I think I just saw an archangel, and he was taking my dad to his final resting place."

"Honey, I love you, but I think you had a nightmare," Christine said as she tried her best to comfort her obviously distressed husband. "Go back to sleep. We can discuss this in the morning."

Perhaps she was right. Maybe it was just a reaction to the subconscious stress that had been lingering in his mind since he had started getting those unsolicited letters from Dwight.

Kyle wondered if he would ever be free of the torment that Dwight had constantly brought into his life. Yet, as much as he hated to admit it, the thought of Dwight dying brought great relief.

Kyle rolled over on his side and did his best to put the strange experience out of his head.

Christine rubbed his back until she was certain he had finally managed to fall back to sleep. She hurt for him in ways no one else would ever understand. Her heart ached knowing how deeply Kyle's father's wounds had scarred him emotionally. Somehow, he had managed to deal with the hurts from his past and build the incredible life they lived together. And, she recognized that the source of his strength was rooted in his unwavering faith.

Kyle was up early the next morning and managed to slip out of the house without Christine or any of the kids knowing he had departed.

What was that all about? he thought to himself as he navigated the challenges of rush hour traffic. Whatever it was, he wasn't shaking its impact anytime soon. The experience was as real to him as anything he had ever encountered.

The new day at the office started off with the usual routine. The superficial morning greetings soon subsided as everyone went about the business of the day. Other than a fresh pot of coffee, everything remained pretty much the same.

Kyle settled in and went to work on an assignment. His email inbox dinged notifying him that he had a new incoming message. When he opened the email, his stomach dropped, and he began to see the words on the screen as though he were looking through a tunnel.

"Dear Kyle, I know it has been many years since we last spoke, but I wanted to reach out to you and make you aware of some news with regard to your dad," read the message from one of Kyle's dear female cousins, Jean.

Despite the unfortunate family circumstances that had put distance between them, Kyle trusted her. Jean had always been kind and supportive. They had shared many wonderful experiences together with their grandparents and cousins. They had made many cherished memories in their early years.

Kyle looked away before he continued reading. His jaw tightened. He could hardly swallow as tears began to pool in the corners of his eyes. He knew immediately that the angel had been preparing him for this moment. What news would be revealed? It had been 35 years since Kyle had stood in that living room prepared to end his father's life. Was today finally the day that outcome would become a reality?

"I regret to inform you…."

Kyle wasn't sure he was prepared to read what was next. He reread the last line in the email.

"I regret to inform you that your daddy is dying. He has COPD, cancer, and other serious cardiovascular issues. Hospice has been called in, and they are not sure if he will make it until the weekend. His dying wish is to see you." I simply wanted you to know. Feel no pressure from me or the rest of the family. We understand what you've been through. Please know this, I love you. We love you. You have been deeply missed. Regardless of your decision or what coming days may bring, you are always welcomed, and we would love to see you."

Kyle sat at his desk overwhelmed with emotion. The last 12 hours had presented intense revelations that had put his mind and emotions on overload.

He immediately picked up the telephone and called Christine.

"Are you sitting down?" he asked before filling her in on what had just happened.

Christine listened in complete silence as Kyle unpacked every detail.

"What are you going to do?" she asked.

"What do you mean? I owe him nothing. He can rot in hell so far as I am concerned," Kyle said as anger thickened in his voice. "He has made his bed. Now he can sleep in it. If he thinks he is going to waltz back into my life on his deathbed, he is going to be gravely disappointed."

Christine chose her next words carefully, "Rot in hell? But I thought you had forgiven him? And, well, what about the angel?"

The conversation went silent for the next 30 seconds until Kyle started to weep. The pain, hurt, and fear he had been carrying since he was a little boy was coming to the surface. So much regret. So much that could have been but wasn't. Kyle pushed honest and grieving words through the silence, "I have forgiven him. This is just so hard. I'm not sure I can do this."

"I love you, baby. You are so strong. You have been through so much. How can we deny what has happened since last night? It's not an accident or a coincidence. There has to be a reason. There has to be a purpose," she said with a tender and caring voice. "Why don't you call Todd. I'm certain he will go with you if you decide it is best."

Kyle whispered his thanks, overcome with how much she meant to him. He gently hung up the telephone. He loved having Christine in his life. She had served as his confidant and counselor so many times before. He knew in his heart that she was right.

Something very unusual was taking place. He had more questions than answers, but if he was to find closure, it would require a huge leap of faith. Faith had gotten them this far. There was no reason to give up now.

Kyle hadn't realized it, but Dwight had returned to Oklahoma about the same time Kyle had returned from Washington D.C. Amazingly, they had lived within 35 miles of each other, and Kyle never knew it. If everything continued as it appeared it would, it would be a 35-mile journey that had taken 35 years to complete.

CHAPTER 47

Todd was a lifelong loyal and trusted friend. He agreed to drive Kyle to the reunion with his dad.

"I can't promise what will happen," Kyle said grimly as the SUV neared the small duplex where Dwight lived. "This could be an ambush—he might see it as his final hoorah. And, I'm not sure how I might react. If I start to pound his face, please step in and keep me from going to jail."

As they stepped toward the screen door that covered the entrance to the house, Kyle was overwhelmed with emotion. He was sweating as his heart rate rapidly increased. He was on the verge of a panic attack, but he knew he had to push through. He had to face his fear. He had to face the giant that had been terrorizing him for so many years.

Now was the day of reckoning.

Tension permeated throughout Kyle's body. He felt like an innocent man on death row taking his final steps down a cold, dark hallway to die by lethal injection. His clammy hand reached out and tapped on the door of his would-be executioner. The world closed in all around him. A raspy voice answered the knock, slithering from the shadowy room beyond the darkened glass and sending chills down Kyle's spine. It had been years since he'd heard that haunting, unmistakable voice. The sound of Dwight's voice struck Kyle like a dagger, driving fear deep into his heart and burrowing into his soul.

"Hello? Come in," Dwight called out, straining to force the air from his lungs in a desperate attempt to be heard. Kyle took a deep breath, looked at Todd, grabbed hold of the door handle, and with every ounce of courage he could muster, he stepped inside. He was overwhelmed by the stench of stagnant urine mixed with a month's worth of chewing tobacco spit that had gone unattended. He nearly gagged as he made his way into the steamy, musty, overheated apartment. The air was heavy with the stench and chill of death. Part of him expected to hear gunfire or at best, cussing and verbal attacks. Kyle never envisioned what would happen next.

As Kyle entered the room, he observed the back of an old man's bald head and without warning, Dwight spun around in the swivel recliner and leapt from his seat.

Kyle stepped back in alarm as Dwight fell to the ground and grabbed Kyle behind the knees.

Holding onto Kyle's legs, Dwight began to wail and weep profusely. As he held tight, he repeated over and over again, "I'm sorry. I'm sorry. I'm so, so, sorry. I can't believe you have come. I am so, so sorry. Please, please, please, forgive me for all that I have done."

Kyle fell to his knees meeting his abuser face-to-face. For the first time in his life, he felt a deep but awkward connection with his dad.

Together they cried and embraced. They held each other tight as their bodies shook from the shock of the reunion. Two broken hearts reunited. Both the breaker and the broken were receiving mercy and grace.

Dwight was skin and bones. His body was frail and weak. He had grown a scraggly beard, and the sides of his head were covered in white curly hair as a nasal cannula, attached to an oxygen tank, protruded from his nose. He was dying and might only have days, if not hours, to live. He was a mere shadow of the lean and muscular young man that had once caught Anna's eye so long ago.

Kyle sat in front of him, knee-to-knee, holding Dwight's hands in utter amazement that this moment was taking place.

"Man, is this what I am going to look like when I get old?" Kyle said with a hesitant laugh as he attempted to help break the intensity of the interaction.

As much as they tried, all they could do was cry. It was the only emotion that matched their shattered hearts.

There were sad tears, as they thought about all the time that had been lost, and there were happy tears as they considered the power of the moment.

In preparing for the meeting, Kyle had wondered what they might talk about. Going down memory lane would be a train wreck. He didn't have one single good memory about Dwight. Not one.

When Kyle was 12, Dwight gave him a nice pocket watch as a sort of rite of passage. For some reason, Kyle had held onto the watch for all those years. He wasn't sure if it was because it reminded him of the one his Grandpa Liam carried or because it represented a hope that someday, somewhere in time, things might be better with his dad. Kyle decided to bring the pocket watch with him and see if Dwight recalled the gift.

Pulling the watch from his pocket, he placed the pocket watch in Dwight's hand.

"Do you recognize this?" Kyle asked.

"I sure do!" Dwight said with enthusiasm as he pushed the words out, gasping for breath. "I gave this to you on your twelfth birthday."

Kyle looked down at the watch being held in the withering hands of a dying man. The face of the watch was visible, and the watch hands had stopped at two o'clock.

Then a thought hit him, and he shared his thought with Dwight. "Look at the watch. It stopped at two o'clock. I think it might be a sign that you and I are getting a second chance."

Kyle wiped away tears and continued. "Would you do me a favor and wind and reset the watch to the current time?"

Dwight took the watch from Kyle's hand and did as he asked.

"Let's make a deal," Kyle said. "Let's forget about the past and start focusing on the future. I don't know how much time you have left. You might have three hours, three days, three months, or three years. Whatever time we have, let's make the memories great."

"Deal!" Dwight said, locking eyes with Kyle, his gaze filled with deep admiration and love. He felt the weight of forgiveness for all he had done—and the undeniable warmth of love being returned.

"What does a guy like you do all day? I can't imagine how frustrating it must be sitting here just wondering if each breath is going to be your last," Kyle said with sincere boldness. "I mean, let's be honest, it's not like you have family and friends lined up out the door waiting to see you."

Dwight accepted the frank conversation. He, too, was a straight shooter, and he appreciated this trait in Kyle. He couldn't help but see a bit of his own influence rubbing off on his son.

"Well, let me start with this. It might surprise you, but I spend a lot of time reading my old King James Bible," Dwight shared with a gentle and honest heart. "You see, I had one too many bar fights and a couple of guys took to pounding my face into the dirt. One of them stomped on my neck and fractured my spine."

Kyle sat quietly as Dwight continued.

"They left me for dead. Somehow I managed to find a way to get in my car and try to make it to the hospital. I never made it there on my own. I passed out and drove the car into a ditch. I found myself coming in and out of consciousness until I woke up with paramedics putting me on a stretcher."

Dwight paused and took a big breath, his breathing shallow and labored.

"Sitting there, trapped behind the steering wheel, my life passed before me, and I realized I had been such a terrible person to so many people. Especially to you, Timmy, and your mother."

He paused again, this time locking eyes with Kyle, searching for any trace of unspoken thoughts on his face.

"It was then and there, in that ditch, that I decided that if I ever came out alive, I would do things differently. I turned my life over to God and found Jesus at the bottom."

Kyle couldn't believe what he was hearing. Dwight had come to faith? Was this a different man than the one that had sent those disturbing letters? Was Dwight truly softer, kinder, empathetic, and not nearly so narcissistic? Had he truly changed? It was too soon to know for sure, but Kyle continued to listen intently with guarded emotion.

"So, that's what I do. That and watch game shows on television," Dwight went on to say. "Oh yeah, I also read the dictionary and keep a little journal based on what comes to mind as I reflect on the words I read.

Kyle thought to himself, *"So this is where a life of selfishness leads you. Sitting in a worn-out old recliner, reading your Bible, watching games shows, and reading the dictionary. How pitiful. Truly sad in every way. Such a loss of potential."*

"Do you have that dictionary handy? Do you mind if I take a look?" Kyle asked with curiosity.

"No problem. It's right here," Dwight said as he reached for the dictionary and handed it over to Kyle.

Based on how tattered the cover was, it was clear that the dictionary had been put to use.

Kyle flipped through the well-worn pages until the dictionary seemed to pause on a certain page. Kyle looked down and saw a word circled on the page. What were the odds that he would stop flipping through the dictionary on this particular page only to find this word circled among all the others.

Reconcile.

Of the thousands and thousands of words that were in the dictionary, what were the odds that he would randomly turn to this page and find this word circled on the page? It was the only word circled in the entire dictionary.

Kyle had come to forgive his dad, many years ago, but this day was about much more than forgiveness, this day was about reconciliation.

The definition on the page read: *Reconcile, to restore to harmony after an argument or disagreement.*

Not everyone would have this privilege. Not everyone could safely reconcile with a perpetrator. Time and space may not make it possible or perhaps the person had long since died.

Everyone might not be in a position to reconcile, but everyone could forgive. Failing to forgive gave the wrongdoer ongoing control. Forgiveness released the victim from the chains of the past.

Kyle recognized the blessing of finding forgiveness *and* reconciliation.

The words Dwight wrote on subsequent pages said it best.

"The best things parents can pass onto their children is showing love to others, plus caring, sharing and forgiving. I don't gauge myself on the activities I can do, but on my faith and love."

If Kyle hadn't read it for himself and seen it in Dwight's own handwriting, he would not have believed these words were Dwight's. Dwight had lived an awful life, but if ever there was proof that following Jesus could change the heart of a sinner, Dwight's turnaround was all the evidence that anyone should ever need.

Kyle spent most of the afternoon getting to know his dad. There were still signs of the old Dwight. But it was clear he was becoming a new man. As Kyle stepped out onto the porch of the duplex, the sun was setting on the horizon.

The symbolism wasn't hard to see. Another day was ending. The page had been turned. A new chapter and a new beginning would soon be rising. If only there was more time.

In coming days, Kyle called his immediate family together to meet with Dwight.

"Dad, are you serious? You want us to come and meet with you and your dad? Is it safe?" Lori-Ellen questioned with sincere concern. "What has changed?"

"I know it sounds crazy, but a lot has happened in the last few days. I have a lot to catch you up on," Kyle shared with assurance. "You are not going to want to miss this."

Similar conversations were had with each of the kids. Christine was onboard with the plan once she paid a personal visit to meet Dwight. She wasn't ready to accept the idea of introducing her children to the man they had been hiding from for so many years until she had the absolute confidence that he wasn't a serious threat.

On the day the family was to meet Dwight, Christine prepared a celebration feast fit for a king. The house was filled with the smell of comfort foods. Fried chicken, mashed potatoes, and corn on the cob, which made everyone's stomachs growl. She couldn't help but reflect on the stories Kyle had told her about how Dwight had pushed Anna's homemade meals onto the floor on more than one occasion. Something told her Dwight would be on his best behavior today.

The family waited anxiously for Kyle and Dwight to arrive.

"What do you think he will look like?" Ben asked the group.

"Do you think he will be mean to us?" Raelyn inquired.

"Guys, trust me. Dwight is harmless. He is weak, feeble, and near death. I can promise you it is taking everything he can muster to be here today. Do your best to make him feel welcomed," Christine said as she pulled a chocolate cake from the oven. She knew Dwight loved chocolate, and she wanted him to feel right at home.

"They are here!" Rosemary announced as she ran from the front window to the kitchen.

Everyone tried to relax and act normal as they saw Kyle opening the front door. It took considerable effort, but Kyle managed to carry Dwight through the entry way as everyone gathered in the front room to celebrate the prodigal father's homecoming.

Each child introduced themselves and either gave Dwight a hug or shook his hand. He was an emotional mess. Seeing his grandchildren for the first time was simply more than his frail body could handle. It was more than he could have ever hoped for. Dwight became so overwhelmed with the love and attention that soon after he left the gathering, he had to be rushed to the hospital emergency room for breathing treatments.

The family introductions didn't stop with Dwight. One of the greatest joys came at Thanksgiving when Kyle, along with his entire family, was reunited with everyone from Dwight's side of the family, as they celebrated the holiday and gave thanks for the reunion of all reunions. Kyle's children were soon interacting with their great aunts and uncles as rooms full of cousins and other extended family gathered to introduce themselves.

They were discovering parts of their heritage that they had often wondered about and were thrilled to be living out. The house was filled with love, acceptance, and inspiration as energy and excitement filled the air. No one could quite believe what was happening before their very eyes. The family was together again!

The only thing that could have made the reunion better was for Kyle to have been able to share the moment with his grandma and grandpa Sanderson. They had long since passed away, but they were anything but forgotten.

Kyle also wished Timmy had made it. He wished Dwight could see that Timmy had survived their childhood and was an incredible man, a successful businessman with a wonderful wife and two kids. But Timmy's journey with his dad was his own, and Kyle understood more than most just how difficult forgiveness and reconciliation could be.

* * *

Dwight's health made a turn for the better. Having family and loved ones in his life invigorated him and gave him a reason to look forward to another day of life.

Kyle began caring for Dwight's daily needs, buying him groceries, cleaning his house, and taking Dwight on car rides in the country. Caring for Dwight also meant frequent visits to the doctor. On one such visit, the doctor presented some troubling news.

"Dwight, you have lost too much circulation in your left leg. If we don't reroute your arteries, we will have to amputate," the doctor shared with all seriousness. "In your condition, I'm not so sure you would live through either surgery."

"Well, I'd rather die than be a cripple," Dwight replied. "Are there any other options?"

"Not really. You can wait until we have to amputate, or we can go with the bypass surgery."

Dwight looked at Kyle and said, "Don't get old, Kyle. It sucks." Dwight then turned to the doctor and said, "Let's go for broke! I'm not about to start hopping around like a one-legged sailor. Surgery it is!"

They arrived at the hospital at five o'clock in the morning. Dwight was wide awake, and Kyle was a bit foggy-headed. It hadn't slipped Kyle's mind that this might be the last few hours he would be spending with the man who had played such a vital role for who he had become.

It wasn't that Dwight had served as a great example, for what it meant to be an awesome husband or parent, in fact, he had served as an example for what not to be.

Nonetheless, even bad examples could serve a purpose if something could be learned from their lives.

It was almost as if Kyle had met a different man. The last two years had gone by so fast. Here was a man that not too long ago wasn't expected to live a couple of days let alone two full years. What might life have been like if the Dwight, Kyle knew now, was the Dwight of old? Where might life have taken him?

While everyone is born with a unique set of DNA and a defined personality, much of whom they are is shaped by the life experiences they have along the way. Who they ultimately become is a mix of nature and nurture that is heavily influenced by choice.

Everyone had someone they could blame for the state in which they found themselves, but all things considered, there wasn't much that couldn't be overcome by making the right choices and adopting the right attitude.

That being said, Kyle realized that no one was truly a self-made man. Everyone had someone to thank for helping them become who they were. He knew it was true in his life.

Kyle was grateful for the many people who had impacted his life. The least of which was not his Grandpa Liam. Liam had stood beside him, took up for him and defended him when he was a little boy and most vulnerable.

How could he have ever survived without his loving childhood neighbors, Mr. and Mrs. Brown? The safe haven they provided in the middle of the night, as his father's violent outbursts ravaged their lives , could never be overlooked.

There was Coach Wilson, the father figure who encouraged him after one of the most embarrassing times of his life following an infamous basketball game. All the dads of the guys in his huddle group showed Kyle what it meant to lead as a family man. They demonstrated what it meant to challenge and discipline their children all while providing support, care, and concern.

He would not be who he was if not for the investment his spiritual mentor, Pastor Catt, had made in his life. Pastor Catt made the teachings and principles of Jesus come to life. He learned that faith wasn't a crutch but the secret to being all who you were meant to be. The greatest revelation was that a relationship with the Creator was possible, and he was the father to the fatherless. He could be trusted, was relevant, practical, and real.

Then there was Ollie and Nita. Kyle and Christine had learned so many things about marriage, child-rearing, and loving life from them. When it came to their approach to life, it was caught not taught. It was made to stick.

Certainly, his own children had taught him how to love, extend mercy, and grant a whole lot of grace. More than once he had needed to ask for their forgiveness. He had fallen short on several occasions, but they always forgave him and made sure he knew they were proud to call him dad.

His mother Anna had taught what it meant to be a survivor, to work hard, to believe in yourself, and most of all to love unconditionally. No one had impacted him more than Christine, his girlfriend, bride, and the love of his life. Who would he be without her? She loved him wholeheartedly, believed in him when doubters were wrong, stood by him when he felt all alone, and modeled patience for him in ways that no one would ever believe. As he had said many times before, he simply couldn't imagine life without her.

It was true, nobody lived a perfect life. Everyone had their fair share of stink. And while some may end up smelling better than others, everyone had the opportunity to make a difference in the life of another. How much of who Kyle had become was influenced by Dwight? That was a great question. As much as Kyle hated to admit it, who he was had been greatly influenced by who Dwight was not.

"I can't believe it has come to this, but I'm sure glad I was able to be here with you," Kyle said as he helped Dwight into a wheelchair. "I bet you come out on the other side of this wanting to go two-stepping."

"You might be right. Even if this is the end of the ride, the last stop has made it all worth it," Dwight said as he patted the top of Kyle's hand as Kyle guided the wheelchair into the surgery center.

The nurses had Dwight prepped and ready in no time. Dwight was flirting with each and every one as usual.

Kyle laughed inside. *Some things never change. Even looking death straight in the face, Dwight is a player to the very end.*

This wasn't a time to be smiling, but seeing the old bag of bones being a bit ornery helped lighten the mood as the surgeon came in to whisk Dwight away.

"I love you, dad," Kyle said, fighting back tears as he did his best to stay strong in front of the man who had taught him how to never back down from a fight.

"You stay strong in there. Don't back down. As soon as you get better, you and I are going to grab a slaw dog with chili."

"I love you, Bud. Thanks for being here with your old man," Dwight said as he reached out with one arm to give Kyle a hug. "It means more to me than you will ever know."

Kyle shared a brief prayer with Dwight and then watched as they wheeled him away.

Dwight signaled with a thumbs up, followed by a wave as they pushed the gurney feet first into the operating room.

Kyle kept his eye on the clock. The doctor expected the surgery to last three hours. At the four-hour mark, Kyle assumed things must be going fairly well or they would have already come out and shared the bad news.

After nearly five hours, the surgeon finally appeared. Based on the look on his face, the news wasn't going to be good.

"Well, he made it. He is a tough old coot. It took me longer than expected, and that's why I am a bit frustrated," the doctor said as he removed his surgeon's cap. "I expect him to make a full recovery."

Kyle waited in the private hospital room for Dwight to arrive. They spent the next few days complaining about hospital food and trying to outsmart the TV guests on Dwight's favorite game shows.

In just under a week, Kyle was once again escorting Dwight through the hospital. This time there was no need for a wheelchair. Dwight was stepping out on his own with a walker, albeit extremely slow. As they approached the automated doors to the parking lot, Dwight stopped right in the middle of the electronic doors causing them to slide back and forth repeatedly. Dwight gave the clanging doors no regard.

Kyle was rapidly growing uncomfortable as Dwight simply was oblivious to the traffic jam he was causing.

About the time Kyle was going to insist that Dwight move along, Dwight turned his head toward Kyle and delivered comments that Kyle would never forget.

"You know, they think I should be dead by now. But you and I know God has given me more time with you," Dwight said as he stepped forward unblocking the right of way.

Those words would linger in Kyle's mind for years to come. More time. More time with you.

For most of his life, time with Dwight was the last thing Kyle had ever desired, but it had become the desire of his heart in recent days. My, how things had changed.

CHAPTER 48

In coming months, Kyle continued to stop by and check on Dwight at the nursing home. It had been three full years, and they had beat the odds in more ways than one. It was becoming clear that Dwight's health was declining. Rides in the country were no longer possible. Dwight was confined to assisted living. Despite the limitations, Kyle did make good on the chili slaw dog. At the time, he didn't realize it would be the last meal he would ever share with his dad. Except for the chocolate-covered peanuts that he brought Dwight as a special treat.

On one of his regular visits, Kyle picked his feeble daddy up from his recliner, changed his clothes, and placed him in his bed much like a mother would a baby in a crib.

"I'll see you in a few days Dad. I am heading back to Washington D.C. for the National Prayer Breakfast. The President will be speaking, and I don't want to miss it," Kyle said as he stood at the doorway. "I love you. Be good, and if you can't be good, be better!"

"Thanks for coming. Come again. I know you will," Dwight said as he closed his eyes, and Kyle turned out the lights.

It would be the last time Kyle would ever see his daddy alive.

The regrettable text message came while Kyle and Christine were at a dinner in Washington D.C.

Dwight had taken a turn for the worse. It appeared he had a stroke and was struggling to communicate. He was likely in his final hours.

Kyle contacted his kids and his good friend, Todd, and asked them to sit with Dwight. Kyle didn't want his dad to die alone.

They made it just in time. Kyle asked Todd to read Dwight's favorite scripture passage from the Bible, Psalm 23.

Ike gently played some of Dwight's favorite tunes on the guitar as the rest of the children gathered around their grandfather's bedside.

It wasn't likely that Kyle's airplane would arrive in time to say his goodbyes, so he placed a call to Lori-Ellen and asked her to put Dwight on speakerphone.

"I love you Dad. I wish I could be there with you. It's okay. You don't have to wait on me. I'm so glad we have had the last few years together. I love you," Kyle said as the tears erupted and his heart broke.

The stroke had left Dwight with the inability to speak. But being the fighter he was, he pushed as hard as he could for his voice to be heard. No one could be certain, but everyone agreed, Dwight moaned and cried out to Kyle, "I love you."

In a matter of minutes, Dwight was gone. Kyle was disappointed and sad that he hadn't been able to be at his dad's side. Nonetheless, he was confident that Dwight knew he was loved. What better way to confirm that love than to know that your son had sent his children and his close friend to be with you as you made the transition to the other side.

CHAPTER 49

The mood was somber yet filled with anticipation as Kyle and his family drove over the long viaduct that connected El Reno to the rest of the world.

Oddly enough, not only was this the town where Kyle had come into the world, it was the town where Dwight had died. It seemed fitting. Yes, there had been plenty of heartache, trouble, and pain. Those words sounded like lyrics from one of the country and western songs Dwight often sang with his acoustic guitar when he was at either end of his bipolar personality.

The chapel of the funeral home served as the setting for Dwight's memorial service. Kyle wasn't too sure if Dwight had ever stepped into a church. Even his parents wedding ceremony had been held in the house of a friend. Nonetheless, Kyle knew in his heart that it wasn't church membership that changed a man and secured his eternal destiny. It was about coming to know Jesus in a personal way, recognizing who Jesus was, admitting he needed what Jesus had to offer, and yielding his way to the Lord's way. Dwight wasn't perfect, but in the end, he had gotten that right, if nothing else.

As Kyle stood to lead the service, he looked into the crowd to see friends and family. The support was comforting as he began to speak truth about the man who had been his birth father, the man he had feared for most of his life, the man who ultimately found faith and was granted mercy, grace, forgiveness, and love for a life ill-lived.

Kyle pulled a poem from his suit jacket. He had written it on the airplane ride back from Washington D.C. on the day that Dwight had died. The room fell silent as the paper crinkled when Kyle unfolded it, then cleared his throat, and stepped to the microphone.

Never Goodbye

He was born in the country where the prairie grass grows.
Where tall cotton is picked and winter wheat blows.
There were five of the kids, and he was the runt.
He was full of energy and known for his stunts.
Try as they might, to wrangle him in,
he was like a wild donkey, loose from the pen.
Liam and Naomie showed no favor or harm.
They put him to toil, plowing the farm.
He would work hard by day and chase coons by night.
He was born to wander and taken to flight.
Short in stature but full of spite,
he would bloody your nose if you got in a fight.
His dark curly locks and big olive eyes,
broke ladies' hearts and magnified their cries.
He was a charmer for sure,
a smooth talker no less.

The farmers' daughters liked him
but called him a mess.

He moved from the country to work on the dock,
raising a family until the troubles did knock.
Hard times they came and his world out of control,
the demons taunted him and fought for his soul.
There were years of darkness, not a glimmer of hope,
but he kept pushing onward never to mope.

His health started failing but his mind stayed intact,
as he battled for oxygen through a mobile air pack.

Then one January, much to his surprise,
a visitor came knocking, it was one of his guys!
It was quite a reunion, full of joy and tears.
The prodigal returned, after all of these years.

They agreed to look forward and not to look back,
to capture new memories and keep things on track.
Three winters they journeyed as they played and had fun,
the old man, his boy, the father, and son.

Life is shorter than we all care to count,
but when with those we love, it's the perfect amount.
God brings us together and then calls us home. This is certain,
sure as the Pope lives in Rome.

Life isn't easy and is chockfull of knocks,
but when we have Jesus, we're solid as rocks.
Dwight has left us, but it's never goodbye.
He is jamming with the angels, with his guitar on high.

If applause would have been appropriate, then a standing ovation would have followed. No one could believe how truth had been spoken yet honor given so graciously for the one who had passed. Everyone in the room knew all too well what life had been like for Kyle and the entire Sanderson family.

Too many funerals looked the other way and presented the deceased as someone hardly anyone recognized. Truth be known, there are few saints at funerals. If Dwight's life stood for anything, it stood for the power of reconciliation. No matter how bad life can get, it can always be put to use for good. Dwight was no saint, but Kyle knew his dad, like himself, had accepted a gift of forgiveness that forever secured his eternal fate.

CHAPTER 50

"I'm glad you were able to reconnect with your dad and share at his funeral," Anna said as she stood by Kyle casting a fishing line into Lake Arcadia, the grandkids splashing in the water by the bank. "I'm not saying I wanted to spend any time with him, or that I even cared to attend his funeral, but I am glad he found faith and made amends with so many that he had hurt."

"Let's be honest, mom. He was a mess, and we all knew it. We are lucky to be alive," Kyle said as he spoke about Dwight as a realist. "What was intended for evil ended up being used for a whole lot of good. Look around you. If it weren't for you making good choices, none of these kids would even exist."

Anna smiled at the thought of all that had come since that lonely day she stood her ground in the doctor's office and made the choice that had no doubt impacted the future.

"Mom, I have a question that has been bugging me for years. Why didn't Riff tell Dwight to take a hike when he found out you were pregnant?" Kyle asked with all sincerity.

"Well. Things were different back then. If a girl got pregnant out of wedlock, it was expected that she would get married to the baby's father," Anna explained.

"I get it, but Dwight was so much older than you. You were only 15 years old, and he was a grown man. He should have been held responsible. The truth is, the law calls what he did statutory rape," Kyle said without trying to make his mother feel uncomfortable.

"I need to share something with you that I didn't know until a few years ago. I hope it doesn't change your perspective about my dad or yours," Anna said as she stepped closer to Kyle and lowered her voice.

Anna went on to reveal that Riff had lived a secret life. He was not all that he had pretended to be. When Riff was a teenager he and a friend offered to take a young girl home from a dance. But, rather than take the girl home, they drove her to the countryside and raped her. Riff claimed he was innocent, and it was the other boy that had savagely raped the young girl.

Since Riff was underage, he ultimately got off with a lighter sentencing and only did a short time in prison. He managed to hide his past in part because the court clerk had misspelled his name on the court documents. Background checks failed to reveal his time in prison because of the error. Without the clerical mistake, it would have been very unlikely that Riff would have ever got the job with the bank.

When Anna turned up pregnant, Riff feared his past might come back to haunt him. Had he instead refused to allow Anna to marry Dwight, questions might start being asked and Riff's past might come to light. Riff didn't want to risk losing his job or his stature in the community, so he insisted that Anna and Dwight get married so as not to draw attention to himself.

Kyle couldn't believe what he was hearing. How might the future have been different if Riff had stepped into his role as a dad and put the best interest of his daughter above his own career aspirations?

"Wow! That is absolutely unthinkable. You have had to put up with some amazingly selfish men in your life," Kyle said as he expressed his disbelief. "I'm proud of you mom. You are truly a survivor."

"I'm proud of you, Kyle. Look how far you have come," Anna said as she kissed him on the cheek.

What a bombshell to end the day with, Kyle thought to himself as he started to bring the day to a close.

Kyle knew he had not been appointed as judge or jury, but he couldn't help but wonder what might have been if people close to him had made better choices.

What if Riff had done the right thing as a teenager? What if Dwight had proved to be an honorable man and not violated Anna? What if Riff had realized two wrongs don't make a right? What if Anna hadn't made the best choice? What if Dwight had put his family first? What if Anna had never opened her own hair salon?

There were so many "what ifs" that could have taken Kyle's life in any number of directions. He couldn't go back and change the bad decisions others made that impacted his life. What he could do was navigate the challenges he faced in life by seeking guidance from the Creator and wise counsel from others he had grown to trust. He hoped that by doing so his life choices never caused harm to anyone or caused anyone to doubt his love for them.

Not every day was like today, but today he was surrounded by multiple opportunities to love. Today he would choose to put the yellow house and the pain of the past behind him and take hold of the opportunity to make yet another lasting Sanderson family memory with those he loved.

"Load up everybody! It's time for us to head home and take our rollercoaster ride," Kyle said as he announced that the day's activities were coming to an end.

The kids were older now, but they could still hardly contain their excitement because they knew exactly what Kyle meant when he mentioned the rollercoaster ride.

There had been a long-standing tradition that at the end of the day at the lake, Kyle would take a special route home where a designated hump in the road proved to be very entertaining if the vehicle could hit a certain speed at the just-right time.

Kyle exited the gate, revved the engine, and stepped on the gas pedal throwing gravel from the back tires of the GMC Suburban. The kids screamed with excitement as they anticipated what lay ahead just down the road. Anna covered her head with her fishing hat pretending she was scared and unaware of what was about to happen next.

Christine and the kids screamed as Kyle hit the desired spot in the road at the perfect rate of speed.

The vehicle's suspension released, and all the passengers defied gravity as they were left floating in space for a brief moment inside the cab of the vehicle. They were literally flying down the roadway. The Suburban's shocks wailed as they took the brunt of the vehicle's prevailing landing back to earth.

Much to Kyle's surprise, a welcoming party had arrived just in time to greet the space travelers. Seeing the entire expedition in living color, a patrol car quickly illuminated a rooftop full of flashing lights. This would not be the kind of escort provided to dignitaries and heads of state.

"Well, this has never happened way out here. I wasn't expecting this today," Kyle said as he pulled the vehicle over to the road's shoulder as the kids giggled into the bends of their elbows.

"License and registration please," the tall law enforcement officer said insistently as he looked into the car peering over the top of his dark Ray-Ban sunglasses.

Kyle immediately cooperated and was embarrassed to have gotten the family in such a mess.

"Hmm. I think I might recognize the name on this license as someone who has a bit of a criminal past," the officer said with a serious tone.

Kyle had been embarrassed, but now he was nervous and definitely stressed.

"Seems I recall a time when you were stopped for illegally transporting a push mower from the back of a motorcycle. Am I right?" the officer said as he started to produce a grin. "You don't have any fresh produce or fryer rabbits in your cooler do you?"

"Officer Bullard? What in the world? Surely not?" Kyle said in absolute surprise as he recognized the officer who had stopped him as a teenager pulling a lawn mower from the back of his motorcycle. "What are you doing on patrol out this way?"

"I retired from the police force back home, and I am now semi-retired as the police chief here at the lake," the officer explained. "Is that your momma back there? Anna, how in the world are you?"

"I'd be doing better if this outlaw son of mine wasn't offering unauthorized rollercoaster rides," she said as Officer Bullard and everyone else broke into laughter.

"I tell you what I'm going to do, Kyle. You caught me on a good day. I'm going to let you off with an unwritten warning so long as you promise to obey your momma. Fair enough? You understand?" Officer Bullard asked as he winked at Christine and handed Kyle back his license.

"Thanks, Officer Bullard. Be safe out there," Kyle said as the officer put away his citation pad. "Next time we come out to the lake, I'll drop you off some fresh okra for old times' sake."

Kyle reentered the roadway and pointed the SUV in the direction of the setting sun. The yellow house had shaped him, its walls holding the echoes of a boy who had once felt small, powerless. For so long, it had been more than just a place—it had been a shadow he couldn't escape, a weight he carried even miles away. But the yellow house was behind him.

As they headed down the road, Anna sat in the backseat teaching her grandchildren to let their hands ride the wind—gliding gracefully over distant fence posts. Kyle exhaled, feeling lighter than he had in years. Life had come full circle.

EPILOGUE

Everyone has a story.

I'm Ray Sanders, and I am the boy in the yellow house.

This is my story.

Though many of the names have been changed, I lived out this story. I survived horrific abuse at the hands of a man who should have shown me love, but instead taught me what it was like to live in constant daily fear. I watched my mother and brother survive this same abuse, often fearing for their lives because of who my father was.

The boy in the yellow house could have easily grown up to be a man in an orange jumpsuit in the big house.

But that's not how this story ends.

Throughout my life, there have been people who invested in me. People, who saw my potential, believed in me, and encouraged me to recognize I was meant for more. These ordinary heroes taught me that it mattered less where a person started, but what mattered most was how they ended.

I was a victim of childhood abuse. But I am not a victim now, I am a victor because people cared enough to use their influence to make a difference in my life.

That's my story.

Maybe you have lived a life similar to mine. Maybe you are living it now. Maybe that's your story.

There is hope, and not just the hope of forgiveness and reconciliation, but the hope of a life filled with joy, adventure, love, and inspiration even if reconciliation never happens.

I hope you have found hope and inspiration in the pages of this story.

—Ray Sanders.

ACKNOWLEDGMENTS

Thanks be to the greatest storyteller who ever lived, sweet Jesus, my Lord and Savior, and the one who has forever changed my life.

This little book would have never come to life without the unwavering encouragement of my dear family and friends.

To the love of my life, Stephanie. You have always believed in me, encouraged me, and loved me unconditionally. Thanks for letting Jesus use you in my life.

To my wonderful children, Lauren-Elaine, Olivia-Christine, Joshua, Isaac, Emily-Rose, and Sophia-Rae. You have taught me more about life than you will ever know. And to the grandbabies, you bring Papa Bear so much joy! I pray you will learn great life lessons as you turn the pages of this book.

To my mother, Patsy Ann. You have been the anchor through many storms. Your love never fails. I am forever grateful you chose life!

To my dear friends, Randy and Amy Davis, Brian and Vickey Banks, Oliver and Anita Powers, and Michael and Terri Catt. I am who I am because each of you have invested your lives in me. Thanks for the encouragement.

To Anita Powers and Elizabeth Evan, thank you for your tireless input, incredible encouragement, and amazing edits!

For all of you who have uttered these words, "You need to write a book," thank you!

SPECIAL THANKS

There are so many friends that have taken special interest in this project. Each and every one has played a unique role in making The Boy in the Yellow House what it has come to be. I will be forever grateful for the input, insights and edits they have contributed.

Anita Powers
Brian and Vickey Banks
Elizabeth Evans
Emily-Rose Hill
Marty Hardell
Patsy Ann Kolar
Michael Gooch
Randy Peck
Sammy Holmes
Matthew Miller
Sophia-Rae Sanders
Robert Shelton
Alan Klein
Doug Hall
Wade McCoy
The team at Lucid Books,
Megan Poling, Carol Jones, and Alisa DeMarco

No one gets to where they are without the influence and inspiration of others. I owe a debt of gratitude to those who helped me become the man I am today.

Mr. and Mr. Brown
Coach Daniel Wilson
Joan Harper
Rev. Michael and Terri Catt
Oliver and Anita Powers
Rev. Charles Draper
Dr. Robert Haskins
Douglas Coe
Bill Counts
Dr. Anthony L. Jordan
Cowboy Charlie
Darrel Lightner
Stephanie Sanders

HELPFUL RESOURCES

The National Domestic Abuse Hotline

☎ 1-800-799-SAFE (7233)

💬 Text "START" to 88788

🌐 thehotline.org

Pregnancy Hotline

☎ 1-800-712-4357

💬 1-800-712-4357

🌐 optionline.org

Suicide Prevention Hotline

☎ 1-800-273-TALK (8255)

💬 Text "HELLO" to 741741

🌐 suicidepreventionlifeline.org

Substance Abuse and Mental Health Services Administration

☎ 1-800-662-HELP (4357)

🌐 samhsa.gov

Suicide and Crisis Lifeline

☎ Call 988

Hope is Alive (Help for addicts and their families)

☎ 1-844-3-HOPE-NOW

🌐 https://www.hopeisalive.net

Alcoholics Anonymous

🌐 aa.org

Celebrate Recovery

🌐 celebraterecovery.com

Faith in Jesus

☎ 1-888-JESUS20 (1-888-537-8720)

🌐 needhim.org

ABOUT THE AUTHOR

 As a passionate communicator, Ray has been the editor in chief of an award-winning weekly news journal, the host of a prizewinning radio program, and continues today as an avid blogger at **RaySanders.com** where he often shares insightful stories and experiences from his faith, family, and travels.

Readers and audiences are discovering Ray has a unique ability to draw from real-life challenges, humorous experiences, and wild adventures that inspire, motivate and challenge people of all ages.

He regularly posts original quotes, photos, and insights certain to cause readers to laugh, cry and think about deeper aspects of life. He has a unique way of turning the everyday into something insightful.

Ray has served as CEO of multi-million-dollar organizations, led international leadership initiatives, community development efforts in remote regions of the world, and served in a nonpartisan role with the United States Senate.

Along with his wife, Ray founded Edify Leaders, a globally-focused organization passionate about inspiring and mobilizing leaders who use their influence to impact the world for good.

Nothing thrills Ray more than spending time traveling the world with the love of his life, his girlfriend and wife, Stephanie. Together they have six children and eight grandchildren and counting!

www.ingramcontent.com/pod-product-compliance
Lightning Source LLC
Chambersburg PA
CBHW061517020726
47502CB00006B/2111